**Going . . .**

AN

"Antiques addicts will enjoy the 'trash 'n' treasures tips."

—*Publishers Weekly*

"Charming . . . a laugh-out-loud-funny mystery."

—*Romantic Times* (four stars)

"A delightfully charming cozy . . . Barbara Allan is a terrific storyteller who knows how to grab and keep reader interest."

—*Harriet's Book Reviews*

ANTIQUES ROADKILL

"Brandy, her maddening mother, her uptight sister, and all the denizens of their small Iowa town are engaging and utterly believable as they crash through a drugs and antiques scam on the Mississippi. Anyone like me, who's blown the car payment on a killer outfit, will love the bonus of Brandy's clothes obsession."

—Sara Paretsky

"If you're either a mystery reader or an antiques hunter, and especially if you're both, *Antiques Roadkill* is your book! This is the start of what's sure to be a terrific new series. Grab it up!"

—S.J. Rozan

"Cozy mystery fans will love this down-to-earth heroine with the wry sense of humor and a big heart."

—Nancy Pickard

"With its small town setting and cast of quirky characters, *Antiques Roadkill* is fun from start to finish. Dive in and enjoy."

—Laurien Berenson

"Brandy and her eccentric mother, Vivian, make a hilarious and improbable team of snoops as they encounter the seamier side of the antiques trade in this delightful debut. *Antiques Roadkill* will certainly make you think twice about those family treasures in your attic."

—Joan Hess

"Terrific. It's funny, witty, irreverent. From the opening page to the very last, the distinctive voice in *Antiques Roadkill* pulls you in and never lets go."

—T. J. MacGregor

"Acclaimed husband-and-wife mystery writers Max Allan Collins and Barbara Collins create a fabulous and intimate voice for this novel's heroine, a flawed but funny 30-year-old who takes us on a spirited journey to a place where family wishes are honored, no matter how eccentric the request, and offbeat characters are the norm."

—*Romantic Times* (4½ stars)

"Enormously entertaining."

—*Ellery Queen Mystery Magazine* (3 stars)

# Antiques Maul

By Barbara Allan:

*Antiques Roadkill*

*Antiques Maul*

*Antiques Flee Market*

By Barbara Collins:

*To Many Tomcats*
(short story collection)

By Barbara and Max Allan Collins:

*Regeneration*

*Bombshell*

*Murder—His and Hers*
(short story collection)

# Antiques Maul

A Trash 'n' Treasures Mystery

Barbara Allan

KENSINGTON BOOKS
KENSINGTON PUBLISHING CORP.
http://www.kensingtonbooks.com

KENSINGTON BOOKS are published by

Kensington Publishing Corp.
850 Third Avenue
New York, NY 10022



All Kensington titles, imprints and distributed lines are available at special quantity discounts for bulk purchases for sales promotion, premiums, fund-raising, educational or institutional use.

Special book excerpts or customized printings can also be created to fit specific needs. For details, write or phone the office of the Kensington Special Sales Manager: Kensington Publishing Corp., 850 Third Avenue, New York, NY 10022. Attn. Special Sales Department. Phone: 1-800-221-2647.



ISBN-13: 978-0-7582-1194-1
ISBN-10: 0-7582-1194-5

First Hardcover Printing: September 2007
First Mass Market Paperback Printing: September 2008
10 9 8 7 6 5 4 3 2 1

Printed in the United States of America

*For the Mull siblings,*
*in lieu of royalties*

"Human beings are the only creatures on earth
that allow their children to come home."
Bill Cosby

"Double, double toil and trouble;
Fire burn and cauldron bubble."
William Shakespeare
The Witches in "the Scottish play"*

*Mother refuses to call it by name—
bad luck in the theater, you know

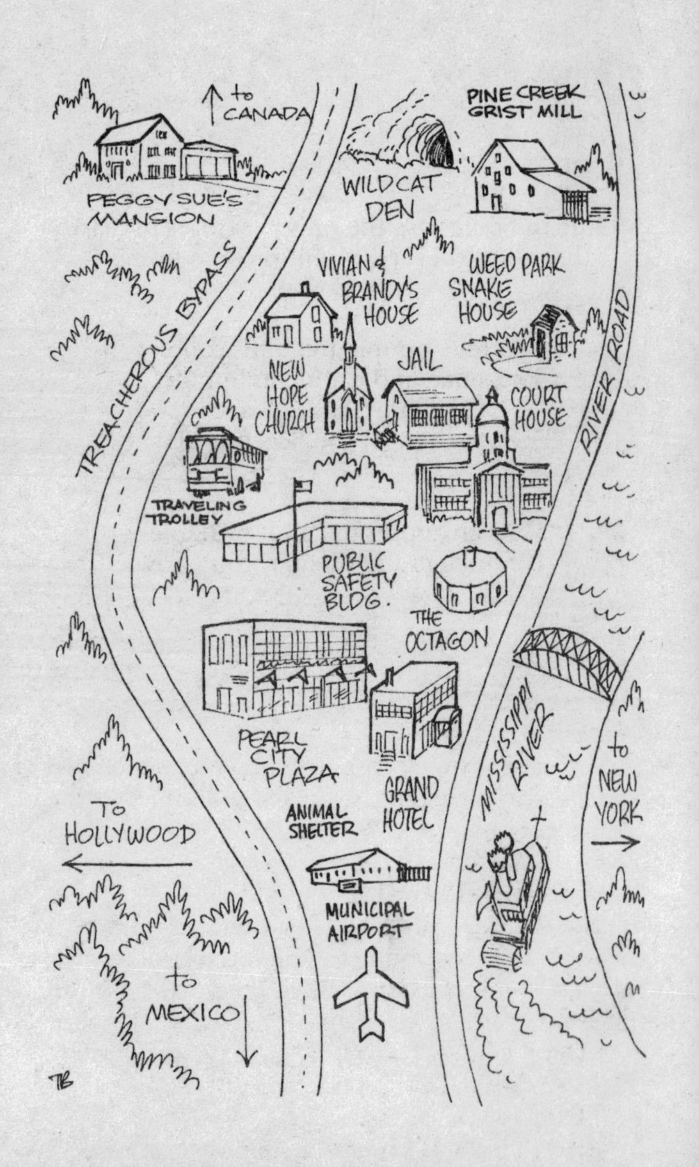
to CANADA
PEGGY SUE'S MANSION
PINE CREEK GRIST MILL
WILDCAT DEN
VIVIAN & BRANDY'S HOUSE
WEED PARK SNAKE HOUSE
TREACHEROUS BYPASS
RIVER ROAD
NEW HOPE CHURCH
JAIL
COURT HOUSE
TRAVELING TROLLEY
PUBLIC SAFETY BLDG.
THE OCTAGON
PEARL CITY PLAZA
GRAND HOTEL
MISSISSIPPI RIVER
to NEW YORK
To HOLLYWOOD
ANIMAL SHELTER
MUNICIPAL AIRPORT
to MEXICO
TB

# Chapter One

## Them's the Rakes

With me toting the box of collectibles, Mother and I entered the unlocked back door and stepped into the darkness of the antiques mall. We had set up our booth yesterday and were here, bright and early, to do some pricing on the various treasures and trash we were foisting upon an unsuspecting public.

I moved to an electric panel on the wall nearby and began switching switches, illuminating the large room, section by section. When I turned back to Mother, she was heading up the center aisle toward the front of the store.

Soon I was hurrying after her and then, as I rounded the row, bumped full-force into Mother, who had doubled back, knocking the wind out of both of us.

"Dear, please," she said gasping for breath, "please don't . . ."

"Don't what?"

"Don't look. It's horrible. Simply grotesque."

Despite her agitated state, and the melodramatic words, Mother seemed atypically untheatrical.

Now, I ask you . . . if somebody tells you not to look, especially if it's "horrible," and "simply grotesque," what is any reasonable person going to do?

Right.

Not only are you *going* to look, but you *have* to look, you *must* look. . . .

Murder wasn't the beginning. The beginning was on a lovely afternoon, not long before. Autumn in Serenity is my favorite time of the year, and this particular autumn was living up to all my expectations.

The trees lining the streets and dotting yards are at their most brilliant—leaves of scarlet, orange, and golden yellow, shimmering in the warm afternoon sunlight. We were in the throes of a glorious Indian summer, yet the nights were cool enough to wear the new fall fashions (specifically, a recently purchased bronze leather jacket from Bernardo).

Still, fall has its inherently melancholy side, a bittersweet, contemplative time—mulling what might have been . . . and then the realization that, given a second chance, you'd probably do the same dumb things all over again. . . .

After ten years of marriage, I was recently divorced (my bad), and had come home to live with my seventy-plus-year-old mother in the small midwestern town on the banks of the Mississippi River where I'd grown up. I had brought with me my share of the spoils of the marriage: Sushi, a white and brown shih tzu, who was spoiled. Roger had custody of ten-year-old Jacob back in Chicago, also spoiled.

Some might think that our newly formed household unit made quite the dysfunctional family . . . Mother bipolar, Sushi blind with diabetes, me zoned out on antidepressants. But *I* think we functioned just fine . . . as long as we all took our medication.

On my return to Serenity several months ago, we'd become unexpectedly involved in a couple of juicy local murders and performed what my mother insisted on describing as "amateur sleuthing." On this fall day, thoughts of that remarkable set of experiences were among my contemplations, sure; but I figured that adventure was a one-shot.

I had no idea, on that crisp autumn afternoon, that a sequel was looming. . . .

Dressed in a brown Juicy Couture hoodie and Blue Cult jeans, orange Puma running shoes, my honey-blonde hair in a ponytail, I leaned on my rake, inhaling deeply, taking in the crisp, clean, humidity-free air, then exhaling with a self-satisfied sigh. Slacking on the job, I listened to the tuneless high-pitched song of the cicada bugs while watching an ever-growing number of birds perched on an electrical wire argue over who was going to lead them south for the winter.

Robin chirped, "I have seniority, so I'm most qualified."

"Hell you say!" Bluebird retorted. "You got us lost over Arkansas last year, remember? Practically got sucked into that jet's nether regions!"

Swallow interjected, "Well, I'm not flying all the way to Capistrano again. That about busted my feathers! I thought my darn wings would fall off. . . . Cancún is far enough."

Blackbird scoffed, "It's still hurricane season down there, you dolt. . . . You wanna get blown into raven munchies?"

Crow crowed, "Think *I'll* fly to Miami, then catch a steamer across the Atlantic to Europe. Heard those Italian birds are swee-*eeet*. . . ."

Swallow was saying, "Hey, Robin! What's the matter? Suddenly you don't look so good. . . ."

"Yeah," Robin answered, "I don't feel so good either. Maybe I'm gettin' that bird flu that's been going around."

"Yikes!"

"Let me outta here!"

"Been nice knowin' ya!"

And the fine-feathered friends scattered in a flap of wings.

Here I thought *my* life was stressful.

Sushi, stretched out lazily under a nearby oak, lifted her small furry head and yapped at me, as if to say, "Get back to work!" While Sushi couldn't see, she could hear my inactivity.

"Yeth, Maaath-tur," I said in my best Midnight Movie manner, and proceeded to corral some sneaky leaves with my rake, foiling their escape on a lucky puff of wind.

A gray squirrel (meaner than their brown cousins) decided to come down from its nest at the tippy-top of the oak. The squirrel planted itself a short distance from Sushi and—thinking the little fur ball no threat—began to taunt her.

"Na-na-na-na-na-na," the squirrel chattered, dancing back and forth just out of Sushi's reach.

"I wouldn't *go* there," I warned.

Sushi sat up slowly, resting on her back legs, head tilted to one side.

The taunter danced closer.

"Na-na-na-na-na-na."

With lightning speed, Sushi struck at the source of the noise; as the startled squirrel whirled to retreat, the canine caught that long bushy tail with her little sharp teeth and clamped.

The squirrel screeched (wouldn't you?) and I commanded, "Let him go, Soosh."

She reluctantly obeyed, and the squirrel scurried back up the tree to its nest—a little bit wiser, I think.

Mother—wearing a voluminous blue caftan and one of her large red hats to protect her delicate Danish skin from the rays of the sun—made a typically grand entrance (even though, technically, it was an exit) as she floated down the front porch steps, one part apparition, one part aberration.

"My goodness," she asked, "what's all the ruckus?" Her eyes, already magnified by her large thick glasses, were owl-wide.

I told her.

Mother gazed up, waggling a finger in the squirrel's general direction. "You'd better spend more time gathering acorns and not picking on a poor defenseless little doggie."

Soosh looked toward Mother's voice with a cocked head.

Then Mother added upward, "The winter of your discontent is *coming*, you know!"

The squirrel said nothing; he was just a bit player in Mother's production.

"Brandy," Mother said, eyes narrow yet huge, "how does a nice glass of chilled apple cider sound?"

I despise cider. "Great!"

I was not trying to make Mother feel better. I was merely willing to take any excuse to forestall further raking. Already I had a blister going between my right thumb and forefinger. Besides, the wind was picking up and all the leaves would blow into the neighbors' yards if I could just be patient.

I leaned the rake against the tree, retrieved Sushi, and followed Mother up the wide steps, across the expansive porch, and inside.

Some months ago, I had tried to talk Mother into building a ranch-style house after our old three-story stucco had been destroyed (which is another story) (available at your favorite bookseller's), pointing out that in the days to come she might find the steps a hardship.

Mother flatly refused.

"A *ranch*-style?" Mother screeched. "*Here?* On *this* property? Why, that would be committing architectural blasphemy!"

"Huh?" I asked. Okay, I'm not quite as articulate as Mother.

Mother gazed at me with haughty sympathy and benign contempt, as if I had a can of spaghetti on my face and was using the meatballs for brains.

"Because, my dear girl, that style would *not* complement the array of structures along our street."

"Array of structures—other houses, you mean."

Mother puffed up. "Why, a single-story home among these two- and three-stories would look like a . . . a stumpy, filed-off tooth next to the other teeth in the block's bright, shining smile."

I didn't point out that the logical extension of her metaphorical spiel indicated that many *other* teeth in that "bright, shining smile" could stand some veneers or capping, or even a few Crest bleach-strips.

But Mother was on a roll. "And as for climbing the stairs when the distant day arrives that I am indeed old and gray . . ."

She *was* old and gray! Indeed!

". . . should the effort take me half an hour to accomplish, what then? What *else* would I have to do?"

For a romantic, Mother could be awfully pragmatic.

The new house—a virtual replica of the original three-story one—went up in record time. I asked around and found the fastest and best builders, hired them, and unleashed my secret weapon: Mother hanging around the construction site, driving the contractors crazy.

You'd have been done in six weeks, too. Maybe five.

I trailed Mother into the house and on through to the kitchen—the only room that had been modified and modernized from the old blueprints—and put Sushi down, watching her find her way to the water dish.

Mother, getting the apple cider out of the fridge, asked, "Brandy, darling, when can I expect these *clothes* to come down?"

She was referring to a new pair of Citizens of Humanity jeans, a plaid L.A.M.B. jacket, and a tight Theory pencil skirt (all a size smaller than I had on), which were hanging on various cabinet doors, blocking the way to forbidden foods.

"Five more pounds from now," I said.

"Good," she sighed. "Because it's most inconvenient to get into the cupboards."

"Which," I said, "is the point."

Mother continued: "And last night I came downstairs for a glass of warm milk, turned on the kitchen light, and nearly fainted from fright! Why, in my sleep-addled state, I thought we had burglars!"

Albeit chic, female ones. Standing on the kitchen counter.

"Although, Brandy, I must admit, this new diet method of yours does seem to be working."

I beamed. "Good! Then you *can* tell I've lost some weight?"

Mother frowned, as if my question had been a non sequitur. "Not *you*, dear, *me* . . . I've shed ten pounds."

Here I'd dropped only a measly three.

Bottom line on dieting: After age thirty (which I had just reached) the only way to lose weight is to go through a divorce (not recommended) or finally get around to having your impacted wisdom teeth taken out.

To drop the poundage, and keep it off, you must make a "lifestyle" change: i.e., *You can no longer eat as you used to.* And the sooner you get that through your thick skull (and thicker waistband) the better.

Here's what I do now (besides hanging too-tight clothes over Temptation's Portal): I eat what I want, but only half portions. Get it? Half a steak, half a baked potato, half a roll, half a piece of pumpkin pie with half a dollop of whipped cream . . .

"*Getouttamyway!*"

I pushed Mother aside and lurched for the blue-jeans-covered cabinet that contained the sweets.

"Brandy, no!" Mother said, in that firm voice I'd heard a thousand times; she raised a properly scolding finger. "Stick to your guns."

"Just *half* a cookie!" I pleaded.

After all, I knew she didn't care about my weight. She just wanted me to lose poundage so she could have her precious kitchen cupboards unblocked.

Mother patted my arm. "Come now, dear . . . drink your apple cider . . . that will fill you up. Let's go out on the porch."

I scowled . . .

. . . but followed her.

We sat in white wicker chairs, our drinks resting on a matching wicker table between us. Sushi trotted over and got up on her hind legs to sniff at what we were having. No fool, she turned up her little wet nose, then found a pool of warm sunshine on the porch floor to settle down in.

I broached a touchy subject with Mother. "Have they decided who's going to be the next permanent director of the Community Theater Playhouse?"

"Permanent" directors at the playhouse came and went.

Mother—after a lifetime of performing on the stage, and decades as Serenity's Community Theater doyenne—had begun to direct a play now and then, and had thrown her red hat into the ring of contenders.

Mr. Manley had been the director for several years until he ran off recently with the Serenity Symphony's lady bassoon player in the middle of the run of *South Pacific* (rumor had it they *went* to the South Pacific) (nothing like a dame) (nothing in the world), leaving their respective spouses adrift. Not to mention a big hole in the wind section.

Mother's sky-blue eyes turned cloudy gray. She said softly, "I'm afraid Bernice Wiley got the position."

"Oh. I'm sorry, I know how much you wanted it. . . ."

We lapsed into silence.

I didn't know much about Bernice. She and Mother formed a friendship after the flamboyant woman had moved to town a few years ago. Of course, from time to time, during our weekly phone calls, I would hear Mother mention Bernice this, and Bernice that. Mother always spoke highly of the woman and their common interests—a mutual love of antiques and the theater—but I still got the feeling that the two had an adversarial side to their relationship.

Perhaps this was because their personalities were so much alike—maybe *too* much. . . .

The tension between them had become more evident this summer, during a production of *Ar-*

*senic and Old Lace,* in which Mother and Bernice performed the leading roles of the two murdering old ladies.

I attended a performance and thought Mother was wonderful—she really is excellent, for a local-theater performer, in her over-the-top way. I'd complimented her but also made the mistake of confessing that, for some reason, I couldn't seem to keep my eyes off Bernice.

Mother practically spat, "That's because that scene-stealing shitheel kept upstaging me!"

Since swearing was not generally Mother's style (though when it was, "shit" always played a leading role), I knew I'd struck a sore nerve.

"How so?"

"Oh, Brandy," Mother said, and looked to the sky for support, "how *can* you be so *naive*?"

"Hey, I'm not an expert on theater techniques. I haven't been in a play since the third grade."

"Yes, and if your little drawers hadn't fallen to your ankles, you'd have gone on to explore your full potential as an artiste, I know."

"Thanks, Mother."

She gestured regally. "Even so, didn't you notice that every time *I* had a line, La Grand Dame Bernice would scratch her nose, or twitch her rear, so that the audience's attention would be diverted to *her*?"

"Oh." Not a very sporting thing for a so-called friend to do.

I took a sip of my cider, which was better than leaf raking (just), and said cheerfully, "You're in the *next* play, though—what is it again . . . ?"

"*Harvey*," Mother said glumly. "And no, I'm *not* in it."

"Why in heavens not?" The play was one of her favorites, or anyway the James Stewart movie version was.

Mother sneered. "Because Bernice didn't cast me in the role of Elwood P. Dowd's *sister* . . . *that's* why! She cast *herself!*" Mother swiveled toward me in her chair. "I ask you, who other than *moi* is as qualified to play the part of a scatterbrained neurotic old lady?"

I said, "No argument."

"*Thank* you! And *who* could best perform the scene where the sister, by mistake, is committed to the insane asylum?"

"That would be you, again."

"Of course!" Mother said. "But Bernice offered me the part of the busybody friend—with only one little scene and hardly any lines—a role I can *not* relate to at *all!*"

There I could not go; Mother is listed under "Gossip" in the Serenity Yellow Pages, or anyway should be.

Instead, I asked, "So . . . what are you going to do?"

She responded, "I already have. This morning. I quit."

"The play, you mean?"

"No, dear. The *the-a-tuh!*"

This was dire, drastic news, indeed.

"Oh, now, Mother," I cajoled. "Don't be so hasty. . . . Anyway, didn't you always say there were no small roles, just small performers?"

"Then let them go find some small performers! Because the Serenity theatrical scene has seen the last of Vivian Borne!"

Trying not to get tripped up over her "scene"

and "seen," I said consolingly, "Surely there'll be other roles. . . ."

"No," Mother announced defiantly. "I'll find something *else* to do with my time and talents."

Which was what I was afraid of.

Mother needed an outlet like the theater for her energy and antics; without one, her mental health might falter . . . and, consequently, mine.

An idea struck me.

"Mother," I said hopefully, "what do you think about the two of us renting a stall in that new antiques mall?" One had just opened downtown.

Mother frowned in thought. I held my breath. Notions either immediately hit her or missed entirely.

Cautiously she said, "I *might* be interested. . . . But what do we have to sell? We have no inventory."

We had a house full of antiques, mostly family heirlooms that thankfully had gone unaffected when the house blew up (another story) (favorite bookseller's). But none of these were anything either of us wished to part with.

"We'll do what all the other dealers do," I responded with a shrug that I hoped masked my desperate enthusiasm. (Mother never falls for a hard sell—telemarketers have *her* on their "no call list.") "We'll hit the garage sales, estate auctions, and—"

Mother interrupted: "That's *precisely* the problem, Brandy, dear. Those markets are saturated—not a bargain to be found anymore, not for a hundred miles around! We'd never make any money at it."

"I guess making money *is* the point," I glumly

had to admit. "But I liked the idea of a project we could do together, too. . . ."

Sushi, bored with sunbathing, wiggled over, her little nails clicking on the porch planks. She always started begging for her dinner three hours early.

Mother stood and collected our empty glasses.

I asked, "How much cash do we have left over from the house insurance?"

"A couple thousand at least," Mother said, frowning just a little.

"Would you be willing to use it for seed money for our new venture?"

Surprisingly, Mother didn't hesitate. "Yes. Certainly. *If* we can find enough antiques and collectibles—at a good price—to fill a booth *and* make a little money."

And she disappeared inside.

That sounded like a tall order. I reached down for Sushi, saying, "I might have an idea. . . . Would you like to go for an adventure, girl?"

Taking Sushi along was always an adventure.

In the foyer closet I plucked from a hook a rhinestone-studded leopard dog-carrying bag (which used to have pink balboa feathers, but Sushi kept sneezing so I removed them). Then I decided against it and, from another hook, got a front-carrying baby harness—pink with rattles and pacifiers and diaper pins (I hadn't had time to redecorate it in a doggy theme) but provided a more comfortable ride for Soosh. I strapped it on my chest and placed the pooch inside, facing out.

Finally I went to find Mother.

She was upstairs on her bed. Since Mother

rarely succumbed to afternoon naps, I surmised she must be depressed. The sooner we got our booth up and running, the better.

I ran my fingers over her brow, and her blue eyes fluttered.

"Soosh and me're going for a long walk, Mother. Be back for supper, okay?"

"That's nice, dear," she murmured, and closed her eyes again.

Naps and melancholy—something really *did* have to be done. . . .

### *A Trash 'n' Treasures Tip*

Dealers in antique malls shouldn't expect to make a fortune. A rare few do, some others do nicely, but many only break even and the unlucky lose money. But it's a wonderful way to thin your own collection and get advance looks at (and dealer discounts on) the treasures in other booths—just don't go broke snatching up bargains.

# Chapter Two

## A Piece of the Auction

I could have taken my car for the five-mile trek downtown, but the day was so beautiful . . . and those last five pounds so ugly. . . .

Woman and dog left the house and started down the street, Sushi a comical hairy growth on my front.

Elm was one of Serenity's most venerable avenues, boasting grand old one-of-a-kind homes set back from the lavishly tree-lined street. Most houses were decked out for Halloween, sporting carved pumpkins, spiderwebs, bats, white-sheet ghosts, life-size skeletons, and witches. Some home owners went a little overboard, planting fake tombstones in their front yard . . . but it was all great fun for the trick-or-treat crowd, who—with All Hallows' Day only a week away—were champing at the bit to get chomping at that candy. I swear you could feel the collective kid excitement hanging over the town like a ravenous cloud.

Here's my weirdest Halloween kid story, which is probably only frightening to me.

Once I went trick-or-treating with an older girl. Her name was Suzanne, and she seemed determined to get all the candy she could in the amount of time the city fathers granted us to ring doorbells. She ran all over town, almost literally, with me huffing and puffing to keep up, and we went places I'd never been before. By the end of the evening, Suzanne and I had so much loot that I had to call Mother to come get us—which she was none too happy about. And me, I was so pooped, I flopped into bed without sampling so much as a munch of my goodies.

In the morning, I discovered that Mother had somehow disposed of half of my candy!

"Whadja do *that* for!" I screamed.

"Too many sweets will rot your teeth," Mother retorted, "and will make you ill. You wouldn't want to miss school, would you?"

Was that a trick question? Certainly wasn't a treat. And why did I have the sneaking suspicion half my haul had gone down Mother's gullet?

But wait, as the infomercial shills say, there's more. . . .

Eight months later I was playing over at Suzanne's house when we went up in her hot, humid attic, looking for a stack of board games her mother had stowed away. There, in a corner, beneath a cobweb, was her huge sack of Halloween candy—*untouched!*

"Why didn't you *eat* this stuff?" I asked her, astonished.

She shrugged and said, "Ah—I don't really like candy."

I couldn't process that. Still can't.

Somehow I managed to ask, "Well . . . can *I* have it?"

She shrugged again. "I guess . . . but it's probably rotten by now."

My friend was right.

And, so, in her way was Mother: That night, she had to rush me to the emergency room to have my stomach pumped.

On the other hand, I did get to skip school the next day, so the effort wasn't a total loss.

I'll stop with the Halloween reminiscing or we'll never get downtown.

Serenity, with a current population of twenty-five thousand, had once been settled by the peaceful Mascouten Indians, who thought the valley between two bluffs on the Mississippi River would be a nice place to raise a family. In the early eighteen hundreds, some Germans moved in, and Scandinavians . . . and the Mascoutens moved over.

Later, in the 1950s, Hispanics migrated from south of the border to toil in the rich corn and tomato fields. Nobody moved over for them, exactly, but room was made. And twenty years or so after that, refugees arrived from Vietnam—and most recently, displaced African-Americans from the effects of hurricane Katrina, all searching for the American dream. And pretty much finding it, if they were willing to work, which most were.

A word about our Native American ancestors:

Every once in a while, some well-meaning citizen would petition the city council to change the name of Papoose Creek, or the community college's baseball team (the Indians), and even would go so far as to demand the removal of the bronze statue of the Mascouten Indian chief (who has guarded the riverfront park entry for a century) because he/she deemed these demeaning.

Well. Whenever this happened, my proactive mother would get her beaded, fringed Indian Princess Iowana outfit (from her stint on a local TV show in the 1950s) (Iowana was an area dairy) out of moth balls and show up at the next council meeting. The last item on every month's agenda was called "Citizen Speak," and anyone with a beef could talk, even vegetarians.

Mother would make her regal entrance from the back of the room. The pews—which could seat several hundred (and usually contained only a bored newspaper reporter, and a few high school students required to attend for a civics class)—would be packed, word having spread (by Mother, of course) of her appearance.

Princess Iowana would begin her speech slowly, head held high and proud, seeking the eyes of each council member (plus the "eye" of the local cable TV camera).

"So," she would say, "you want to erase all evidence that *my people* once laughed and loved, lived and died, here on the riverbanks of this great town. . . ."

At the "my people," a few titters would break out among the nonbelievers; with her blue eyes, fair hair, and light complexion, Mother would have been a likelier representative of the Vikings who settled in America.

But the skeptics soon came around, as Mother

disappeared into her part . . . and at the end of her performance (which kept getting longer each time, well past the five-minute allotment), even the disbelievers would have tears in their eyes, rising with the others to give Princess Iowana a standing ovation.

Sometimes, even the petitioning do-gooder would apologize to the city council for making trouble.

Funny thing—over the years Serenity did such a good job being an American melting-pot, no one kept track of the Mascoutens. Long-standing rumor had it, however, that one elderly reclusive woman living in town was *part* Mascouten. So the first time Mother planned to speak to the city council she tried to solicit this woman's help beforehand.

But the native American descendant refused, as the meeting was at the same time as her favorite TV show, *T.J. Hooker*, and even though Mother promised to tape it for her, the woman still refused to go. And, furthermore, if Mother didn't stop bothering her, the Mascouten old maid would call the cops. Possibly even T.J. Hooker himself.

Mother had been suitably outraged. "*T.J. Hooker*? *Star Trek* I could understand. . . ."

Apparently, for an actress like Mother, right or wrong fell on the side of which William Shatner program you preferred.

I turned down Fourth Street and power-walked past the beautiful stately courthouse—a Grecian wedding cake of limestone and marble—Sushi thumping lightly against my chest. In the next block awaited the modern redbrick

Safety Building, housing both the Serenity police and fire departments, the latter's huge garage door open wide, fire truck and emergency vehicles at the ready, brass pole poised for some good-looking fireman to come sliding down . . .

Yes, it had been a long time since I had a real date.

I entered on the police department side, walked quickly through a small, perfunctory waiting area, and up to a ponytailed female dispatcher who was monitoring (what else?) monitors and computers and such. I spoke into the little microphone embedded in the bulletproof glass.

"Brandy Borne to see Chief Cassato," I said.

Barely acknowledging me, but giving my pooch a mildly disapproving glance, the woman said crisply, "Take a seat."

Backstory: A few years before my divorce—and after Mother landed in jail for a few days after a particularly bad spell—I came back to Serenity and spent some time working with the chief on bringing qualified teachers from NAMI (the National Alliance for the Mentally Ill) to teach the boys in blue how to recognize the mentally disabled, and how not to treat them like hardened criminals.

I returned to the waiting area and chose the hard plastic mismatched chair that looked most comfortable. I sifted through some public information pamphlets on a scarred end table, but had already read them before. Sushi was panting, so I stood, went over to the water fountain, and gave her a drink, then had one myself.

Then I noticed something else in the room

that sorely needed some H-two-0: the corner rubber tree plant.

I found an empty soda can, filled it, and was in the process of giving the plant a good dousing when the chief stuck his head through the forbidden door to the inner police sanctum.

"Still solving other people's problems, Brandy?" he said, with the mildest of smiles.

I grinned sickly.

He motioned to me.

I put down the can and followed the town's top cop, who was in his midforties, barrel-chested, with gray temples, a bulbous nose, square jaw, and bullet-hard eyes.

Tony Cassato was a man of mystery to most everyone in town. He came from the East Coast about three years ago to head up our police department, and hardly anyone knew anything about him . . . even Mother.

Besides its button mills, lumber mills, and grain mills, Serenity was also famous for its rumor mills. One rumor had the chief ratting on the New York mob and, after having plastic surgery to change a Gary Grant–ish face, was sent to Serenity in the witness protection plan. Another story circulating said the chief had to trade his stressful, big city job for small-town life because of a nervous breakdown.

Another possible scenario could be that Tony Cassato applied for the position, was found to be the best qualified, and landed the job on merit. But that story has never gotten much traction around here.

As we walked down the tan-tiled corridor, its

gray walls broken periodically with pictures of bygone police days, the chief asked (in his charming, decidedly eastern accent), "How are you doing these days?"

"Fine. Great. Wonderful."

Why was I overcompensating?

"And your mother?"

"That, I'm afraid, is why I'm here."

He raised his eyebrows.

Most people in Serenity, should you mention that you've dropped by on account of my mother, would raise their eyebrows.

At the end of the hallway we entered his office, which was nothing fancy . . . could have belonged to anyone in middle management. Tony sat behind his paper-cluttered desk, and I took the visitor's chair, removing Sushi from the carrier and putting her on my lap, so she would be more comfortable.

Tony leaned back in his chair, tented his fingertips, and waited for me to begin. Like a doctor preparing to hear where it hurt.

"Mother has quit the theater," I announced.

"Why?"

Briefly I told him about her losing the director's job to her friend, then said, "I'm worried that without an outlet like acting on the stage, she might take her acting elsewhere . . . like to the streets, if you know what I mean."

He nodded. "Prying on the phone with friends is one thing—doing it, out and about, something else again."

"Exactly. I've suggested to Mother that we rent a booth at the new antiques mall in Pearl City Plaza . . . and I think hunting for antiques and collectibles to stock it with should keep her busy enough . . . but finding merchandise around here has gotten very competitive."

The chief sat forward with a grunt. "Tell me about it. We broke up a fight at a tag sale on Morning Glory Circle yesterday afternoon."

Mother hadn't told me about that! She was slipping; further evidence of her depression.

"That's exactly what I mean . . . I don't know how Mother and I are going to make a go of it."

Tony frowned. "Where do I come in?"

I adjusted Sushi on my lap. "Well, remember once you told me about the Crime Control Act, and that the government has the right to seize *any* property at the site of a criminal act . . . ?"

The chief was nodding.

"And that this property was sold at federal auctions?"

"Right."

"That means antiques and collectibles can get confiscated right along with contraband."

"It happens."

I shrugged. "I was thinking, maybe Mother and I could snag some bargains at those auctions . . . it's not like a lot of people know about this."

He shrugged but his expression said he was giving me serious consideration.

"I mean," I said with a half smile, "I'd hate to bring home a steamer trunk and find a body in it."

The chief didn't return my smile, just said, "Let me do some checking. . . . I'll let you know where and when any federal auctions are being held in the Midwest. Might give you girls a leg up on the antiques front."

"Thanks!"

"Glad to help. After all, you helped me, not so long ago."

I stood. Chief Cassato was a busy man and I didn't want to take up too much of his valuable time; after all, he had crooks to catch and capers to foil and fights at tag sales to break up.

Sushi, however, had other plans, and began yapping in earnest.

"What does *she* want?" the chief asked, adding quickly, "As if I didn't know."

I sighed. "Is Rin-tin-what's-it around?" Couldn't recall the drug-sniffing canine's name.

"Rudy was taken out to the high school this morning. I'll see if he's back."

Rudy? Sushi and Rudy. Rudy and Sushi? Didn't exactly roll off the tongue; maybe if I panted it . . .

While the chief abandoned us, my eyes searched his office. Other than a couple of duck-hunting prints, no evidence presented itself as to this mysterious (and not unattractive) man's life after working hours.

Soon Tony returned.

"Lunchroom," he said, not mincing words.

I thanked the chief and told him I'd find my way. By the time I entered the lounge, Sushi had worked herself into a frenzy.

Two uniformed officers were seated at a dinged-up dining table, both brown-bagging it. One was Brian Lawson—another attractive cop—and the other I'd never seen before.

Rudy was on the floor by the table, his large brown head resting on one paw, eyes closed, most likely pooped from sniffing kids' lockers. But the German shepherd still had enough of his olfactory perception to get a whiff of Soosh; he lifted his head, and—I swear—groaned!

I lowered Sushi to the floor and she followed *her* olfactory perceptions, scampering over to the canine (or in cop terms, K-9), and started crawling all over him, making a complete fool of herself. (I will point out that I was too restrained to do the same with Officer Brian Lawson, despite a crush I was nurturing). Rudy, however, was a gentleman, and put up with her shenanigans.

I saw Brian give the other cop an ever-so slight "beat it" look, and his fellow officer did so, giving *me* a not-so-slight sly grin.

Was this middle school?

I assumed the vacated chair and looked at Brian and asked, "Does your partner know something I don't?"

"I don't think so, Brandy."

"I mean, if you want to talk, I'm in the book. Even have an answer machine, should you miss me. And my cell number could probably be pried out of me, knowing your keen interrogative skills."

He laughed in an aw-shucks way.

"I was afraid," he said, "you'd consider me a kind of unpleasant reminder."

Officer Lawson had been a participant in those juicy murders I mentioned (not the murderer—he, as a cop, took one of the cop roles) (typecasting, courtesy of Mother).

"Not much about that experience I care to linger over," I said. "But we could always have some *new* experiences."

He flashed a nice smile, full of teeth and sex

appeal. "That would be fine with me. What was that cell phone number again?"

By late afternoon, Sushi and I had left the police station, having wasted enough of the time of two law enforcement officers, one human, one not; I didn't feel like making the trek home on foot, so instead strolled over a few blocks to Main Street to catch the Traveling Trolley, which was really a bus reconditioned to gas from an old electrical car.

The trolley was the brainstorm of the downtown merchants to bring patrons to shop at their stores rather than out at the mall—free to the public, as long as a person was going to, or coming from . . . that's right . . . downtown.

Sushi seemed subdued as we waited for our free hitch, probably thinking lovey-dovey doggy-style thoughts about Rudy, while I watched an elderly woman in navy blue slacks and a tan coat crossing the street in my direction, trying to use a U-shaped walker with one hand while talking on a cell phone with the other.

When she jostled into the curb, I should have felt more sorry for her. But steering with two hands applies to walkers as well as cars. . . .

Still, I helped the lady on to the sidewalk, and she stood next to me, apparently also waiting for the trolley.

I'd just like to know . . . at what stage do old folks lose the ability to censor themselves? I mean, they just blurt out whatever comes into their minds.

She said, "*My!* You've certainly dropped the weight after the baby."

I responded, "This isn't a baby—it's a dog."

The woman leaned in for a closer look, her cataracts almost as bad as Sushi's. "Well, thank goodness!" she said. "Here I was thinking you'd given birth to just about the ugliest baby I've ever seen!"

"What a lovely thing to say," I said, smiling.

Soosh just growled.

The trolley arrived, and the silver-haired, bearded gent driving assisted my new acquaintance with her walker up the few steps, then turned to me.

"No pets on the trolley," he announced. "Sorry."

Hmmm. "What about Seeing Eye dogs?" I asked.

"In that case, of course. But, young lady, you're obviously not blind."

Liking the "young" part if not wild about the "lady," I said, "Well, the *dog's* blind and *I'm* her Seeing Eye human."

And giving him no time to think about that, I climbed aboard.

The wonderful smell of Mother's beef stroganoff greeted us when we arrived home, and I thought Sushi was going to swoon and faint—Rudy and stroganoff in the same day! Heaven on earth. . . .

In the kitchen, I mixed a little of the stew with Sushi's dry dog food (was a woman in Japan right now feeding a pet named Dry Dog Food sushi?) and put it in her dish. That way, Soosh would be sure to eat right away . . . so I could give her the insulin shot. (It's not good to have a diabetic animal who's a finicky eater.)

After dinner—at which I was anything *but* a

finicky eater, forgoing my one-half portion rule—I did the dishes (well, the dishwasher did the dishes . . . but I put them in). Then I retired to the seclusion of the music/library/den room to catch up on my e-mail on my laptop, which hadn't been tended to for a few days. Usually this amounted to an hour or so of deleting unwanted spam, but to my surprise, I had one from Jacob.

The e-mail read

> Mom, I guess I could come for a little while to see Grandma and you. My year-round school has a vacation break soon.
>
> Jake.

I sat back.

He hadn't written "Dear" Mom; he put his grandma before me; and he didn't sign off "Love" Jake . . . but still . . . hearing from him was . . . hearing from him.

You see, though I'd sent Jake many missives via both snail- and e-mail, this was the first message I'd received from my son since the divorce.

Could this be a warming trend along with the Indian summer?

I was alive with excitement about his visit . . .

. . . but also, I have to admit, a little trepidation.

If I was the kind of writer who wrote things like "Little did I know how much trepidation I'd have felt, had I but known the danger I'd be putting him in," that's what I'd write right here.

But lucky for you, I'm not.

*A Trash 'n' Treasures Tip*

If you can't wait around all day at a local auction for a particular item of interest to go on sale, ask the auctioneer to move it up in the schedule. But don't try this at a federal auction; you'll get your head bit off.

# Chapter Three

## A Hunting We Will Hoe

My sister, Peggy Sue, was old enough to be my mother. Born in the 1950s, pretty, pretty, pretty Peggy Sue was named after Buddy Holly's hokey if infectious rock 'n' roll song.

Mother always claimed the idea to call sis Peggy Sue came to her in a vision shortly after giving birth; but Father, who kept a diary (a holdover from his World War II correspondent days), penned that a pimple-faced but pretty nurse's aide was singing the rock 'n' roll tune as she pushed a groggy Mother-on-a-Gurney out of the delivery room, still wearing saddle shoes from a sock hop. (The aide, not Mother!)

Then, after eighteen years passed with no more children, Mother and Father thought they were done with child-rearing, Mother having entered menopause. But (as she has told me so often) when Mother began gaining weight and filling out around the middle, she trundled to the family physician, Dr. Swayze, thinking I was a fibroid tumor gotten out of hand (I've been called worse).

According to Mother, when Doc Swayze gave her the news, she fainted dead away, hit her head on the examining table, and had to get twenty stitches. (Mother always exaggerates, as you'll learn; it was probably only fifteen stitches.)

I don't know what Father thought about my surprise arrival—there was nothing recorded in his daily musings, which stopped just before I was born. Shortly thereafter, he departed for the Great Beyond, courtesy of a heart attack. Guilt feelings that somehow my unexpected (unwanted?) presence may have contributed to my father's premature exit had haunted me for years.

Of course, I'm over it now. Aren't I? And my marrying an older man couldn't have anything to do with daddy issues. Could it?

Mother came downstairs looking normal (relatively speaking) in emerald-green velour slacks and jacket, her silver, wavy hair pinned back in a neat chignon. But the blue eyes behind the thick, large glasses were a little wild, even for her.

"Hurry up, Brandy," she commanded, in a manner both regal and hysterical. "You know how Peggy Sue hates it when we're late! And she's been so thoughtful to have us over for dinner before we leave for the auction."

I found it prudent not to point out that I had been ready for an hour. *And* had packed the car.

Not wanting to add to the palpable tension, I said simply, "Okay," and scooped up the pooch, who had been dancing at my feet, knowing something was in the air. When Mother had pronounced that fateful word, "dinner," Sushi had practically done a back flip.

With the inside automatic light switches set (which fools no one into thinking we're home) and the house locked up, we headed out into the crisp fall evening, the kind perfect for burning leaves, if the city hadn't banned it.

I had a little trouble backing out of the driveway, what with a U-Haul hitched to my new used vehicle, a burgundy Buick.

Mother, seated next to me with Sushi secured on her lap, said, "Brandy, dear, whatever direction you want to go, turn the opposite way."

This was helpful advice, as long as I ignored her contradictory and (of course) theatrical hand gestures, though I did wonder if her words about turning opposite to my instincts might also work in my rudderless life about now. . . .

Peggy Sue lived in an upscale housing development on the outskirts of town with her husband, Bob (a CPA), and their only child, Ashley (a senior in high school). To get to this promised land, we had to cross the Red Sea of a treacherous bypass.

One of the first built in the state—cleverly routing business away from our fair town—Serenity's bypass was designed with too great a curve factor for drivers to properly see the oncoming, fast-moving traffic, and had no "safe zone" between the four lanes where terrified souls might hole up after a misjudged crossing, waiting for their sobbing to cease and another dangerous opportunity to present itself.

The bypass was originally conceived with no traffic lights to slow people down as they sped around our little burg . . . but over the years, in response to the number of traffic fatalities, several lights had been installed—just not at our juncture. Apparently, the intersection where we now sat idling hadn't racked up enough of a body count to warrant a light. Patience. (Or is that patients?)

I squinted to the left into the setting sun, wishing I hadn't blown off my appointment for new contact lenses. Choosing between shopping and my eyesight was no contest. Mother looked to the right, but I had little confidence in her vision with those thick, trifocal glasses.

I saw an opening in the steady stream of traffic.

"Now!" I exclaimed.

But Mother shouted, "No!"

So I braked, the car shuddered, and so did I. We waited. Another car pulled up behind us wanting to cross, and the pressure mounted. In my mind the *Jaws* theme played counterpoint to the *Jeopardy* final round music.

Teeth bared, eyes glittering, Mother said, "*Now!*"

But I exclaimed, "No!"

Then, several long moments later, Mother and I *both* yelled "*Now,*" and I hit the gas. . . . Whether the decision was a good one or a bad one, at least we'd made it together.

And you thought life in a small heartland community lacked in excitement.

Nearly across, I was feeling relieved, until a car horn blasted and brakes squealed. I looked in my rearview mirror to see a figure in a pickup truck giving me a high five, the one-finger variety.

I guess I hadn't allowed for the U-Haul.

I sank down in my seat and said to nobody, "Sorry. . . ."

Mother sniffed, "Serves him right. He was going too fast, anyway."

Probably, but that would have been a small consolation had we been hit.

Dusk had fallen, or crept in or sneaked up or however it gets here, and a huge harvest moon popped up on the horizon like a big orange Necco wafer as our little caravan pulled into the Mark Twain housing addition. As soon as we had made the turn, Sushi knew where she was—don't ask me how, doggie radar, I guess—and she began to shimmy and shake with excitement. We rumbled down Aunt Polly Lane, went left on Tom Sawyer Drive, then right on Becky Thatcher Road, and finally arrived at Peggy Sue's modern monstrosity of a house on Samuel Clemens Court.

Get back to me, if you sense a theme here. . . .

I pulled into the long driveway and parked in front of the first of the Hasting household's three garages. As Mother opened her car door, Sushi jumped out (blindness be hanged) and began running and sniffing all over the thick, green grass. There wasn't a lawn anywhere that she liked to pee and poop on better than Peggy Sue's, much to my sister's dismay.

I, however, had made sure Soosh was running on empty before we'd left home, and it was comical to see the darling trying to squeeze out even one little chocolate drop to mark her return—much as I hated to spoil her fun.

From the car I gathered up Sushi's pink bed, and a tote bag containing her special dog food, insulin, and syringes, and followed Mother up the curved walkway, which was lined with colorful fall mums. The wonderful, smoky smell of burning leaves wafted toward me. The leaf-burning ban was restricted to inside the city limits—which was designated by the bypass; the ban was partly in consideration of those afflicted with asthma, but mostly due to an old couple who accidently burned their house down.

Bob opened the front door as if he'd been poised there waiting for us.

Mother gave her son-in-law a cheerful "Hello!" and brushed past him, stepping into the house; her level of interest in Bob was minimal, because somebody as cheerfully self-centered as Mother doesn't have much left in the gas tank for a mere in-law. I, however, stopped short, startled by Bob's appearance, although I hope I didn't show it.

Peggy Sue's husband looked thinner than usual, face more gaunt, with less hair on his head than I'd remembered, and suddenly seemed way older than his fifty-plus years. Unless Bob was recovering from a recent bout with the flu, my brother-in-law was in desperate need of a vacation.

I gave him a hug with my usual greeting, "Hi, handsome . . . what's new with you?"

He grinned, showing some of his old spark. "Not much . . . work, work, work. . . ."

The two of us had a nice, comfortable rapport due to our mutual standing: We were both at the mercy of my sister.

"You should get some extra help at the office," I scolded.

He shrugged good-naturedly. "That's a problem."

"Yeah? Why?"

"I'd have to pay them."

"Generally how it works," I returned, while keeping an eye on Sushi, who was navigating the front stoop.

Bob shook his head and grinned, changing the subject. "That dog's amazing . . . she remembered every step."

I smiled. "We *were* underfoot around here while they rebuilt our house, remember?" As if he could forget. "And, anyway, Sushi is a regular canine memory expert. Watch . . . she'll go straight to where her water dish used to be."

Which the little dog did, trotting down the long gleaming hallway toward the kitchen.

Chuckling, Bob shut the door. "I'll remind Peg not to rearrange any of the furniture while we're taking care of her." He was the only one on earth who could call my sister Peg and get away with it.

To the right of the entryway yawned a formal living room, tastefully and expensively decorated, a wonderful room for entertaining. So, of course, nobody ever went in there except Peggy Sue's cleaning woman. To the left, a formal dining room, also exquisitely furnished, the perfect place to share a sumptuous meal. Nobody but the cleaning woman ever went in there, either.

Nostrils flaring, I followed the delicious aroma

to the kitchen, where Peggy Sue was retrieving a pan from the stainless steel oven in a kitchen so modernized and gadget-arrayed that it would make Martha Stewart's mouth water. Like mine was at the sight of Sis's homemade lasagne.

Peggy Sue—wearing a tan/light pink plaid jacket and matching wool slacks (my guess: Burberry), pearls, and pumps, her brunette hair perfectly coifed—looked like a high-power broker, and not the homemaker and sometime volunteer that she was.

I'm not knocking my sister. If you got it, baby, flaunt it, flaunt it! And by "it," I mean green stuff, and I'm not talking broccoli.

Peggy Sue announced, "Dinner's ready." To her husband she commanded, "Call Ashley."

And Bob left the kitchen to get my niece, who, like every teen, was holed up in her bedroom. Back in my day, my bedroom was where Mother would send me for punishment, a sparse little chamber overseen by Madonna and New Kids on the Block posters, with no TV and no phone. Today a girl being sent to her room meant banishment to a barren landscape populated only by computers, flat-screen TVs, and iPods.

The horror.

Ashley arrived in short order. Tall, slender, brunette, and as beautiful as her mother (which was saying something), my niece could easily have earned my resentment for the comfortable, coddled, privileged, lucky, painless ride she'd had in life. But I imagined that having Peggy Sue for a mother had its drawbacks, and since I'd come back home to live, Ash and I had connected more and more, like sisters. Or like I would imagine sisters connect, when one of them isn't Peggy Sue.

Soon chair legs were screeching on the tiled floor as everyone took their proper place at the table that separated the kitchen area from the great room with its overstuffed leather furniture, huge flat-screen TV (turned off), and fireplace (roaring). Over the fireplace hung a huge portrait of the family, Photoshopped into sheer perfection.

Utensils clanked, glasses tinkled, and everyone made yummy sounds as they dug into the Caesar salad, garlic bread, gourmet olives, and lasagne.

I said to Peggy Sue, with the stiff awkwardness that I call my own, "Thank you for fixing dinner for us, Sis. It's delicious, and Mother and I really appreciate it."

Peggy Sue waited until she had completely chewed and swallowed (unlike me) before she said, "Chicken cacciatore would have been a healthier choice . . . but you wanted lasagne, so lasagne you got . . . even though it's heavy and fattening."

Wouldn't "thank you" have been sufficient?

The eighteen-year spread between sisters—both in age and social attitude—conspired against us ever being on the same wave length. For as long as I can remember I seemed to be a constant disappointment to my painfully perfect older sister. And my ramshackle self must have been a crushing blow to her.

Is it possible to love someone but not like them?

Ashley filled the strained silence by announcing, "I'm going to see *Rocky Horror Picture Show* on Halloween night with some of my friends?" (She was an up-talker, treating sentences like questions. The first couple of times are endearing, and the final few instances are guaranteed to induce teeth grinding.)

Mouths stopped midchew at this unusual opening dinner-table gambit.

Peggy Sue slowly set her fork down and looked pointedly at her daughter. "I wish you wouldn't."

Ashley shrugged. "Why? I've never seen it and everybody says it's a hoot?"

"It's not a hoot. It's a disgusting, perverted movie. Encouraging all sorts of deviant behavior."

Sis had said much the same thing about *Brokeback Mountain*.

Ashley was raising one well-shaped eyebrow. "Really? Have *you* ever seen *Rocky Horror*, Mother?"

"No, and I don't have to," Peggy Sue said with measured distaste, "to know it's . . . inappropriate."

"How psychic of you."

"I'm not psychic—I am merely . . . attuned to the youth culture."

I was staying out of it. It wasn't my place to mention that *Rocky Horror* hadn't been "youth culture" since the eighties.

Ashley must have picked up on something in my silence, because she was gazing across the table at me with a mischievous twinkle. "How about you, Aunt Brandy?"

"Huh?" Yes, I'm always ready with a sharp and witty comeback.

"Have *you* seen it?" Ash found no greater joy in life than to pit me against my uptight sister.

Which put me in a tight spot.

I owed Sis a great deal. Starting with my childhood and her taking care of a little dirty-faced Brandy *and* a then not-so-stable Mother . . . all the way to the favor she was doing us, not just feeding us a decent meal but dog-sitting Sushi while Mother and I went antique hunting.

I was pretending to study my Caesar salad. "Well, what do you know!" I pointed at the lettuce. "Am I crazy, or does that look just like Jesus? You can see his eyes, and his beard. . . ."

Mother was leaning for a look, while Peggy Sue's expression turned horror-struck and Bob tried to disguise his amusement.

"We really should save it," I said. "This is way better than the pope in a pizza, or that Virgin Mary grilled cheese sandwich that sold on eBay for—"

"*Well,* Aunt Brandy?" Ashley pressed with impish glee. "*Have* you seen *Rocky Horror*?"

I sighed, shrugged, fessed up with a nod, adding, "Frankly, I'm surprised to find anyone who *hasn't.*"

The first time for me was with my BFF, Tina (you'll meet her later); we'd been out one night in our college days, celebrating a test we both squeaked through, rewarding ourselves by imbibing a bottle of champagne on empty stomachs, and both tipsily thought the crowd lined up at a theater was there to see the latest Sylvester Stallone *Rocky* picture (although the people waiting were dressed kinda funny—but it *was* a college town, after all).

The picture hadn't been about Rocky at all, but our experience sure was. . . .

Two hours later, Tina and I stumbled out of the theater sopping wet, with hot dog pieces in our hair and soggy toast down our blouses. The really weird thing was that for quite some time I tried to make it work as a Rocky movie—I thought sure Rocky was going to box that guy in the gold shorts for the heavyweight championship.

Later we saw it, fairly sober, three or four more times; but never had as much fun.

Mother piped up: "Well, *I* have seen the flick. Quite entertaining, really. Catchy tunes! Some girls and I used to go to the midnight show, in Davenport—we each had our own roles!" She bolted to her feet, pushed back her chair, and ("put your hands on your hips!") began to dance in place while singing, "Let's Do the Time Warp Again!"

To make Mother stop, Peggy Sue threw her hands up and caved: "All right, all right—you can go!"

Ashley smiled. She glanced at me and I glanced at her, and my smile said, *Nicely played.*

Mother sat down, imparting these words of wisdom to her granddaughter, "Do take a newspaper to cover your head, dear . . . or sit in the last row."

No one could put an end to a discussion like Mother. After the dishes were cleared (by me) and washed (by the dishwasher), I gave Peggy Sue a quick refresher course on how much dog food and insulin Sushi needed while Mother and I were away.

Then I kissed Soosh on her mouth (I know, yuck) and bade them all good-bye, never once considering that any of these humans I was related to might deserve a smooch.

While Mother made one last trip to "the little girls' room" (as she insisted on calling it), Sis corralled me in the entryway.

"You *will* use good judgment on what you buy." It wasn't a question.

"Of course," I said.

She raised a forefinger and somehow managed not to waggle it. "Remember, Mother is on a fixed income, and if these antiques don't sell . . ."

"I realize all that."

Peggy Sue frowned. "You don't have to be defensive."

"I'm not." I wasn't.

"Need I mention the fake Grandma Moses painting you once bought?"

Okay, now I was.

"I got my money back," I sputtered. "Anyway, Peggy Sue, this isn't about money."

"Isn't it?"

"No, and anyway I have four thousand dollars, thanks to that incredibly rare Indian head penny I found."

My ex-husband had paid off the monthly alimony a while back in pennies, trying to get my goat; Mother and I had gone through every one of them (my father having been a coin collector), and henceforth I've encouraged my ex to continue payment in pennies, though so far it's only been that once.

"If it's not about money . . ."

"Peggy, this is about keeping Mother occupied in a productive way. She's reeling from this blow Bernice dealt her."

"Ah. The theater director position."

"Yes. Idle hands are the devil's playground."

"I see." Nothing condescending; she really did seem to. "Thanks for looking after her."

"Hey, she's my mother, isn't she?"

Mother appeared, tugging at her girdle. "Shall we go, Brandy, dear? Good-bye, everyone! Farewell!"

Peggy Sue, Bob, and Ash all echoed Mother—well, not the "farewell," just the "good-bye"—and then we were out the door and into the cool night and off to the Emerald City, leaving our blind Toto behind.

The federal auction Mother and I were attending the next morning was being held in Rockford, Illinois—not exactly Oz, but not bad—a three-hour drive by interstate. Mother had brought along a Nero Wolfe book on CD that was about the right length for us to find out who the murderer was before we got back home. (If the story was too long, she'd make me drive around until it was finished, so I hoped she calculated correctly.)

Mother popped the first CD in, settled back with a self-satisfied sigh, and said, "I love that man." (Nero, Archie, or Rex? I didn't ask.) Then she promptly fell asleep.

I drove through the night, stewing about a number of things, mostly my strained relationship with Peggy Sue, my stalled relationship with Officer Brian Lawson, and my shattered relationship with Jake. Therefore I paid only intermittent attention to the CD.

About an hour into the trip, Mother woke up with a snort. "What happened?" she asked.

"What do you think happened? You fell asleep."

"No . . . No! I mean, what happened in the story, dear? Did Nero Wolfe leave his house?"

Since I hadn't been listening, I made a bunch of stuff up, based on eleven or twelve other Nero Wolfes we've listened to.

Mother frowned and murmured, "Not Stout's best," and went back to sleep.

Sorry, Rex.

At about eleven that night we finally pulled into the Holiday Inn on the outskirts of Rockford. After some fancy maneuvering in the technically full parking lot, I invented a spot (or two) for our U-Haul-bearing vehicle, and then Mother and I checked in.

The check-in was uneventful, Mother being too tired to indulge in theatrics. Our room was spacious with two beds, and within minutes we had stripped down to our skivvies (me scanty pink lace; Mother long pink thermal) and dove under our respective covers.

Unfortunately, Mother—even after all of her car napping—fell asleep faster than I did, and began to snore so loudly the windowpanes rattled. I wish that were a joke.

Whenever we were on the road together, I considered it a race as to who got to sleep first. If I didn't beat Mother to the punch, the snorefest would make slumber a challenge for me, no matter how bushed I was.

And I would just like to know . . . how can a person still hear with a thick feather pillow clamped against one ear, and the other ear pressed against a six-inch mattress?

So I got up a couple of times and poked Mother with my finger, but she only rolled over and snored with renewed vigor and as much personality as she brought to her stage performances.

About two in the morning, deciding against murder or suicide or murder/suicide, I grabbed my covers and stomped into the bathroom. In the tub I made myself a bed, pulled the shower curtain closed, snuggled in, and finally, finally, *finally* fell asleep.

I'm not exactly sure what happened next, but apparently Mother came in to use the toilet and I must have stirred and made a noise, because she shrieked—which startled me!—and I jumped up, grabbed hold of the shower curtain, which fell down over me, and then Mother began beating my head with a hairbrush while screaming, "Rape! Rape!"

Actually the second one was sort of a question.

I tried to fend her off, hollering over her shrieks and the shrieking *Psycho* strings in my brain, "It's *me* . . . it's *me*!"

But my words must have been muffled by the curtain because Mother ran gracelessly out of the bathroom, waving her arms in *Oh, Lordy, Miss Scarlet* fashion.

Stunned, I heard the front door open and click shut. I tumbled out of the tub, got onto my bare feet, and ran after Mother, catching her halfway down the hallway by reaching out and grasping the tail of her thermal top like a relay baton, stopping her short.

She whirled, relieved it was me. "Brandy! Thank God you're all right! There was a big, hairy man in our bathroom!"

"That was *me*, Mother, in the tub."

And please, if you believe anything I've told you, believe this: I am neither big nor particularly hairy. And certainly not a man.

Her wild expression turned quizzical. "Well, my goodness . . . whatever were you doing in there, pretending to be a rapist?"

"I was not pretending to . . . I was trying to escape your big, hairy *snoring!*"

The quizzical expression turned dismissive. "Don't be silly, child . . . you must have been dreaming. You know very well that I don't snore."

I put my hands on my hips. "Are *you* kidding me? You sound like a pig rooting out—ohmigod! We're locked out of our room!"

We stood in the cold hallway gaping at each other.

"*Will you shut up out there!*" requested a loud if muffled voice from a nearby door.

This—or anyway the first word or so of it—scared us into leaping into each other's arms. If only somebody'd been there with a video camera, we'd have made it onto one of those funniest video shows.

We stepped apart, and Mother said, "You must go down to the front desk and tell them what happened."

"*Me?*"

She frowned but her eyes were big—somehow they seemed bigger without the magnifying glasses. "This is *your* doing, Brandy . . . and besides, you look better in your scanties than I."

I had a bit of trouble picturing Mother in my "scanties." I protested, "But you've got more coverage!"

"*Shut* up *out there!*" another door said.

This called for a time-out, and drew our attention to the end of the hallway where an elevator began to groan.

I groaned, too, and then Mother and I goggled at each other with the shared thought: *Where are we going to hide?*

A bell dinged.

Too late.

The elevator door slid open and a security guard stepped out.

Mustached, beefy, wearing more clothes than us, the man approached, his stern expression turning amused as he neared us. Mother and I kept our ground, and what little dignity we had left. I held my hands, fig-leaf style, as if naked, not nearly naked. . . .

"Young man," Mother said in her most grandiose theatrical voice, "we seem to be locked out of our room."

"Yes, I know," the guard responded. "Several guests called about the racket."

As he fished out a pass card from a pocket, Mother asked ridiculously, "Do you need to see some kind of identification?"

An eyebrow raised on the guard as he looked us over, in a manner that might have been inappropriate if Mother hadn't just suggested we might be carrying ID in our drawers.

Then the guard smiled. "That won't be necessary . . . I noticed you both when you checked in."

Mother preened. Touched the side of her face. "Why, thank you."

He didn't say "you're welcome," too busy sneaking peeks at the younger idiot in the pink scanties.

Safely back in our room, Mother remarked cheerfully, "Well, wasn't *he* nice?"

"Yeah . . . he's probably used to dealing with all kinds of drunks and dopers in the middle of the night."

"Well, we must have been a pleasant surprise, then!"

Rolling my eyes, I retrieved my covers from the bathroom and quickly jumped into bed hoping to beat Mother back to sleep.

For once, I won the race.

When the alarm clock shrilled at 7:00 AM, I about had a heart attack. Catching my breath, I shut it off and looked over toward Mother, who wasn't in her bed.

Nor was she in the bathroom.

I was beginning to worry, when the door to our room opened and Mother, dressed again in the emerald outfit (it's her favorite) entered, carrying a tray with coffee, fruit, and muffins.

I said, reaching for the steaming java, "How nice!"

"Yes, and it was free!"

"Really? Complimentary breakfast came with the room?"

"No," Mother replied munching a muffin. "Not exactly. There's a convention of morticians downstairs having a buffet, and I just got in line and pretended to be one of them. Made use of my improvisational skills, blending in."

I nodded, making a mental note to send the Morticians of America—if there was such a thing—a donation. I mean, flowers would be redundant.

After hurriedly checking out, we followed the directions Chief Cassato had provided to an old armory on the south side of the city where the federal auction was being held.

A good football field long, the massive brick and mortar structure gave no indication of its military past (or, for that matter, present) other than a few cement barricades around the front entrance. An orange-jacketed guy directing incoming traffic stopped us and we paid him five dollars for the privilege of parking a quarter of a mile away from the building. Mother and I should have rolled out of bed a lot earlier.

We got hit up again entering the building—ten bucks!—and then once more when we signed up for our white-numbered bidding card.

Despite my Prozac, I was getting annoyed, mentally calculating how much money this venture had cost us so far, what with hotel and gas, when I glanced over at Mother, who was taking in the aisles and aisles of merchandise with big, wide kid-in-a-candy-store eyes.

Mother started to move away from me and I yanked her back by the sleeve of her jacket.

"And where do you think you're going, young lady?" I asked sweetly.

She looked at me with feigned concern. "Have you been taking your medication, dear?"

"Yes . . . have *you*?"

"Of course! But we must shake a tail feather if we're going to see everything before the auction begins. . . ."

I put a hand on her shoulder. "I realize that, Mother, but we also need to stick together. We'd never find each other in this crowd if we got separated—understand?"

"You are not dealing with a child!"

"Mother . . . we need to be on the same team. Lots of competition . . ."

She drew in a breath and nodded firmly and I held out my hand, which she took, and together we began the hunt for the wonderful treasures that would make us a fortune and transform our lives.

However, as we jostled by each exhibited lot, I soon began to realize that Mother and I might just be in over our heads . . . way over.

This was no ordinary auction.

The items for sale, in fact, were quite extraordinary: Cadillacs and Hummers, exquisite artwork by names you would recognize, beautiful homes (displayed by photos), and even a helicopter!

Nor was an ordinary crowd in attendance. The women were well dressed, the men nattily attired. The younger participants appeared to be corporate minions, dispatched to do a boss's bidding, some with a cell phone at either ear.

I'd been thinking flea market and found myself in the middle of a James Bond movie.

But Mother didn't seem fazed by either the well-heeled people around us or the high-ticketed items up for sale. And as we walked along she began to announce loudly her best guess as to how each item got confiscated . . . that is to say, under what circumstance they were pinched by the feds.

"Bank heist." Black Caddie. "Securities fraud." Picasso painting. "Drug deal." Miami condo.

I tried to shush her. Guess how much good *that* did.

Among the unattainable (by us, anyway) were little pockets of antiques and collectibles that could possibly be within our reach, and we would pause and examine them, making notes in our booklet, and agreeing upon a ceiling price for each—as if Mother would keep her word. . . .

As auction time approached (noon) the excitement and tension in the air intensified. While a few undecided bidders dashed up and down the aisles for a final look, everyone else had already left for the auction arena, which was located in one far corner.

Even though Mother had gone ahead to get us seats, I should have known better. The lucky hundreds who had their butts in chairs must have camped out all night, or had some insider's advance ticket.

As I approached the cordoned-off area, I spotted Mother standing along the periphery with a mass of others; judging by Mother's pained expression, the corns on her feet were killing her. I squeezed through the crowd to be next to Mother, who then did a despicable thing.

To an older, silver-haired gent seated next to where we were standing, Mother leaned over and whispered, "Sir, I believe something fell out of your pocket."

She pointed helpfully to a wadded-up bill a few feet away in the aisle.

The old gent fell for Mother's cheap dodge, scrambled off his seat, his eyes on the green, and Mother slid into his place.

All is fair in love and war . . . and nabbing a seat at an auction. To the gentleman's credit, he didn't call Mother on her trickery. Instead, he took her standing-room-only place beside me, a tiny bemused smile on his face, a now-unfolded one-dollar bill in his hand. He was a candy bar or maybe a soft drink to the good, and shy of one chair. . . .

I looked away, pretending not to know Mother. She could have at least given the old boy a five-spot!

After instructions by the auctioneer—a tall, thin, black-suited Ichabod Crane type—the auction was off and running.

The atmosphere was fast, tense, and a little scary. I watched in amazement at the frantic pace and pitch at which the first item—a silver current-model Mercedes—was sold. This must have been what it felt like on the floor of the New York Stock Exchange the day Enron tumbled. I could barely keep up with the bidding, my own card limp in my hand.

When the woman seated directly in front of Mother won the car, and stood and edged for the aisle, I sprang into action, beating a paunchy middle-aged man for her vacated seat in a round of musical chairs.

Settled in, I checked my booklet. Next on the docket was an item Mother and I wanted: an old brass steamer trunk with wood trim and leather straps.

By way of reminder, Mother slapped me on the back of my head with her booklet, making me regret taking the seat in front of her.

"I'm *on* it!" I snarled over my shoulder.

As Ichabod opened his mouth to begin the bidding, Mother's voice carried over the crowd. "*Oh my, I do hope they got the bloodstains out. . . .*"

Funny how I won the bid with very little competition—paying less than budgeted.

A good half hour passed before the next item Mother and I coveted came on the block. The rolltop desk was small enough not to be cumbersome, but large enough to have all the wonderful cubbyholes and drawers that make such a piece special.

Again, seconds before the bidding began, Mother gave another pronouncement. "And to think that very desk was used to write the ransom note . . . that poor dead child. . . ."

I was afraid that might attract some sick collector, but maybe Mother knew best . . .

. . . although the auctioneer didn't seem to think so, addressing her with a frown. "Madam, you're going to have to keep *quiet*, or be escorted out."

Mother shot back, "*I have Turrets syndrome! Shit! I can't help it! Doody!*"

For a moment the auctioneer was at a loss for words. Then he managed, "Well . . . *try.*"

And the bidding began.

I had competition this time, but I hung in, flashing my card, and one by one the opposition fell . . . except for a man seated at the end of my row.

He was about thirty, dressed in an expensive black suit and blue shirt, open at the collar, and had dark pomaded hair, piercing eyes, and a two-day stubble, whether facial fashion statement or just a guy needing a shave, I couldn't say. With each upping of the ante, we eyed each other, until he bidded beyond my limit, and I fell unhappily silent.

Mother poked me in my back with a stiff finger, though the comment she gave was anything but confidential: "Keep going, dear . . . we simply *must* get Grandmother's desk back! Crapdoodle!"

As people around us snickered—the auctioneer again frowning at Mother—my competition suddenly leaned forward in his seat, looked my way, and seemed to signal me with a nod. I flashed my card, topped his current bid by one dollar, and he graciously fell silent.

Grandmother's heirloom rolltop desk where the ransom note was written (that poor child) was ours!

As the long afternoon wore on (Mother's Turret's syndrome with its very limited range of obscenities miraculously cured) (or anyway in remission), we continued to score, while well-heeled bidders went after bigger fish, letting the minnows go.

By five o'clock we had purchased: a Moser cranberry glass dresser set; a lyre banjo clock (even though a reproduction c. 1930, it was lovely); an amber-faceted vase (because Mother likes anything amber); some old tinware, including a black-and-yellow-decorated tea caddy; a pair of round Stickley lamp tables (I might talk Mother into keeping those); a box containing various metal and glass candlesticks (Mother likes to burn candles); and (my favorite) a Weller pottery vase depicting an Indian's face.

Since we had depleted our cash, I turned around to Mother and mouthed, "Let's go," even though I was mildly curious to see who would bid on the frozen bull semen coming up next.

We were two happy girls who settled our bill (under budget, but barely) and happier yet to discover that all of our treasures fit snugly into the trailer for the trip home.

As I pulled slowly out of the armory parking lot Mother said, "You have an admirer."

I glanced at her curiously. "Who?"

"That man who bid against you for the desk."

I snorted, and asked, "Whatever made you think he could possibly be interested in me?"

"Because I saw him write down our license plate number."

I knitted my brow, not knowing what to make of that. Seemed like a funny—no, disturbing—way for an "admirer" to get information on me.

But I dismissed it, my mind moving on to one last treasure I had yet to pick up that night . . . not an antique, but something of relatively recent vintage and yet very, very precious to me.

My son, Jake.

*A Trash 'n' Treasures Tip*

As a dealer, buy antiques and collectibles that you wouldn't mind having in your own home . . . because if they don't sell in your shop, they will be.

# Chapter Four

## Close But No Cigar Store Indian

Hauling our trailer full of treasures, Mother and I pulled into the I-80 rest stop at about seven in the evening, right on schedule.

Before we left the auction in Rockford, I had celled Roger in Chicago, and we timed it for the trade-off of Jake, both of us agreeing to meet halfway (which is the best one can hope for with an ex).

Jake's school is year-round, which I'm totally against. Granted, the students get a few weeks' vacation every couple of months (like now), but it's just not the same as having that long stretch of summer through which to recharge your batteries, get good and bored so you don't mind going back to school, and, in the case of one girl I knew, reinvent yourself.

Kids called her Fat Freda (not me!) (okay, maybe once). Cruel as such name-calling is, Freda had a certain amount of bad karma due her, because she had developed (likely as a defense mechanism) a withering mastery of sarcasm. Put-downs apparently weren't enough, because during the three summer-vacation months between our junior and senior year, Freda dropped fifty pounds, got a nose job, had her teeth capped, cleared up her zits, and dyed her mousey brown hair a surfer-girl blonde. The first day back at school in the fall, everybody was like, "Hey, who's the new babe from California?"

Of course, when the kids found out it was Freda, they treated her terrible again—because despite the otherwise radical transformation, she forgot to change her sarcastic personality—but she did have a couple of nice days on top, just the same. Plus the attention of some male admirers who didn't rate personality all that high on their female scorecards.

The wind was spitting raindrops into my face as I got out of the car, leaving Mother behind. I could see Roger and Jake seated inside the modern glass-and-concrete bathroom oasis, which also included a small vending-machine food court. They were alone as I entered, bringing leaves swirling in with me.

Roger stood as I approached.

"Brandy," he said coolly, with the kind of nod you reserve for the barest of acquaintances.

Tall and slender, face tanned, brown hair touched with gray on the temples, Roger—ten years older than me—was wearing black dress slacks, a gray sweater topped by a black jacket with Ralph Lauren logo. His familiar Polo cologne wafted toward me.

He looked like hell—the lines in his face deep, the loss in his eyes palpable, the . . . oh, hell.

He looked good. Great.

I, on the other hand, didn't. Tired, pale, most of my makeup worn off, clothes wrinkled from the long day of auction adventure and behind-the-wheel road warrioring . . . I wondered if my disinclination to even run a comb through my hair had been subconsciously on purpose.

I mean, I can look pretty good when I feel like going to the trouble. And there'd been other rest stops where I could have stopped, spruced up, changed clothes. Right now Roger might have walked out of a *GQ* spread. I might have been the trucker who delivered *GQ* to a supermarket newsstand.

Was I—the dump-*er*—trying to send a weirdly self-serving message? Like, "See, you're better off without me." While he—the dump-*ee*—seemed to be saying, "Just look at what you're missing."

"Hello, Roger," I said, and gave him just enough of a smile to maintain the thin veneer of former-spousal civility.

Then I gazed at my son, who had remained seated, having just finished up a Kit Kat bar. I worked not to seem too damn puppy-dog eager in my smile and in the tone of my voice as I said, "Hiya, Jake."

Our son had on a Chicago Bulls sweatshirt and cargo pants that had more pockets than a closetful of regular slacks.

"'Lo." The boy's eyes didn't meet mine.

Jake, at age ten, had changed very little since I'd seen him six months ago, and for that I was glad. Having been a stay-at-home mother, I'd witnessed every stage of his existence . . . every new tooth, every mole, every inch of growth . . . and it hurt, no longer being a part of that, an emotional ache that even Prozac couldn't dull.

Our son was a handsome kid, a true collaboration of us both: Roger's thick brown hair, straight nose, cleft chin . . . but my blue eyes, often smirky mouth, and (I have to admit) ornery disposition.

Roger set a hand on Jake's shoulder and asked, "Got everything, son?"

"Yup."

I looked at the two huge duffel bags on the floor, which seemed a lot for a week's stay—had Jake belatedly inherited his mother's jones for clothes? Taking a closer look, I noticed sharp angles poking at the canvas that indicated objects within that were not apparel.

Roger had always been able to read me easily, and now was no exception. "Jake brought a few things from home to keep busy."

"Good. Good idea." After all, there wouldn't be anything to do down in Dogpatch, where the young 'un's mammy lived.

Soon we were outside, the wind whipping our hair and clothing, as Roger stashed Jake's bags in the trunk of my Buick. Then he put his hands on Jake's shoulders and gave him a long, hard look and a slow, knowing smile. "You know what we talked about."

Jake met his dad's eyes but his voice had about as much enthusiasm as a customer service clerk at Best Buy. "Yeah."

"You be good."

"I will."

Then Roger gave his son a hug. "Need anything, just text me on your BlackBerry."

Jake had a BlackBerry? How busy could a ten-year-old's schedule be? My day planner at his age would have been breakfast, school, lunch, school, supper, TV, bed. Or during the summer: breakfast, no school, lunch, no school, supper, TV, bed.

I held the rear car door open and Jake climbed into the back. I shut him in and stood there awkwardly wondering what else I should say to my ex.

Roger saved me the trouble, by asking with genuine concern (probably for Jake), "You *will* drive carefully? You look terrible."

"Thank you."

"No, I mean . . . Brandy, you look tired. Is Vivian up to driving?"

"She'd love to, except for the part where she doesn't have a driver's license anymore. You'd really rather entrust Jake to my mother than to me?"

"I wasn't looking for a fight. I'm just worried about you, that's all."

Worried about Jake, he meant. Which wasn't a bad thing. But I wished my ex weren't viewing me like a recruiting officer preparing to ship his son off to war.

"Roge, I'm not looking for a fight, either."

"I know."

"Really, I'm fine . . . just a . . . a long day." I made a stab at conversation. "Mother and I got some great antiques for our booth . . . at the federal auction?"

But Roger had quit listening, his eyes moving to Mother behind the car window. Until that moment, he had not acknowledged her presence, other than mentioning her to me as a potential preferred driver; now he gave his former mother-in-law a halfhearted wave, and Mother waved back, a little too animated.

Roger wasn't trying hard enough, and Mother was trying way too hard. There was no love lost between them. Here, in a nutshell, is the story of their relationship during our marriage: Mother thought Roger encased me in a shell, and Roger thought Mother was a nut.

Which just goes to show how two opposing factions can both be right.

I crawled in behind the wheel, then slowly drove out the exit ramp, Roger following in his BMW. After a few miles another exit appeared, and as my ex veered off to make his turnaround back to Chicago, I gave a sigh of relief. Having Roger back in my life for ten minutes had been much, much too long.

While I drove, Mother returned to the Rex Stout CD, now and then exclaiming, "*He* did it!" or "*She* did it!" Oblivious (I almost said "cheerfully oblivious," but scratch *that*), Jake played his lighted-up Game Boy with the music up not loud exactly, but maintaining a frantic, increasingly irritating presence. I could have asked him to use earphones, but I didn't want to start nagging right out of the gate.

As the sprinkles built to a downpour, I switched on the wipers, which screeched on the windshield like pterodactyls seeking prehistoric worms. Suddenly I was aware of a splitting headache, and realized that I'd stupidly left my migraine medication at home, even though this weekend had all the elements of a three-day marathon headthrobber: bad food, poor sleep, an exhausting day, and an emotional family reunion.

I asked nicely, "Say, Jake, hon . . ."

No response.

". . . would you mind turning that down a little?"

No response.

Mother said, "Darling . . . Grandma is trying to hear who the murderer is."

"Sure, Grandma."

The volume decreased.

So that's how it was going to be.

About midnight, we finally reached Serenity, and I was fighting serious nausea. Both Mother and Jake were asleep, the Rex Stout story concluded, murderer nabbed, video game won.

I wheeled into our drive, shut off the engine, threw open the car door, fell to my knees as if praying to Mecca, and retched instead. And retched some more. When I finished up with a flourish of a little choking sob, Mother and Jake were standing over me.

"So she's still doing that, huh?" Jake asked sleepily. He might have been asking if Sushi was still wetting on the carpet.

Mother answered, "I'm afraid so, dear. Not as often as in the past, because the medication is better. But on a day like this? Well . . . I only hope you don't inherit your mother's migraines. . . . Now be a good boy and help Grandma in with our bags."

They did so, while it was all I could do to stumble inside, fumble down my meds, fall into bed, and hope sleep came before my stomach rejected the pill.

Delirious, I dreamed about going into a shoe store where the UGGs were on sale 75 percent off, but I couldn't find a single pair in my size. Not a single pair. *Not a single pair!*

Talk about a nightmare!

Finally, thankfully, something or someone shook me awake. A hand on my shoulder . . . that's what it was . . . a hand. . . .

I opened my eyes and stared up into a wonderful mirage: the sweet if sullen oval of my son's face, my son who didn't live with me anymore . . .

Then the mirage said, "Grandma's making Yummy Eggs," and the face disappeared.

I closed my eyes again and imposed a new method I'd read about recently, designed to prevent constant nightmares. I mentally returned to the dream and changed the outcome: This time I found lots of boots in my size, and even cheaper.

So there!

I sat up slowly, searching for signs of the migraine, which seemed to be gone, or at least beaten back into a corner of the cave I call my mind.

Mother knew very well that her trademark Yummy Eggs (so named, many moons ago, by a sick little Brandy) were the only thing I could stand to eat coming out of a bad headache.

*Yummy Eggs*

*For a single serving follow these directions: Soft-boil one egg in simmering water. Toast one slice of bread. Scoop the egg out of its shell into a cereal bowl, then salt and pepper and dot with butter. Tear the toast into small pieces, add to the eggs, and mix.*

That's the first and last page of *Brandy Borne's Coming Out of a Migraine Cookbook*, not published by Duncan Hines.

I sat by myself in the dining room, listening to the familiar sounds out in the parlor of Jake—who had already had his breakfast—playing with Sushi, who I was pretty sure my son had missed a hell of a lot more than his mother.

Suddenly Soosh let out a *yipe!*

I jumped up and ran into the adjoining room only to find Jake holding a black and silver gun, and Sushi on her side, her brown and white fur turned . . .

. . . purple?

"What have you *done*?" I yelled, rushing to the whimpering dog's aid.

My son looked genuinely distressed and was bending down himself by the fallen beast. "I . . . I didn't mean to. . . ." Jake swallowed. "It just sort of, you know, *happened*. . . ."

I pointed to the gun in Jake's hand. "Just what the hell is *that*? You got a license for that thing?"

"It's just a stupid, you know, paint gun and stuff. . . ."

The thing really did look like a real pistol, not a toy. It would come in handy if Jake ever wanted to rob a convenience store.

And it was then that I said what every mother, even the divorced ones (maybe especially the divorced ones), inevitably say: "Wait till your father hears about this."

"Dad . . . Dad *bought* it for me."

"Figures," I muttered, and continued to examine Soosh, who seemed to be recovering from the sting of the paint pellet. In fact, she was milking the attention shamelessly; next to Mother, Soosh was the biggest ham in the house.

Jake scratched the dog's neck affectionately. "Is she all right?"

"I think so. . . ."

Gently, I got Sushi up on her feet; she was a gooey mess, the purple paint transferring to my hands.

"Give me that thing," I said to Jake.

"I won't do that again. I won't use it in the house, or shoot at any living thing and stuff."

Through my teeth, I said, "Give it here."

He swallowed and handed me the paint gun, but asked, "What about the paint grenade? Can I keep that?"

My eyebrows shot up.

"I *promise* to take it outside."

"Three guesses and the first two don't count."

He sighed. "Oh-kaay . . . I'll *get* it. . . ."

When Jake came back from his bedroom, I stashed the realistic-looking grenade and the realistic-looking gun on the top shelf of the closet.

"For your penance, Jake," I said, hand on hips, "you'll give Sushi a bath—I assume that paint washes off. . . ."

"Yeah. Sure it does. You don't need turpentine or anything."

"Good. Then I want you to help Grandma and me set up our booth this morning." Might as well get everything I could out of this little episode.

"*What* booth?"

"*The* booth, our stall, at the antiques mall. We have a U-Haul to unload and lots of things to arrange."

Jake groaned. "Come on, Mom. I'll give Sushi a bath and stuff, but do I have to go down to that antique shop—"

"'Antiques shop,'" I corrected. "It's not an *old* shop . . . it's a shop with old things in it."

He smirked. "Yeah, right. I bet it is *too* an old shop . . . an old shop with old boring things and dust in the air and stuff that'll make me sneeze."

I glared at him.

He glared at me.

I tried softening my voice. "I'm not punishing you. I'm asking you for help."

"Well . . ."

"We could really use your muscles. Grandma shouldn't lift anything heavy, and I can't do it by myself."

Jake shrugged with his eyes. "Well, okay . . . but it'll cost ya."

"What do you mean by that?"

"I mean, when I do chores for Dad, he gives me something."

Awfully early for him to be playing the Dad card. . . .

"Sure," I said. "You can have a kiss on the cheek or a pat on the head. Your choice."

"I was thinking more . . . a Game Boy game."

"Whoa . . . don't those cost thirty bucks?"

"One I want is forty."

"I'm not made of money like your father."

He shrugged. "Okay. I do know one I want that's only thirty."

Damn that husband of mine. Ex-husband.

I said, "There's a pawnshop with a ton of games just up the street from the antiques mall. Current games and older ones, too."

He was interested. "Old-school stuff? I like old-school stuff."

"That's where that vintage Super Nintendo I bought you for Christmas came from."

His eyes lighted up. "Really? That was a cool gift, Mom."

"You can have a fifteen-dollar game at the pawnshop," I said, and extended my hand.

"Done," he said, and shook it.

"The dog shampoo is under the kitchen sink," I said. "And don't make the water too hot."

While Jake took Sushi into the kitchen—holding her out at arm's length to keep from getting paint on himself—I went off to find Mother, finally locating her outside in the old garage.

The stand-alone structure hadn't been destroyed with the original house, and was mostly used for storing unused items, which included Mother's ancient pea-green Audi. Mother had lost her driver's license for what she referred to as a "silly infraction," which was driving the car through a cornfield on the way to a play one night, hitting a combine, but sparing the cows.

This was, as you may have guessed, shortly before her doctor "readjusted" her medication.

At the moment, Mother was struggling with a tarp at the back of the garage.

"What are you up to?" I asked, startling her and inducing a take worthy of W.C. Fields.

Mother recovered, then said, "I'm retrieving this wonderful antique. . . ."

And she lifted the cover.

I stared at a five-foot- tall statue of an Indian chief in full regalia—feathered headdress, decorative vest, loincloth, and moccasins—with one hand raised in the air in a manner that was usually accompanied, in ancient cowboy movies and on *F Troop*, with "How?"

"What are you going to do with *that*?" I asked, hoping the cigar store Indian wasn't taking up permanent residence on the front lawn as an unusual piece of yard art.

Speaking of which, is there a direct correlation between the age of home owners and the amount of tacky yard art (miniature windmills, fake deer, country geese, gnomes, etc.) found on their lawns?

"Why, dear girl," Mother responded, "I'm going to *sell* the statue, of course . . . in our booth. Don't you know a valuable artifact when you see one?"

Big sigh of relief. "I never saw that before. Where on earth did you get it?"

Mother shrugged. "From a former friend."

"Former friend . . . you don't mean Bernice?"

"I do indeed mean She Who Must Not Be Named. When She Who Must Not Be Named first moved here, She Who Must Not Be Named brought the Indian with her. . . ."

"Look, She Who Must Be Maimed, call her Bernice or I will stick that Indian somewhere and I don't mean in our booth!"

"No need for dramatics, dear. My former

friend, her condo was too small to properly display it—a precious item like that needs just the right place, to show it off, you know—and, well, a while back when I commented on the exquisite craftsmanship, my former friend . . . who was my current friend at the time . . . said I could have it."

Why do I ask? Why do I even ask?

Mother added quickly, "That was back when we were speaking, of course."

I got a sudden snapshot mental picture of Mother and Bernice standing on either side of the Indian, grinning at the camera, with the caption below reading IN HAPPIER TIMES.

"What did Bernice charge you?" I asked.

Mother looked surprised. "Why, not a wooden nickel, dear. . . . In the Midwest, when we say you can have something, that means, take it away! At no cost!"

"That would explain a lot." The garage was crammed with "you can have its," as Mother is incapable of turning down anything free.

I asked, "Shouldn't you offer the statue back to Bernice first, before we sell it? Might be a nice gesture. Smoke the peace pipe kinda deal?"

"I *did* offer it to her," Mother said testily. "I made the magnanimous gesture this morning of calling her."

"Good. Very grown-up of you, Mother. And?"

"And *she* said it just so happens she *did* want the Indian back, that by all rights it was hers and I had no business even considering selling it—not at all magnanimous on her part. So I informed her that she could pick it up at our booth."

"Why not have her just pick it up here?"

"Because, dear, I informed her that the Indian would be available to her . . . for *sale*, in our booth!"

"Ah. And she took this, how?"

The cigar store Indian eyed me as if I might be making fun of him.

"Not at all graciously! She called me . . . I won't tell you what she called me."

I sighed. "An Indian giver?"

"Yes! Yes, can you imagine? What a terrible, horrible, repulsive thing to say."

I had to agree; the phrase *was* offensive.

"After all," Mother huffed, "it was *she* who gave it to *me*, so that would make *her* the Indian giver, wouldn't it?"

My migraine was crawling out of its corner, a bear ready to trade hibernation for the nearest victim. . . .

I rubbed my temples and said, "I'm against putting that distasteful thing in our booth."

Mother looked puzzled. "Why ever not?"

"Why ever not? The unofficial historian of the Mascoutin Indians has to even ask me that? Because it's *racist*, that's why!"

Mother frowned, considering as she studied the Indian, who was keeping his opinion to himself. "Dear, may I ask you a question?"

"Why not? This can't get worse, can it?"

"Did cigar stores exist in the olden days?"

"Yeaaaah," I said slowly.

"And were there Indians?"

"Yeaaaaah."

"*Well?*" Her eyes were huge behind the glasses.

"I, uh, don't get your point."

Mother gawked at my sheer stupidity. "*Must* the unofficial historian give her daughter a history lesson?"

"Apparently."

She sighed in exasperation. "The reason the American Indian became associated with tobacco stores was because it was *they* who first introduced smoking the noxious weed to the early settlers. Consequently, a wooden Indian statue was placed outside a frontier establishment to inform a mostly illiterate public that tobacco was sold inside . . . much the way a red-and-white-striped pole denoted a barber shop."

I ventured, "There's a *difference* between using a striped pole and a Native American as an advertisement."

Her eyes flared behind the magnifying lenses. "Brandy! *Yesterday* can *not* be changed just to suit today. This statue is a wonderful, valuable example of American folk art and should be—"

But before I admitted she had a point, I interrupted, "How much is valuable?"

Mother appraised the statue. "Well, taking into consideration that it has been repainted, and the cigar that should be in the hand is missing . . . I'd estimate, oh, four to five hundred dollars."

New tires for the car.

My political correctness vanished in a puff of smoke signal. "Okay, then. I'll load ol' Chief Big Wampum up. . . ."

Under Mother's watchful eye, I hauled the unprotesting Indian to my car and leaned him into the backseat so that there would be room for Jake.

Then Mother and I returned to the house

where Jake was finishing up with Sushi's bath, gently drying her with a towel, her fur restored to its natural white and brown.

Soosh gave Jake a lick on his face, and he kissed her back. Dogs are forgiving (unlike cats, who will *pretend* to forgive you, then later spray your favorite Jimmy Choos with urine).

We were all gathered in the entryway, getting ready to leave for the antiques mall, when Sushi started in with a hissy fit.

"Mom," Jake said, "she wants to go along."

"Well, she can't. We'll be busy, and she'll be in the way. Not to mention being blind in unfamiliar territory."

"Mom," Jake said again, but with conviction, "Sushi thinks she *deserves* to come with us after what happened. . . ."

I looked down at the yapping, jumping dog whose just-washed hair had tripled in volume, making her look like a bouncing beach ball. Had my son just managed to make me feel guilty for what he had done to her? Is every son the hood in motherhood?

"I'll wear Sushi," Mother announced, as if Soosh were a scarf or a hat. "I'm mostly supervising, after all."

Caving in, I retrieved the baby harness from the front closet and, after letting the straps out as far as they'd go, secured it across Mother's ample bosom. Then I put in Sushi, whose tiny smile seemed to say, "I *knew* I'd win."

We had just piled into my car when a powder-blue Cadillac pulled up in front of the house and an older woman climbed out in an array of endless limbs.

Tall, slender, with striking, shoulder-length, gunmetal gray hair (fixed in a forties Joan Crawford pageboy), she wore black tailored slacks and a tan cardigan over a crisp white blouse. It took me a moment to separate this Bernice from the little stooped-shouldered old lady murderess she had played opposite Mother this past summer.

Mother, seated next to me, became immediately agitated and got out of the car. Sensing disaster, I did likewise.

Bernice strode purposefully toward us. Her expression seemed pleasant enough, although it was hard to tell because of the troweled-on makeup (a hazzard of show business, I suppose).

"Thank goodness I caught you before you left," Bernice said, smiling at Mother. "I want to apologize, Vivian, for my absolute *rudeness* on the phone . . . I'm afraid I was having a personal problem at the moment, and I took it out on you, my darling, which was an inexcusable thing to do to a dear, close friend. . . . You *will* forgive me, won't you?"

I was ready to forgive her, just in hopes she'd stop making speeches.

But I wasn't sure about Mother, who only grunted.

Bernice stepped closer to Mother. "Why, what an adorable dog!" she said with a smile displaying lovely, expensive choppers. "I wish I *could* have a pet . . . but they're not allowed by my condominium association."

"What do you want?" Mother asked coldly.

Bernice's smile vanished, hurt showing in her

eyes. "Why, I've come to buy the cigar store Indian. You were right, Vivian . . . I *did* give the statue to you, wholly and completely, and it's yours to do with as you please . . . and if that means selling it, well, then, I'm willing to pay for it."

Her saddened eyes moved past Mother to the backseat of my car where the leaned-back Indian stared stonily straight ahead. This calculated slice of ham put both Mother and Sushi to shame. Like many stage actresses' performances, Bernice's were better viewed from a distance.

Mother said haughtily, "It will be available this afternoon in our booth at the antiques mall!"

I butted in. "Mother! Bernice is here now, and it will save us hauling the stupid thing downtown."

Mother said, "Brandy, I'll thank you to stay out of this. And it's a precious collectible, an American artifact, not a 'stupid' thing."

I tried again, because Bernice's eyes now had tears in them; these seemed genuine, unless she'd doused her orbs with glycerin when I wasn't looking.

"Well," I said, "what difference does it make if she buys it now, or in a few hours at the shop?"

Mother put her hands forcefully on her hips, jostling Sushi. "It matters a great deal! An immediate sale in our booth today will make us look good . . . plus, I'll see to it Bernice will receive a store discount—perhaps as much as fifteen percent—off the purchase price."

"Oh." I shrugged and looked at Bernice.

Bernice, blinking away the tears, said, "What if . . . if someone else buys the statue before I get there? I have a director's meeting at the playhouse this afternoon that could last quite a while. . . ."

Uh-oh. *Not* the right thing to say.

Stiffening at the mention of the lost director's position, Mother sniffed, "Well, then, you'll just have to take that chance. We all have our priorities."

And Mother abruptly left us and got back into the car.

I said softly to Bernice, "Don't worry . . . I'll put a sold sign with your name on it."

Bernice smiled warmly. "Thank you, Brandy. I would so much appreciate that. I'm . . . I'm afraid I've permanently damaged our friendship, your mother and me."

"Give it time. Offer her a nice role, and all will be forgiven."

Bernice nodded and smiled and clasped one of my hands in both of hers. All of it played a little phony to me. Mother, for all her theatricality, was real. Had Bernice forgotten how to climb down offstage and just live?

I pondered this as I watched the woman return to her car and drive away too quickly, before I got back in behind my own steering wheel.

Jake was the first to speak. "Wasn't much of a fight," he said disappointedly from the backseat.

I looked disgustedly at Mother. "Really! Did you *have* to be so mean? She used to be a good friend."

"Key phrase," Mother said acidly, "'used to.'"

"She was crying!"

"Those weren't *real* tears! Those were *acting* tears!"

How could I argue with that? I'd had my own suspicions.

Mother was saying, "Honestly, Brandy, sometimes you can be *so* gullible."

I started the car, making a mental note to call Mother's doctor about her agitated behavior. (We regularly ratted each other out to our respective shrinks.)

But soon we were tooling along picturesque Elm Street, the recent unpleasantness having vaporized in the bright autumn sun. As we drove by, a woman who was out for a morning walk stopped in her tracks and gawked. Couldn't blame her . . . wasn't every day a pedestrian saw *both* a woman with a fur ball growing out of her chest *and* an Indian chief glide by in a car.

I smiled and waved.

You'd think people would be used to us by now.

*A Trash 'n' Treasures Tip*

Most antique dealers have a "buyer beware" attitude about their merchandise . . . so before laying down the cash, examine the item closely. Mother uses a magnifying glass and, if she finds the slightest defect, demands a deep discount.

# Chapter Five

## Teacher's Pet

With Mother, Sushi, Jake, the Indian, and the trailer in tow, I drove down Main Street, five blocks of regentrified Victorian buildings, quaint retro lampposts, redbrick sidewalks, and the occasional ornate wrought-iron bench.

Most store windows displayed colorful fall and Halloween decorations and merchandise . . . with a glimpse of Christmas waiting impatiently in the wings. Our destination was Pearl City Plaza, at the end of Main, where an antiques mall recently opened in a four-story building built in the 1860s that had been originally—according to Mother, who knew Serenity history—a wholesale grocery business for over a hundred years; since then the building had been occupied by a variety of businesses: a disco, a sporting goods store, an exercise club, a photography studio, a Mexican restaurant, and an antiques shop. Proprietors came and went so fast that townspeople were beginning to say the building was cursed.

But all the bad luck the corner spot had endured did not faze the building's current owner, Mrs. Norton, a retired teacher (I had her for Algebra and got a D, which in this case stood for "deserved") who had transformed the venerable structure into an antiques mall with fifty-odd dealers—and I do mean odd.

I pulled my Buick into the alley behind the antiques mall and, remembering Mother's think-opposite instructions, backed the trailer up to a loading dock on the first try. I got out and so did Mother, sporting Sushi on her chest. We left behind a Game Boy–playing Jake in the backseat to guard the goods, and I did my best not to picture the entire trailer being pillaged while my son's focus remained on the *blips* and *bloops* of his game.

Even though the mall wasn't due to open for another hour, the eternally officious Mrs. Norton wanted us there early (would she take attendance and report tardiness—to the janitor, maybe?) to fill out the necessary paperwork and give us pertinent information regarding what could, and what could not, be put in our booth (which Mother, naturally, would ignore) (risking detention).

We found the door next to the loading dock unlocked, and went on in—Mother, me, and Sushi makes three—then up a short flight of cement steps to the first floor.

Mrs. Norton had done some remodeling since the last tenant, the original wood floor now covered with gray industrial carpet, the once cavernously open area transformed into tidy rows of partitioned booths and glassed-in cases filled with furniture, glassware, pottery, kitchen gadgets, tools, toys, trunks, clocks, and every other antique and collectible imaginable. Because of the time of year, especially showcased were Halloween decorations of bygone days, like papier-mâché masks of witches and ghouls and goblins, wildly cartoony designs that were somehow creepier than the more realistic gory ones of today.

But what really caught my attention were the signs posted everywhere:

CHECK ALL BAGS AT THE COUNTER!

CREDIT CARD OR CASH ONLY!

CHILDREN MUST BE SUPERVISED!

SHOPLIFTERS WILL BE PROSECUTED!

BATHROOMS RESERVED FOR CUSTOMERS ONLY!

And the ever-popular YOU BREAK IT, YOU BOUGHT IT! (Remind me to tell you how to wriggle out of that one.) (If the U.S.A. doesn't have to obey the Pottery Barn rule, why should you?)

Clearly, the former teacher in charge had residual issues from her years in the educational trenches . . . and perhaps did not have the right temperament to deal with antiques shoppers, who can be an eccentric, maddening bunch . . . much less the dealers.

Mrs. Norton stood stiffly—*were* we tardy?—by the circular checkout counter in the middle of the large room. In her early sixties, tall and slender, with straight, chin-length gray hair, and a face turned permanently tired from years of yelling at mischievous kids like me, she wore tailored brown slacks, an orange cardigan, and red-framed half-glasses on a silver chain as a necklace.

I hoped Mrs. Norton wouldn't remember the

irresponsible me (well, the even *more* irresponsible me) of years gone by.

No such luck.

"Hello, Vivian," she said to Mother, then looked at me. "Well, Brandy . . . it's been a while since algebra class."

I sighed inwardly—the "well" alone had conveyed Mrs. Norton's wealth of disappointing memories; no new first impression for me.

"Hi, Mrs. Norton," I responded sheepishly, transported back to middle school, somehow managing not to scuff the floor with the toe of a shoe. "I hope you don't mind that we brought Sushi along."

Mrs. Norton's gaze returned to Mother, settling on her enormous bosom; perhaps she had thought Sushi was a blanket Mother was holding or some funky backpack worn on the wrong side. Or maybe she thought Mother's chest really was that hairy.

Then, suddenly, alarm flashed in the former teacher's eyes; it was as if the overhead sprinklers had all gone off. "Oh! I . . . don't . . . I really . . . this might not be . . ."

A low-slung but nonetheless large dog galloped out from behind the circular counter, having caught wind of Sushi, and the creature screeched to a stop at Mother's feet and began to snarl and snap, flicking flecks of canine spittle.

Mother and I jumped back, my fleeting thought that somehow the two of us dying in an antiques mall seemed fitting. Nostrils flaring, Sushi's reaction to this affront was a crescendo of ear-piercing yapping that sent the pit bull fleeing back from whence it came, clawed paws slowed by the industrial carpet.

Mother's eyes behind the thick lenses were so wide they filled the glass. "My *goodness*! What was *that*? The Hound of the Baskervilles?"

"No, dear," Mrs. Norton said, actually smiling—the woman did like a good literary reference, even if she had been a math teacher. "*That* is *my* dog. . . . His name is Brad."

"Brad?" I asked. This seemed an unexpectedly benign name for such a creature.

"Yes, Brad *Pit* Bull. My niece named him after an actor she adores."

I suppose I should have smiled politely or laughed a little, but I was still congratulating myself for not soiling my slacks over the vicious dog that had been inches away not so long ago.

Mother, ever helpful, said to me, "Brad Pitt, darling. Get it?" Then to Mrs. Norton, Mother said, "Brandy isn't hep to all of the new young actors. She didn't really inherit my thespian interests."

I might not have been "hep" to actors like Mother, but I was hip to the dangers of having a beast like Brad on the loose.

Before I could express this sentiment, which most likely was written all over my very pale face, Mrs. Norton explained. "You needn't be worried, girls—Brad's bark is much worse than his bite."

From the sound of Brad's bark, that left lots of room for his bite to be plenty bad.

But the former teacher was saying, "Brad's really a sweet, gentle creature, though I hope you won't advertise that fact! You see, I keep him here at night to discourage break-ins. . . . I just hadn't gotten around to putting him in the back room before you arrived."

So we were early, not tardy. You couldn't win with this teacher.

"Here's an idea," I said, my skin still feeling crawly. "How about a security system? A burglar alarm would give you all the 'teeth' you need."

Mrs. Norton gave me an I-see-you're-still-a-troublemaker look, sniffing, "Nonsense. I told you, Brad is really quite timid. You saw how your little dog frightened him away."

I wasn't convinced. Little dogs yapping often scare off larger ones. That didn't erase the fact that pit bulls can—and do—kill people, and many towns ban them. Having a cutesy movie-star name didn't make Brad's fangs any duller, or take the kill out of killer instinct.

Mother, not wanting to get off on the wrong foot on our first day, suggested, "Perhaps if we were properly introduced, the animal might take to us."

"Yes, you're right, of course," Mrs. Norton said, then called, "Here, Brad! Come here, boy! It's all right, they won't hurt you."

That was true. The only way I could hurt that dog is if I tripped and fell on him, fleeing in terror.

But Brad Pit Bull did not emerge—afraid of paparazzi, maybe.

"Come on, dear! Brad! Oh, *Braa*-ad!"

Jeez, maybe Sushi had traumatized the tender critter, like that poor bulldog Tom and Jerry made such a nervous wreck out of in the cartoons.

Finally, after many long moments, a tentative

Brad reappeared from behind the counter, his expression more pitiful than pit bull, and cautiously approached our little group.

As Mrs. Norton began the ridiculously formal introductions (somehow I managed not to curtsy), Brad—his confidence bolstered—began to pant and loll his tongue and wag his tail.

When he brushed up against my legs, with what seemed to be shy affection, I took a risk and extended a hand for him to sniff. Which, oddly, is exactly what I'd do if the real Brad Pitt brushed up against me. . . .

"Nice doggy," I said, then drew it back, and counted all five fingers, which I was able to do thanks to the able educational skills of math teacher Mrs. Norton.

"There, now," Mrs. Norton said with a patronizing smile known only to teachers (and their best students), "we're all going to be great, good friends." She bent and gave Brad's collar a little tug. "Come along, Brad! Time to go to the back. . . ."

Once Brad Pit Bull was shut away, Mrs. Norton showed us to our booth, which was nicely positioned near the front entrance. Since we'd nabbed one of the last available stalls, this surprised me (I learned later that was because it was booth 13, and no one else wanted the unlucky number).

Leaving Mother and Sushi, I went back to the car and stuck my head in the rear window.

"Time to pitch in, Jake!" I said, trying to make the load-in sound like fun.

Jake ignored me. The cigar store Indian paid me more attention than my son.

"Jake? Would 'now' be a good time for you? Because 'now' would be a good time for us."

Jake's growl rivaled Brad Pit Bull's: "*I'm just about to beat this game!*"

Rather than start an argument, I began unloading the trailer without him.

But after a few minutes, Jake was suddenly alongside me, giving me the smallest I'm-sorry grin ever given, but soon was helping out with all his youthful energy.

With the aid of a dolly and cart, in less than half an hour we managed to get everything in through the freight doors, and up the few steps with little trouble . . . with the exception of the rolltop desk, which was way heavier than I had figured. We started by taking the drawers in first, but the thing still seemed like deadweight.

But Jake was strong for his age, and I was no slouch, either, and with some extra huffing and puffing, the desk arrived at our booth unscathed (well, maybe a little gouge on the back . . . but that wouldn't show).

While we toiled, Mother sat on the brass-bound trunk and ordered us around, her performance as General Patton blowing George C. Scott's away—thank God she didn't spot the horsewhip in the booth across the aisle.

When everything got into the area where Mother had bidden us put it, she shifted from general to movie director, getting very specific about the placement and positioning of each item in the booth . . . and although she got on my nerves, I had to admit that the woman did have an aesthetic eye for display. For a star performer, she knew her way around props and art direction.

Several times, Mrs. Norton came over to appraise our work, bestowing an encouraging word or two upon her newest pupils. Funny how, after all these years, some part of me was stilling hoping to finally earn an A from my former teacher. . . .

When it came time to install the cigar store Indian in its place of honor, the big lug slipped from my sweaty hands and tipped over in the aisle. And as I righted the statue, I heard an ominous *thunk.*

"What was that?" Mother asked, alarmed.

"I don't know," I said, with a gulp, hoping I hadn't damaged the statue. What a horrible thing to have happen to such a precious artifact—or to the new tires I'd buy when the stupid thing sold.

Mother slid off the trunk, like a coach coming off the bench to personally get into the game. "Sounded like it came from inside," she said, then added excitedly, "Maybe it's the missing cigar!"

Jake—who had been taking a breather on the floor, sitting Indian-style—got to his feet, saying even more excitedly, "Or *maybe* a tomahawk!"

The three of us—four, counting Sushi, still attached to Mother like a friendly, furry tumor—gathered around the statue, scrutinizing it.

"Look," I said, pointing to the small of the Indian's back, between the end of the carved vest, and the beginning of the loincloth. "Is that some kind of . . . compartment?"

Mother squinted. "My goodness, yes . . . a secret compartment! But how does it open?"

"Maybe you pull down on his raised arm," I suggested.

But the appendage didn't budge.

"Or pull up on this feather," Jake suggested, and did . . . breaking it off. "Whoops . . . sorry."

Lips peeled back over his teeth in "uh-oh" fashion, he looked at his grandmother to see just how upset she was with him.

But, since grandchildren (unlike children) can do no harm, she just shrugged. "That's what they make epoxy glue for."

And Mother loved epoxy glue almost as much as duct tape. Stuff breaking never depressed someone who lived to fix things (make that "fix" things) (Mother fixed things in the same sense that the vet had fixed Sushi). I would have to supervise the repair of the feather. . . .

Mrs. Norton appeared so suddenly even Jake jumped.

She said, "Vivian, Brandy . . . would you please come and sign our agreement? I have to open for business, and it's best we take care of this before I unlock the doors."

We followed Mrs. Norton back to the center counter, leaving Jake to solve the latest Nancy Drew mystery ghostwritten by the Borne "girls": *The Mysterious Hidden Compartment in the Cigar Store Indian's Back.*

When Mother and I returned to the booth, we were amazed and delighted to see:

(1) the little compartment open, and
(2) the missing cigar magically restored to the Indian's hand.

"How did you pull this one off?" I asked Jake with a big astonished grin.

"See that little button behind the chief's ear? You just push it."

Jake demonstrated, the action closing the compartment, then repeating the action, opening it again.

I peered inside the hole, which was deeper than it was wide. "Was there anything else stuck in there?" I asked. "Gold coins? Loose diamonds? Deed for Manhattan?"

Jake shrugged. "Do you *see* anything?"

I didn't, but stuck my hand in just the same, remembering all of the horror films I'd seen where doing something like this hadn't turned out so well.

Same five old fingers returned, empty. A small wooden shelf down there, perhaps six inches below the slot, had nothing to offer, except maybe splinters.

Mrs. Norton having unlocked the front door, the aisles began to fill up with customers, all with their own agenda. Some were avid antiquers, on the hunt for a particular piece or collectible to add to their ever-growing collection. Others were simply browsers, letting happenstance lead them to the object(s) of their desire, otherwise just enjoying a stroll down memory lane.

In and among these regular folks were dealers, trolling for underpriced items that would end up in their own booth here or elsewhere, or their own shop in or out of town, marked at a higher price. You could distinguish them by their set jaws and frantically moving eyes, and a humorless single-minded approach, all of which would serve them well if they ever needed to stalk a lover who spurned them.

Since Jake and I had completed our task of setting up the booth to Mother's liking, and with Sushi squirming in her captivity, we left the booth to Mother, for her to price the merchandise, which only she could do anyway.

But before going, I made a SOLD sign with Bernice's name on it and stuck it to the Indian.

"Call me on my cell when you're ready for a ride," I told Mother, removing a squirming Sushi from her chest.

"No need, dear, I'll catch the trolley. I could be here quite some time."

And Mother turned her attention to a particularly gullible-looking woman who was checking out our booth. The kind who says, "Oh, *this* is nice!" and, "This is *just* what I've been looking for!" A bonus Trash 'n' Treasures tip: Don't do that.

As Jake and I left, I heard my black-widow-spider mother saying to the caught-in-her-web fly of a customer, "This rolltop desk once belonged to Mamie Eisenhower . . . a dear, close friend of mine. . . ."

Outside, Jake asked, "Who's Mamie Howitzer?"

This may have been the first time the First Lady of the 1950s had been confused with an attack gun.

"Eisenhower," I corrected. "A former First Lady with the worst haircut and tackiest clothes in American history . . . set women back decades."

Future generations must know such things—

those who don't learn from history are doomed to repeat it.

At home, while Jake went upstairs to use the bathroom, I took Sushi outside for a similar break, then we came back in and I refreshed her water dish, giving her a dog treat for good conduct in the face of adversity (Brad Pit Bull) (and us).

When Jake, his cargo pants pockets lightened of some of their load, returned from upstairs, I asked, "How 'bout going down on the island with me and picking out a pumpkin for Halloween?"

"Naw, Mom. That's kid stuff. And, anyway, I'm kinda tired."

"It's not kid stuff! Pretty, pretty, pretty please. . . . *you* can pick it out this time."

He sighed. "*Fine* . . . if it makes you happy."

It did. I might even let him carve it.

The Island—as locals still refered to it—was not really an island at all, rather a sandy stretch along the Mississippi River where the soil was perfect for growing vegetables and fruits, specifically melons. (It was also long rumored to be a favorite dumping ground used by Chicago gangsters who also like the soft, sandy soil for the burial of former associates whose own melons were in less than perfect condition.)

I took the Treacherous Bypass to the River Road and headed south. Jake, in the passenger seat, remained silent, Game Boy not in sight. I was thinking about the booth and wondering if we could make a go of it, when he blurted, "Dad has a new girlfriend."

When I didn't respond, he said, "Well?"

I looked at him sideways. "Well . . . what do

you want me to say . . . 'Is she pretty, is she nice, do you like her?' "

"I *don't* like her . . . she's bossy."

"Is that supposed to make me happy?"

"I don't know. Does it?"

"No," I lied.

After another moment Jake asked, "Why did you leave Dad, anyway? And don't give me that bull hockey again about growin' apart and stuff."

Actually, Roger and I had started out apart, due to the difference in our ages, and had grown closer . . . until I blew it.

This time I didn't lie.

I said, "Jake, I did something that hurt your dad. He can't forgive me for it. I can't even forgive me for it. So there's no place to go but apart."

I knew this was dangerous. I knew Jake was old enough to probably read between the lines, and I sat there quietly praying that the next words out of my son's mouth wouldn't be along the order of "Then you were a dumb slut, right, Mom?"

Either Jake didn't read between the lines, or didn't want to; anyway, thankfully, he didn't press for details.

Instead he asked, "Can't you take it back, what you did and stuff, or . . . ?"

"I'm afraid not."

"Well, then why did you *do* it?"

I gave that some thought. "Remember what you said when you shot Sushi with the paintball?"

"Yeah . . . I said I didn't mean to. That it just sorta happened and stuff."

"That's right. Sometimes we do something stupid, and we don't really mean to."

Like I didn't mean to get tipsy and go to bed with an old boyfriend at my ten-year high school reunion . . . it just sort of happened. And stuff.

Unfortunately, the stain it left wasn't the paintball variety that can get washed out.

Jake was saying, "But *Sushi* forgave me. . . . Why can't Dad forgive *you*?"

"Maybe . . . maybe because people aren't as forgiving as dogs."

"Sometimes," he said, then stopped. Finally he finished: "Sometimes I think dogs are smarter than people."

No argument there.

I turned off the River Road and into the gravel drive of one of the many fruit and vegetable stands dotting the lone stretch of highway.

This one had an eye-catching green and red watermelon standee (with a bite taken out of it) to lure customers in, and the "stand" was actually a rustic western-style building, half of which was an open-air produce store—selling vegetables in season (potatoes, tomatoes, acorn squash, butternut squash, and the odd assortment of colorful gourds) while the other half of the building was a year-round restaurant, serving that same wonderful produce, along with the biggest and bestest pork tenderloin sandwich *either* side of the Mississippi.

I eased my Buick up to a flatbed wagon piled high with pumpkins of various sizes, including some huge ones whose growth hormones had gone seriously awry, worthy of an old fifties sci-fi flick—THE PUMPKIN THAT SQUASHED SERENITY!!!

Jake and I climbed out of the car into an uncomfortably muggy day, too warm now for my Juicy Couture sweatshirt. As we approached one of the wagons, I removed the long-sleeved top covering my sleeveless T, and tied it around my waist.

Jake pointed to one of the pumpkins. "*That* one."

His choice was rather smallish, lopsided, and had no stem for a handle.

I frowned. "Don't you want to look them all over? And find just the right one?"

"*That's* just the right one—right there."

"Gosh, I think we could do a *little* better. . . ."

"You *did* say I could pick it out, didn't you?"

That I had; and the fact that Peggy Sue often let me choose something, then would be disappointed in my selection, was not lost on me. However, Jake was just being obstinate. He was purposely picking a lousy pumpkin just to challenge me.

I said, "Okay, pick what you want . . . but let's go in the corn maze first."

A sign announcing the labyrinth carved in the adjacent cornfield had caught my attention. Especially the "free" part.

Jake wrinkled his nose. "Uh, let's not and say we did."

"Oh, come on . . . it'll be *fun*." Somewhere in the back of my mind I recalled that never in the history of man had actual fun followed a parent making that prediction. "Anyway, I bet I can get through it *before* you."

Now I was challenging Jake, and he couldn't resist a dare, even a lame one like this.

He said, "Last one out's a rotten pumpkin!"

We ran into the maze together, but at the first fork in the road of tall, dried cornstalks, went in opposite directions.

With each juncture, I continued going left—it seemed like a plan—but I kept dead-ending. And it wasn't long before a hot and sweaty Brandy was sorry she ever suggested navigating the maze, much less making a race out of it.

Finally I burst through the other end.

No Jake.

I waited five minutes, then ten minutes. I went back, retracing my steps, calling his name . . . but Jake didn't answer.

Frustration turned to anxiety, and I began visualizing my son at a younger age, wandering the paths in tears.

Finally I made my frightened, downcast way back to the entrance, with visions of the FBI and milk cartons in my frantic parental brain.

And there, in the car, sat Jake, head bent, playing his Game Boy.

"Didn't you hear me *calling*?" I said, lashing out at him as I approached his rolled-down window.

"No." He didn't look up, my tone having no effect.

"How long have you been here?"

"A while." His thumbs danced on the control buttons; the sound *bipped* and *booped* and *bopped* and *beeped*.

I gleeped, "I told you to meet me at the other *end*. . . ."

"Come on, Mom! I got tired of waiting, is all, so I came back here. . . . Some guy's looking for you."

"Who?"

"I don't know . . . some guy. He said he'd be in the restaurant."

I wondered if it could be my law enforcement dreamboat, Brian . . . but if so, how could he know where I'd be?

I asked Jake, "Will you be all right out here?"

"What am I, a baby?"

To me he was, and would be, forever.

"Of course not," I said. "Sorry. Cut me a break—I'm a mom."

"And I'm thirsty. Bring me something to drink, will ya?"

Inside the restaurant, whose decor sported a watermelon theme that overdid it some, I slowly scanned the tables and booths where farmers and family types were having a late lunch (or early supper). I didn't see Brian, or any other man I knew . . .

. . . at first.

Then I recognized a face that was vaguely familiar and then jogged back into full focus: piercing eyes, sharp nose, sensual mouth, dark hair, fashion-statement chin stubble. My admirer—stalker?—from the federal auction was seated alone in a side booth, the man who had bid against me for our now legendary rolltop desk.

In the moment before he spotted me, something about his good looks took on a cruel cast that disappeared when he did see me and a dazzling smile blossomed, and now the cold eyes sparkled, and I might well have been a long-lost friend.

Wearing a Locoste orange-and-yellow-striped

ruby shirt, and well-worn jeans, he stood as I approached.

"You're looking for me?" I asked.

"Yes. Brandy, isn't it? Will you join me?"

I might have told him to stick it, or I might have fled in fear; but I was a single woman who knew a good-looking man when she saw one, and this was a public place with lots of farmers around to defend a lamb like me.

So I slid into the booth, across from him.

"Something to drink?" He already had coffee, black.

"Iced tea would be nice."

He motioned to a young waitress who had *Tweety-Bird* tattooed on her neck.

(I remain among the minority of my generation who refuse to have a permanent etching dyed into their skin. *However!* I nearly changed my mind about the art form after a girl I know had her eyebrows, eyeliner, and lipstick tattooed on. Think of the time she saves getting ready every morning! It might've worked if the guy's hand had been steadier with the needle . . . but as it turned out, her eyebrows give her a perpetually startled look.)

After Miss Tweety-Bird had taken my drink order, my friendly stalker extended a manicured hand, perhaps not unintentionally showing off a Rolex watch that probably cost more than my used Buick.

He said, "Troy Hanson . . . from the auction the other day?"

I took the hand—warm, not sweaty (his, not mine). "How could I forget?"

He displayed those perfect teeth, which would

have been charming except that the longer-than-normal incisors seemed predatory.

As if reading my mind, he said, "I'm not a predator, if that's what you think."

I waved that off with a smile, but said nothing, keeping my options open.

The smile disappeared. "I *do* have a good reason for tracking you down."

"Okay. Let's hear it."

"I'm a picker."

"*Excuse* me?" I didn't know what he meant by that and wasn't sure I wanted to. Was he also a grinner, a smoker, and a midnight toker?

"I mean to say," he said quickly, "that's what I do for a living . . . find and purchase antiques for clients. For example, the owner of this restaurant might hire me to buy these"—he gestured to the wall of our booth where several forties and fifties vintage watermelon-oriented advertisements were nailed (several in worse racial taste than our cigar store Indian)—"to give the place a certain nostalgic look."

"You work for various . . . businesses?"

"Sometimes," he said. "I'm also hired by individuals, like the one who wanted me to get a particular antique at that auction yesterday."

"Ah—the rolltop desk."

"That's right." He looked down at the coffee cup held in his hands. "And I shouldn't have let it go."

"Why *did* you?"

Troy (I'll call him by his first name because he was that good looking) glanced up, smiled one-sidedly. "I honestly don't know. . . . In most instances, at an auction like that? I can be quite ruthless, I assure you."

"Oh, that is reassuring."

"But . . ." He shrugged, laughed silently. "I guess I was in a funny mood that day." He smiled and his eyes met mine in that unmistakable *you are hot, lady* look. "And there was something about you, and that woman you were with, that was so . . . so . . . what is the word?"

"Pathetic?"

He laughed. "I was going to say endearing. A peculiar combination of naive and relentless."

"I'm naive, and Mother is relentless, generally. Sometimes we trade off."

He waved off my flip comment. "Anyway, I tracked you down to—"

"By tracked down, you mean followed me."

He frowned in embarrassment. "I'm not proud of myself. But I would like to ask if you would consider selling the desk to me, at a profit. Whatever you think is fair."

"It's that important to you?"

He nodded. "You see, it would damage my reputation as a picker if word got around that I wasn't reliable."

"Surely your clients know you can't win everything you bid on."

"Yes. But I was authorized, for a desk of that style and vintage, to go higher than it actually went. I shouldn't have allowed you girls to charm me so."

"Yeah, well, Mother and me, we're pretty much charm personified."

"You are to me."

Not knowing how much of this was B.S., and how much was him thinking he might make a bonus on the sale with the little lady seated across from him, I shrugged and said, "Sure, you can have the desk . . . but there's one caveat."

"What's that?"

"The rolltop is already in our booth at the antiques mall . . ."

His dark, calculating eyes betrayed alarm; he must have really wanted it bad.

". . . but I'm sure the desk's still there, because, knowing Mother? She's overpriced it."

Another wave. "I'll pay whatever it's tagged. . . . Where is this mall located?"

"It's a new one, back in Serenity." I told Troy how to get there, then noticed the wall clock. "But you'll have to hurry . . . they close in about twenty minutes."

"Then you'll excuse me if I go . . . ?" He tossed a tenspot on the table.

"No problem," I said. "And thanks for the drink."

He didn't stay long enough for "You're welcome."

And as quickly as he left, Troy's true interest clearly was in that desk and not in my bodacious bod; oh well. I hailed Tweety Bird, and got Jake a Coke to go.

Halfway home I'd realized we'd forgotten to get the damn pumpkin.

*A Trash 'n' Treasures Tip*

Some dealers will fabricate a fantastic story about an antique just to sell it. For instance, if you're told a rolltop desk was once owned by Mamie Eisenhower, or Mamie Van Doren for that matter, ask for proof before buying it.

# Chapter Six

# Let Sleeping Dogs Die

The next morning I awoke early, brushed my teeth, threw some cold water on my face, and stumbled down to the kitchen to fix myself breakfast. It was the kind of morning where your first thought is: *I think I have just enough energy to survive. . . .*

Mother, however, was up and dressed, and already had a frantic demeanor that said this was going to be a long day.

"Brandy, dear," she said, so chipper the pope would have wanted to shake her by the shoulders, "I was rooting around, out in the garage?"

"That's nice."

"And I found some more simply delightful items that I think would really spruce up the old booth."

The "old" two-day-old booth.

"Wonderful." I yawned. "We should do that when we get around to it."

"No better time than the present!"

One good cliché deserves another.

I said, "There's no rush."

Mother's eyes went wild behind the huge glasses. "Oh, but, actually, there is! Brandy, we mustn't dawdle!"

"Please don't say the early bird catches the—"

"Frankly, I have a confession to make. Something I'm truly ashamed of."

I looked over at her with my eyelids at half-mast. This should be good.

"I woke up in the middle of the night, realized that I put too low a price on the amber vase! I want to get down to the antiques mall before it opens, and correct my error."

I closed my eyes and mentally groaned.

But, good daughter that I am, I asked, "When do you think Mrs. Norton will get there?" (I wasn't such a good daughter that I relished the notion of cooling my heels in my Buick outside the place.)

"Why, she's probably there now, if I know the woman, tacking up more signs. Her efficiency is matched only by her energy. Pent-up sexual tension, you know."

This rolled up my eyelids like window shades given too hard a tug. "How's that?"

"Well, these other older women, a widow like Mrs. Norton, they don't have the good sense to make sure their sexual needs are—"

I held up a hand before I could get chapter and verse on how unmarried women mother's age dealt with their sexual needs. "We'll go, Mother. We'll go."

"Good. I'm glad you thought of it!"

Ignoring that, I said, "But Jake isn't up. I don't

think he'll be thrilled by another trip to the antiques mall."

"Just leave the dear boy a note," Mother replied with a shrug. "He'll probably sleep until noon, anyway."

I sighed. "Can I at *least* have my Count Chocula first?"

"If you must."

I must . . . and poured a bowl of the sugary, chocolatey cereal—Jake's and my favorite. And did my best to avoid any images that might be triggered by Mother's sexual needs remark. . . .

When I returned upstairs to dress (jeans, Citizens for Humanity; top, Johnny Was), Jake was still in the spare bedroom, the little devil sleeping like an angel. I left a message telling him where we were, a Post-it stuck to his Game Boy where he'd be sure to find it.

Mother was waiting impatiently for me in the car. She held a cardboard box full of items on her lap, some of which looked strangely familiar.

"Hey!" I said, climbing behind the wheel. "Are those my *Barbie* dolls?"

Mother shrugged. "Why? Were you planning to play with them again?"

I glared at her. "That's not the point! They're mine . . . my precious memories . . . and *I* should be the one to decide if, and when, we're going to sell them."

"They *could* fetch a nice price."

A pause. "How much?"

The Buick could use a new battery and a pre-winter checkup.

"Into the hundreds, I should think. Most are

collector's editions, and you kept them in such lovely condition, in their boxes, why, it's almost as if they'd never been played with."

That's because I preferred to play with Kens rather than Barbies. Some things never change.

Mother asked, "What say we split fifty-fifty?"

"Are you kidding? Seventy-five, twenty-five. They *are* mine, after all."

"Ah, but I did buy them for you."

My eyes narrowed. "I'm sure Peggy Sue gave me *some* of those dolls. What was that awful term you used to describe Bernice and our cigar store Native American? Some certain kind of *giver*?"

She threw up her hands. "All right, all right, you win. Seventy-five, twenty-five it is. You *do* drive a hard bargain, my dear."

I smiled and started the car. It wasn't often I outmaneuvered Mother.

But then . . . why was *she* smiling, too? Could it be that she'd just snagged herself 25 percent of something that was 100 percent mine?

On the way downtown, Mother said, "Some familiar faces stopped by our booth yesterday, dear."

"Such as?"

"Such as your sister's friend Connie."

"Ick. And you can quote me."

"Well, yes, there is no accounting for taste. Although she did display rather good taste herself—she was sniffing around our rolltop desk to beat the band."

"Was our price too high for her?"

"We didn't talk price. She just said, 'Interesting piece. Maybe later.'"

"I guess her money is as good as the next witch's. You said 'faces'—who else?"

"More a familiar face to me than you, darling. Ivan, our ex-mayor? He was doing a war dance around our Indian friend."

"Really? Didn't he see the 'sold' sign?"

"He did, but he made me a good offer."

"Mother! You didn't sell that horrible thing out from under Bernice, did you?"

"I thought about it . . . but no. A promise is a promise. And anyway, his offer wasn't *that* good. . . ."

Mrs. Norton was indeed at the mall, as attested to by a tan Taurus parked in a "reserved for owner" space in the back alley. I pulled into another not-so-reserved one marked PRIVATE, and hoped I wouldn't get a ticket.

With me toting the box, Mother and I entered the unlocked back door and stepped into darkness. I fumbled momentarily for a light switch, found it, and we continued up the short flight of cement steps to the first floor, which was also dark, and eerily quiet.

"Why was Mrs. Norton working in the dark?" I whispered to Mother.

"I don't know. Why are you whispering, dear?"

"I don't know."

Mother called out, in her best olly olly oxen free fashion: "Mrs. *Nor*-ton! Oh, Mrs. Nor-*tuh*-un!"

She got no answer.

I called out even louder, and I *did* get an answer . . .

. . . but not from my former teacher, rather

her watchdog, Brad. Only this was not the sharp bark of a watchdog at all, instead a soft, pathetic whimper.

Brad Pit Bull was crying.

Mother and I looked at each other, eyebrows raised. Where was the mournful mutt's mistress?

I moved to an electric panel on the wall nearby, and began switching switches, illuminating the large room, section by section. When I turned back to Mother, she was heading up the center aisle toward the front of the store.

"Be careful!" I called out. "If that dog is *hurt*, he could be dangerous!"

Typically, Mother ignored me, disappearing at the end of the aisle, heading toward our booth. I hurried after her and then, as I rounded the row, bumped full-force into Mother, who had doubled back, knocking the wind out of both of us.

"Dear, please," she said, gasping for breath, "please don't . . ."

"Don't what?"

"Don't look. It's horrible. Simply grotesque."

Despite her agitated state, and the melodramatic words, Mother seemed atypically untheatrical.

Now, I ask you . . . if somebody tells you not to look, especially if it's "horrible" and "simply grotesque," what is any reasonable person going to do?

Right.

You're not only *going* to look, but you *have* to look, you *must* look. . . .

So I pushed past Mother, expecting to find a

poor injured Brad, and instead I stared down at a poor, much more than merely injured Mrs. Norton.

My onetime math teacher lay sprawled in the aisle near our booth, in a pool of blood, her clothes—the same orange and brown outfit as the day before—torn and shredded, and the same was true of what had been her face.

The apparent culprit was there, too, the pit bull straddling his master, lethal front paws and deadly mouth blood-caked. On seeing me, the beefy animal's whimpering morphed into a deep growl, and I backed up slowly, until he was out of my sight, and I was out of his.

I grabbed Mother by the arm and hustled her back down the aisle and outside to safety.

After allowing herself to be swept along, Mother now glared at me while I pushed with two hands on the door as if its being shut tight weren't enough.

"What's the idea?" she demanded.

"The idea," I said, "is that that pit bull mauled that poor woman to death."

Mother frowned. "I don't know why you jump to *that* conclusion."

I just looked at her.

"It seemed to me," Mother said, "the creature was merely standing guard over its fallen mistress."

"It has blood all over its teeth and mouth. It's a pit bull. Mrs. Norton was viciously mauled to death. What *else* could have happened?"

Mother's frown turned thoughtful; she put a pensive hand on her chin. "Perhaps another dog did it—Mrs. Norton did say the creature was timid. When the other pit bull attacked, Brad cowered in the corner!"

"Mother."

"Yes, dear?"

"Your Red-Hatted League reading group is doing Agatha Christie again, aren't they?"

"Why, yes, dear. We ran out of Rex Stout. What makes you ask that at a time like this?"

"Nothing. But let's say your assumptions are right. You have shrewdly ascertained exactly what was going on in there. Then we were wise to scoot, weren't we? Because, logically, there's another, *really* vicious pit bull in there!"

She was nodding, taking my sarcasm at face value. "Yes. Logically. Not necessarily a pit bull, but . . ."

Shaking my head, I got out my cell phone and quickly told the dispatcher what we'd found. Then Mother and I stood by our car and waited for the sirens to come.

I was shaking, traumatized into silence by the ghastly death of my former teacher.

But Mother wasn't.

"I wonder how long our things are going to be tied up," she mused, glancing toward the massive building. "Every day that goes by we'll be losing money, you know."

I looked at her, appalled. "Mother . . . a woman—a woman we *know* and *like*—has been brutally mauled in there."

"Yes, dear, I saw her," Mother said patiently. "But Mrs. Norton is dead and there's nothing we can do about it."

"That's a little cold, don't you think?"

Mother's eyes behind the lenses were disconcertingly calm. "At my age, Brandy, the past becomes quickly irrelevant and the future most pressing."

"I understand that . . . but can we wait until this afternoon to talk about the future? Let's have a little respect here. . . ."

Mother nodded slowly. "That seems reasonable."

Which was more than I could say about Mother.

A black-and-white police car—siren wailing, lights flashing—wheeled into the alley, stopping abruptly in front of us. From the opposite direction came another screaming siren and a yellow emergency rescue truck, which nosed up to the squad car, and two paramedics jumped out.

The officer reached us first.

I told the stocky, mustached man whose name tag read MUNSON where to find Mrs. Norton, adding, "But watch out for the pit bull."

Mother chimed in: "*Both* of them!"

Munson frowned. "There are *two* pit bulls?"

I shook my head, and whispered, "Mother's just excited. There's only one."

Munson nodded and gestured to the two paramedics. "Stay behind me. . . . I'll shoot the damn dog if I have to."

Again Mother butted in. "Surely that's not necessary! Don't you have a tranquilizer gun, young man?"

Officer Munson, who was forty if a day, looked at Mother like she was a suspect in a one-woman lineup. "Vivian Borne, isn't it?" he said slowly, and smiled, but not in a friendly way. "Mrs. Borne, there's no time to call for Animal Control. . . . That woman may be alive and in need of immediate medical attention."

"Oh, I assure you, she's dead," Mother said. "Who could have that much blood on the outside and be alive on the inside? It's a rhetorical question."

Munson's upper lip curled back; it was sort of a sneer. "Thank you for your diagnosis, Mrs. Borne. But you don't mind if we go in and find out for ourselves?"

"A second opinion is always a good idea," Mother granted.

I suppose I should have either defended Mother from Munson's rudeness, or maybe duct-taped Mother's mouth shut to minimize the trouble she was causing. But words were in short supply for me. I kept seeing Mrs. Norton on the floor and the blood-flecked dog hovering over her. . . .

Drawing his gun, Munson opened the back door of the building and entered, followed by the medics, who in turn were followed by . . . Mother!

I stood gaping for a moment, but I had no choice but to snap out of it and tag along. Mother and I were unnoticed for a while, and our presence didn't get spotted till our little group arrived on the first floor, where we'd have undoubtedly been sent back outside if we hadn't been rudely interrupted . . .

. . . by the pit bull.

Brad came barreling down the center aisle toward us, claws again making his progress awkward over the industrial carpet; that the dog was slightly slowed didn't lessen the threat: Brad's teeth were barred in that horribly blood-smeared mouth. . . .

Officer Munson raised his gun and took aim at the dog, which was a perfectly reasonable thing to do—I would have done the same.

But, just as Brad seemed poised to spring at Munson, Mother lurched forward and shoved the officer's hand-with-the-gun aside.

Some fool screamed (me).

Mother slapped Brad like a frisky first date and bent over and scolded, "*Bad* dog! Bad, bad doggie!"

Brad, stunned, looked around at the rest of us, hoping to find a sympathetic face; and then, finding sympathy in short supply, the animal cowered and whimpered as Mother continued her scolding.

"Now, you be a good dog," Mother commanded, "and go over there and *lie down*!" She pointed sternly to the closest booth.

Brad, staying very low to the ground, like a commando navigating a beachhead, obeyed, crawling under a Heywood-Wakefield coffee table and depositing himself there.

The two paramedics rushed forward to find Mrs. Norton.

A red-faced Munson turned on Mother. "I ought to book you for interfering with a police officer!"

Mother studied him. "Have you had your blood pressure checked lately, Officer Munson? Stressful work like this can be a contributor to—"

Ignoring her, the livid Munson barked into his shoulder microphone: "Ten-seventy-eight."

Mother leaned toward me and behind a hand whispered: "Requesting backup." She knew all the police codes forward and back.

The microphone crackled. "Ten-eighty-sixty?"

"No. Ten-one-hundred."

*Crackle.* "Sorry, sir, is that a new one?"

"*You* must be new—that's a Vivian Borne. . . . I need someone to handle her!"

Mother's eyes widened and her hands clasped in delight. "Brandy! Isn't that *wonderful?*"

"Isn't what wonderful?"

"It would seem I have my very own designated police-code number!"

"I've never been more proud."

One of the medics returned. "You'd better notify the coroner," he told Munson solemnly.

"Ten-seventy-nine," Mother chirped.

I thought the vein on Munson's forehead was going to pop.

"I want you two out of here . . . *now!*" he barked, looking from Mother to me.

What had *I* done? Mother was the one with a police code.

"And wait outside until someone takes your statement . . . understand?"

"Yes, sir," I said meekly.

But Mother's hands were on her hips. "You're a terribly rude young man. I told you Mrs. Norton was dead and you dismissed that. I suggested you didn't need to use lethal force on that poor animal, and then proved you wrong, and saved you from endless reports about firing your weapon on the job. Now I have one more small piece of advice for you."

I was tugging her sleeve. "Mother . . . Mother . . ."

"That dog is innocent! I suggest you policemen start looking for whoever is really responsible. Possibly a suspicious character driving around town with a pit bull in his rider's seat."

Munson's gaze fell upon me. One eyebrow rose practically to his hairline; the other stayed in place, or mostly stayed in place, considering the twitch.

Through another unfriendly smile, he asked: "Do you want to get her out of here? Or should I call Animal Control for *her*, too?"

"Well!" Mother huffed.

But I said, "Thank you, Officer, I'll take charge of her," and I took Mother by the arm and marched her away.

We retreated down the back steps; but before exiting to the alley, I stopped Mother. "Why did you take such an awful risk with that creature?"

"Officer Munson?"

"No! The dog!" I was shaking my head, my voice trembling. "That vicious thing could have mauled you, just like he did Mrs. Norton!"

"Nonsense, dear," she said, and waved off my concern. "Your former teacher was right about her pet . . . Brad the pit bull is timid. A coward."

"Then *why* did he kill Mrs. Norton? He's *her* dog, for God's sake!"

"Brandy, I'll thank you not to take the Lord's name in vain, at a time like this." Mother's brow furrowed. "But you heard what I told that awful young man—I don't think Brad is guilty."

I was getting a warning tingle at the back of

my neck; I didn't want to admit it yet, but I could see where this was going, at least if Mother had anything to say about it. She was letting her theatrical notions turn a horrible tragedy into another murder mystery.

"Saving that dog from a bullet right now," I said, "is a reprieve at best . . . you *know* he's going to have to be put down."

Mother sighed. "I'm afraid you're right. Pity the only witness is a silent one. Poor thing can't defend itself!"

"Uh . . . I think Brad can defend himself just fine."

"With those fangs of his, perhaps, if he weren't so timid. But he can't point at the *real* killer, can he?"

"Mother . . ."

"Such a beautiful animal . . ."

Compared to what? A rottweiler?

"Mother," I said, "listen to me."

"I can hear you, dear. You needn't shout."

"I'm not shouting! Mother, you are not Jessica Fletcher and I am not Nancy Drew. We happened to get involved with something a while back—"

"Those murders, you mean?"

"Yes, yes, those murders. But that's the kind of thing that happens once in a lifetime. You can't go around looking at deaths, however tragic and, yes, grotesque, and turn them into a hobby, like your Red-Hatted League reading group."

She sniffed. "I have no idea whatsoever what you're talking about."

A crowd had gathered in the alley, moths drawn to the flashing lights of the emergency vehicles, and I could see the wheels turning in Mother's head. She loved an audience of any kind, and I warned her, sotto voce, to keep her trap shut. If any reporters were among the gawkers, Mother's theories could find their way into the *Serenity Sentinel*.

A second squad car arrived, blocking the alley further, and uniformed officer Brian Lawson got out. To Mother's dismay, he shooed the bystanders away. This was the closest she'd got to center stage since she quit the playhouse.

"I don't know what you see in that wet blanket," Mother muttered to me as Brian approached, nodding to us both, all business.

"Mrs. Borne . . . Brandy . . . I understand, Vivian, that you found Mrs. Norton?" Officer Lawson produced a tiny tape recorder from his pocket.

"Indeed I did!" Mother said a little too happily, as if stumbling on the corpse of a friend was like finding a prize in a Cracker Jack box.

I sighed. "I'll be over on the freight dock if anyone needs me."

You're probably pretty disgusted with Mother by now, and you won't be surprised to hear that I was, too. In her defense, she'd had numerous shocks this morning and, however ill-advised her intervention between gunslinging Munson and the bloody-fanged pooch, she had indeed shut down a dangerous situation. Still, I made another mental note to call her shrink and make sure her meds were right.

During the interview, Mother was her usual rambling, histrionic self, and more than once Brian had to get her back on point.

When I heard her saying, ". . . and her poor husband got killed after imbibing too much and decided to take a nap on the tracks just as the Rock Island Line passed through," I called out singsongy from my dock perch, "I'm, uh, pretty sure that's not pertinent, Mother!"

Mother threw me an irritated look. "Brandy, the officer asked me what I knew about the woman, so I'm telling him!"

"I know, but that doesn't mean everything from her first tooth to her last meal."

"Dear, I *know* what I'm *doing*!"

I knew what she was doing, too. I was afraid my efforts to keep her on the straight and mentally-balanced narrow were severely challenged by the loss in her life of her theatrical pastime. The other day ex-pal Bernice had seemed willing to bury the hatchet, and not the kind that that cigar store Indian might wield.

Finally I just had to tune her out, and wound up watching a gray sedan try to navigate the congested alley. Then the driver gave up, parked cockeyed, and got out; short, bald, and bespectacled, the man carried a medical bag as he puffed toward us.

Mother spoke first. "Hello, Hector!" she called out pleasantly.

Hector seemed startled to see her. But then, most everyone seemed startled when they caught sight of Mother. . . .

The man's gaze went from Mother to Officer Lawson, who said simply, "First floor."

Hector nodded and entered the building.

Mother called over to me (still keeping my distance on the dock), "That's the *coroner*, dear."

Then in a stage whisper: "He's lost a little weight since the divorce."

"I'll file that with the rest of the evidence," I assured her.

After only a few minutes, the coroner returned, said something to Brian that I couldn't hear, then hoofed it back to his car.

Once again the back door of the building swung open, Officer Munson coming through first, holding it wide for the paramedics who carried Mrs. Norton in a body bag on a stretcher.

As the medics loaded their human cargo into the emergency vehicle, a respectful silence fell over the alley, only to be broken by the finality of the slamming of the vehicle's double rear doors.

Then the Animal Control van arrived.

I hopped off the dock and joined Mother and Brian.

"Regular Grand Central Station," Mother muttered.

"Terminal," I corrected.

"It was Grand Central Station when *I* was a girl."

"It's always been Grand Central Terminal, Mother."

"Dear, a terminal is for airplanes."

"A terminal," I said, "refers to anything that ends at a certain destination . . . be it trains, buses, boats, or planes."

"Or life," Mother sighed.

I searched her face and found, in her eyes, a strain of worry that explained her careening over-the-top behavior. For all her inappropriate remarks, she really was upset about Mrs. Norton's death. The two women had only been friendly acquaintances—I'd overstated it, calling my former teacher a "friend" of either Mother or myself—and finding that ravaged body had taken a toll on Vivian Borne.

The animal control man went in . . . and the animal control man came out, with a sad-looking, docile Brad on a leash, head down, as if he was being sent to his pen for making a mess on a carpet (which I guess he had done, in a way). Finally Brad was shut into the back of the van.

Then, after all the hoopla, everyone was gone, except for Mother, me, and Brian. Even the diehard gawkers had lost interest and faded away.

Mother turned to Brian. "You've been very efficient, very thorough, Officer."

"Uh . . . thanks."

"Is there anything else we can tell you before we go?"

"No, I have enough," Brian said (or was that, "I've had enough"?).

Half bowing, Mother offered magnanimously, "Well, you know where to find us, should anything further occur to you. Brandy, are you coming, dear?"

"Give me a minute, Mother."

"I'll just wait in the car, dear."

"Yes. Do that."

We waited for her to stride out of sight; then Brian asked, "Will you be all right?"

"Yes. No. I don't know. I may sleep with the lights on, tonight, after a nightmare like that. . . ."

He nodded, his brown eyes sympathetic. "I've seen my share of animal-attack aftermaths, and you never get used to it."

I shook my head, shuddered. "Horrible to think a trusted pet could turn on you like that."

Brian said, "I remember a drug bust where there were three pit bulls on the premises. Two, I used mace on, but the third took four bullets before it stopped charging."

I shuddered again. "What *will* happen to the pit bull?"

"He'll go to the animal shelter . . . for now."

"And then?"

He shrugged.

I nodded.

However docile he had been after Mother scolded him, Brad Pit Bull remained a potentially deadly animal.

Brian touched my arm. "Listen, Brandy—if you like, I could, you know, come by later? See if you and your mother're okay?"

I managed a smile. "I'd like that. Hey, it'll give you a chance to meet my son, Jake. . . . He's staying for the week."

Brian didn't *exactly* look like he'd been smacked in the face with a dead mackerel, but he did register some surprise.

Which surprised *me.*

Even though we hadn't gone beyond the flirtation stage, I had taken the initiative to find out that his busted marriage had produced two girls who lived with their mother in Wisconsin. He was a cop, a detective of sorts—hadn't he bothered to look into my past?

"I *would* like to meet Jake," he said, and smiled, redeeming himself a little; and then he walked me to my car.

As I drove down the now-deserted alley, I

glanced in the rearview mirror and saw Brian putting yellow tape across the back door of the building.

*Crime scene*, it said. Was it one? Wasn't this just an accident?

I said to Mother, "You were a little hard on him, weren't you?"

"Who, dear?"

"You know very well who . . . Brian."

"Yes, dear, I guess in a way I was."

"What's the idea, putting him through the wringer like that?"

She shrugged grandly, the excitement of the morning having restored her diva status. "Brandy, any man who's interested in *this* family—and by 'this family' I mean you, dear—ought to know exactly what he's getting himself in for."

I steered the car toward home. "Don't you ever get tired of being right, Mother?"

"Does any mother?"

By noon Mother and I had arrived back home, where we found Jake curled up on the living room couch (Sushi, too), dressed in his usual attire of T-shirt and cargo jeans. He was using his BlackBerry, probably text-messaging his father about how off-the-hook Mother and I were.

Mother suddenly made herself scarce, leaving it to me to tell Jake about Mrs. Norton's demise.

I didn't know where to begin, always inclined to shield my son from such unpleasantness.

I said, "Some sad news at the mall."

The tone of my voice, as much as my words, told Jake to put down the BlackBerry, his blue eyes asking me what this was about.

"You know that lady you met yesterday? Mrs. Norton? The one who runs the antiques mall?"

He nodded.

"Well . . . your grandmother and I found her in the store this morning, on the floor. I'm afraid she was dead."

Jake's eyes grew large. "What, was she shot or something?" he asked, alarm in his voice.

I frowned. "Why would you think that?"

"I . . . I don't know. It just kinda popped into my head."

A result of playing violent video games?

I said, "No. She wasn't shot . . . I'm afraid her dog attacked her."

"You mean Brad Pit Bull?"

I nodded.

"Oh." His eyes left mine to stare out the front window. "That's too bad."

How could I help him process this? For a kid his age, the day after he encountered that pit bull and the nice woman who ran the mall, to suddenly hear one had killed the other?

"I . . . I just hope you won't be too upset about it."

"Okay."

"And if you ever want to talk about it . . ." I patted his knee. ". . . I'll do my best to answer your questions."

"I do have one question, Mom."

"What's that, honey?"

"What's for lunch?"

## *A Trash 'n' Treasures Tip*

Broken porcelain, pottery, and crystal can be repaired. Check with a reputable mender to determine the cost versus the depreciation of the item once fixed. Don't try to do it yourself with epoxy glue like Mother.

# Chapter Seven

## Assault and Pepper Shakers

The next morning I was to meet my BFF, Tina (short for Christina) at Gloria Jean's Java Hut coffee shop at the Indian Mounds Mall. We'd set the shopping get-together up a week before, and despite a certain lingering discomfort over finding Mrs. Norton mauled like that—melancholy tinged with unease—I didn't cancel. Me shopping wouldn't do Mrs. Norton any harm, and it might help get me out of this funk.

As usual, I was in a quandary over what to wear. Tina and I don't try to outdo each other with our fashion finesse or anything, but we did strive to look our best out of a mutual respect for each other (and also to pay homage to the Shopping Mall Goddess for good luck and low prices).

Finally I put on a BCBG tan jacket with epaulets and military buttons, Rock & Republic jeans (rolled up), and a pair of distressed brown Frye boots. To counter the armed forces look, I picked out a girly pink Betsey Johnson rhinestone-encrusted hobo bag and matching hip-slung belt.

Do you ever bemoan the fact that you never have any extra cash for a shopping spree? Here are some ways to save a little money:

(1) Ditch the bimonthly trip to the nail salon for fakes. You're not even fooling the men these days . . . who only wonder what *else* might be fake. Keep your nails filed short (they're in these days) and slap on a little clear polish. (Savings: seventy dollars a month, plus gas and a sitter.) P.S. Do you *really* enjoy breathing in chemicals in a place where nobody gossips? (In English, anyway.)

(2) Stop the monthly visits to the hair salon and go only four times a year. Get a really good *short* cut, and let it grow out; you'll have several different looks over time. And if you've been having a salon color your locks, learn the suicide approach: Dye by your own hand. . . . The salons use the same stuff found at drugstores, but charge three times the rate. (Test a strand first, though. I once ended up with green hair—great for St. Paddy's Day bashes, a downer otherwise.) Savings: approximately forty-six dollars a month.

(3) Stay away from the cosmetics counters. Don't you have enough, already? Use it up! Or throw it out! And this goes for all those hotel amenities of shampoo and conditioner you've been hoarding in the bathroom closet, unless you're actually

prepared to *use* the darn things. (Savings: twenty to thirty dollars a month.)

(4) This is a touchy one, because I know you're as serious as I am about losing ten pounds and getting back into all those expensive party clothes languishing in the back of your closet. . . . But let's face it, unless you're scheduled for a root canal, it ain't gonna happen. Why not take those lovely things (before they're completely out of style) to a resale shop and get some extra cash? (Savings: estimated forty-seven dollars.) P.P.S. Do you know what the worst thing is about a root canal? The *bill*!

(5) Are you still buying fashion magazines off the stand? Fool! You can save up to 75 percent with subscriptions to your faves. (Savings: twelve dollars a month.) Okay, that's stretching it . . . but you get the point.

Now you've got two hundred dollars for shopping, and can come along with Teen and me!

Indian Mounds—so named because of an adjacent Indian burial ground—was situated on gently rolling hills just across the Treacherous Bypass (this much commerce had bought the intersection a traffic light). That the Mounds was an outdoor mall, which is unusual considering our cold winters, didn't seem to deter shoppers. I, myself, love going in and out of the stores in all types of weather, preferring it to stuffy enclosed shopping centers where you get hot and crabby in your coat and draw in the same kind of recycled air that makes so many old people get sick after taking a cruise.

Laid out asymmetrically with winding walkways, the Mounds had lots of benches on which to rest those poor tired little doggies, flower gardens to stop and enjoy color and fragrances, and spurting fountains to gape at in childish wonder. Seated on some of the surrounding benches were hyperrealistic, fully painted statues of humans, so hyper and so realistic that newcomers would sometimes stop to ask them the time.

Which was 9:00 AM when yours truly, the early bird, pulled into the vast, nearly empty parking lot, taking a prize worm of a spot right up front . . . although, even if it had been midday, at the mall's busiest, I *still* would have snagged a close space.

Allow me to explain.

Mother, during one of her "spells" some years ago, bestowed upon me a spiritual Indian guide that she dubbed Red Feather, since Mother was under the impression that red was my favorite color (it's not; yellow is). Mother's guide is Pink Feather, even though she doesn't *own* anything pink.

The purpose of these Native American spirits, according to Mother, is to help guide our lives, since "sometimes the Big Guy Upstairs can't be bothered with trivial matters like finding a good parking space" (her words, not mine—I'm just reporting here).

Pink Feather, when called upon by Mother, does all kinds of good things for her; I've actually witnessed some of these . . . like the time we went into the mall bookstore and Mother asked for the newly released *Miss Marple* DVD box set and the sales clerk said they were sold out and Mother called on Pink Feather to get her one, only to have the clerk say, "*Wait* a moment! That's funny . . . there *is* one here. . . ."

Red Feather, on the other hand, seems to be only good at getting me parking places . . . but, hey, I'm not complaining. A premiere parking spot along Michigan Avenue in Chicago during the Christmas rush is golden!

Among the mysteries associated with this process is Red Feather's willingness to find me a spot to park at a mall that had the bad taste to appropriate the name and general area of a Native American burial site.

As I entered the coffee shop, breathing in the delicious aromas, I spotted Tina, who'd beaten me there, laying claim to the chrome table for two that we felt was "ours" along the bank of windows. Tina always seemed to be able to snag that table for us—maybe she had her own Indian spirit guide (I never raised the issue).

At this hour, Gloria Jean's Java Hut was the only store open, its line of patrons at the counter mostly people who worked in the other mall shops, grabbing a scone and a quick cup of hot joe before reporting in.

Tina had thoughtfully already purchased our drinks: cinnamon mocha frappés with whipped cream and candy sprinkles. (We needed shopping energy, didn't we?) (And don't you dare mention those ten pounds I'm trying to lose!)

She gave me our usual greeting, "Hi, honey!" (à la Judy Holliday in *Born Yesterday*), and I tossed it back with the same lilt.

As I pulled out the other chair, "Heart of Glass" morphed into "Disco Inferno." We were both suckers for old eighties tunes and Gloria Jean's serving up both disco and cinnamon mocha frappés kept us coming back for more.

Tina was wearing an olive-green cropped jacket with three-quarter sleeves, Earl jeans (also rolled up), and *her* Frye boots. (Honestly, we didn't plan it . . . just great minds thinking alike.)

Teen was a tad taller than me (five seven; me, not her), also blond like me (natural; her, not me), with lovely fair skin and features speaking to her Norwegian ancestry. With my own Danish/German background, we were often mistaken for sisters (and I just as often wished we were, but I'd never been given any option except Peggy Sue).

Tina and I first met in high school—she was a junior, and I a sophomore—when some skanky senior girls were picking on her in the hallway and I ran up and told them to lay off in the kind of no-uncertain terms that would make a sailor blush.

We'd been friends ever since.

I asked, "How's Kevin?"

Teen's husband worked for a pharmaceutical company; he was a peach of a guy, always nice to me, never jealous of our close friendship.

"He's not gonna be traveling as much," she said with a smile. "And I'm already looking forward to this winter, cozy evenings by the fire. . . ."

Teen and Kev had been trying to have a baby for a couple of years now; no luck yet, but they seemed to be having a good time trying. She kept herself otherwise busy working at the Serenity Tourism Office, which allowed her flexible hours (like now).

Tina took a sip of her frothy drink, then asked, "And how's the new antiques business going?"

She obviously hadn't heard about the death of Mrs. Norton, so I recapped the events of yesterday morning, going light on the antics of one Vivian Borne.

Tina shook her head. "How awful . . . how terrible. Poor woman. . . . She was a great teacher. I had her, too, you know. Really liked her. Strict but fair."

"Too bad life isn't. Well, it's strict. Just not fair."

She frowned. "Why in the world would Mrs. Norton keep a vicious animal like that around? She seemed more like the Chihuahua type to me. You know, nervous energy attracting nervous energy."

Dogs often did mirror their owners. (I'm not sure what that says about me and Sushi.)

"Tell you the truth," I said, "it's more surprising that the animal went after her that way. He seemed more bark than bite."

"You'd run into the thing before?"

I explained that we had, setting up our booth.

"The mutt seemed devoted to her," I said, "and vice versa. She said she was using the pit bull to protect the mall at night . . . instead of putting in a security system. But I have a feeling that was just an excuse. She liked having the company."

"Certain breeds can turn on you," Tina said with a shiver, "even when you're pretty sure the animal loves you."

"Kind of like men."

Tina didn't disagree. Her eyes narrowed and she leaned forward. "What's going to happen to the antiques mall now?"

I shrugged. "I hope someone else will take it over. Mrs. Norton has relatives, though I don't think in town. I was counting on that place to keep Mother out of mischief."

Tina nodded sympathetically. "La Dame Borne is still reeling from the playhouse disappointment, I suppose."

"Oh yes. She wanted to be director in the worst way, which I'm sure she would have been. But losing her best friend in the process put salt in a very melodramatic wound. Yesterday, when we found the body, and after?"

"Yes?"

I shook my head, sighed. "Mother misbehaved. Started spouting 'murder' again."

"Oh dear."

"Only Mother would look at a mauling by a pit bull and see visions of Agatha Christie."

Tina's smile went lopsided. "Well, hon—she's had the playhouse stage taken away from her. That only leaves the streets of Serenity for her theatrics."

I held up a palm. "Stop. I'll scream or cry or something. Sometimes I think getting involved in that murder last year, however well things turned out, was the worst thing that ever happened to us. Put all kinds of ideas in Mother's head, wackier ideas even than usual."

Our conversation, thankfully, turned to more vital subjects, like the latest season of *Battlestar Galactica,* lawn prep for winter, and—exploring that most important of decisions—whether or not to buy gauchos.

The more trivial our talk got, however, the more distracted Teen seemed. Even as self-absorbed as I can be, I could always read her, so I asked, "You have something else on your mind, don't you?"

She laughed. "I'm that transparent?"

"No more than Barbra Streisand's 1970s Academy Award outfit."

Tina said tentatively, "Well . . . maybe it's none of my business."

"And this has ever stopped you?"

She laughed. "It's just . . . I really do wish you'd get off that Prozac."

I raised my eyebrows. "Why? Most people prefer me mellow."

"Maybe. But, sweetie, mellow is simply *not* you."

I snorted. "And this is bad, how?"

She sighed and sat forward, asking, "How long have you been on that stuff, anyway?"

"Oh, I dunno . . . year, maybe."

Her eyes were slits. "Correct me if I'm wrong, but aren't antidepressants supposed to be used for getting someone through a bad patch? Since when is a *year* a bad patch?"

I shrugged. "Well, maybe I just have a lot of patches, and they're all bad, and they're sorta strung together."

She shook her head. "Honey, you're using that junk as a crutch."

"For what, Teen?"

"You tell me."

But I didn't have to: The medication helped me not to feel anything. Numbed me from the disappointment dished out by Peggy Sue, protected me from the anger administered by Jake, and softened the loathing lobbed by Roger. If I weren't on the stuff, I'd be crying into my pillow every night.

She reached across and took my hand and her eyes held mine. "I think it's time you faced life, sweetie, even if it hurts a little. How else are you going to begin the healing process?"

"Same as always." I jerked a thumb toward the door. "Retail therapy."

Tina smiled sadly, squeezed my hand, then drew hers away. "I won't mention it again."

And she wouldn't. That's how good a friend she was.

Tina stood and heaved a change-of-subject sigh. "Now . . . how about buying some gauchos?"

"I will if you will," I said. "But they'll be out of style before we walk out of the store with our sacks."

And I took the last noisy slurp of my cinnamon mocha frappé with whipped cream and candy sprinkles, and rose to follow my BFF into battle.

The air outside was crisp and cool, putting us in a perfect mind-set for looking at fall/winter fashions.

Tina is the only person I can shop with and not get a migraine. We're veterans of the shopping wars and have the scars to prove it. We'd honed our craft years ago by once hitting nine malls in the Chicago area over two days, and proved our mettle (and our friendship) by still speaking to each other at the end of the trip.

I have some advice (big surprise) on shopping etiquette for beginners, and old hands, too.

(1) No visiting while you shop with a friend or friends. Do your gabbing ahead of time, like we do. The most Tina and I ever say while looking at clothes is "Who shot the couch?" or "Does clown makeup come with this?" Mostly, we grunt.

(2) No talking on the cell phone. Do you know what I do when someone yakking on a cell *dares* to come around the rack I'm sifting through? I start singing "Feelings," nice and loud. With feeling.

(3) Never shop with someone who doesn't have the same taste in clothes as you. Nothing is worse than being dragged into Christopher & Banks when you want to go to Arden B.

(4) Slower traffic, stand to the right! Sure, I like to browse . . . but if I come into contact with a woman on a mission (or on her limited lunch hour), I know enough to gangway. She'll be gone in a nanosecond—and hopefully not with all the good stuff.

(5) Don't be a dressing-room hog. If you can't make your mind up about something, don't buy it. Or, step out of the room and ask the lineup of impatient women waiting their turn; we'll tell you what we think and won't mince words!

October is Breast Cancer Awareness month (*that* got your attention, didn't it?), and Ingram's Department Store—where Tina and I were headed—had come up with a brilliant idea to encourage women to have a mammogram.

Working in conjunction with the local hospital, the department store had the mobile X-ray unit park just outside their back entrance, and offered 20 percent off on everything in the store (cosmetics and jewelry, included!) to each lady who got one.

The weeklong response was tremendous . . . . Because if there's one thing a woman likes more than saving her own life, it's getting a nice discount!

Plus, no anxiety or tears to ruin the shopping day; X-ray results had to be forwarded to the hospital for evaluation and that would take a few days.

As a pianist somewhere in the store mangled "Wind Beneath My Wings" into a crash landing, Tina and I filled out a form at a table just inside the department store. Then we were each handed a card with a number—mine was sixteen, hers seventeen; number eight was being paged at the moment over the store's intercom.

Tina and I split up (as prearranged), her heading for the shoe department, me to the David Yurman counter. I already had one of his rings for my left hand and wanted another for the right. (A word of caution: Don't ever put David Yurman in a liquid jewelry cleaner; it'll take off the signature black. I wish somebody had told *me* that!)

As I tried on rings, the time flew by (not for

the poor clerk helping an indecisive me) and just when I was zeroing in on one with a black pearl, my number got called. *Curse you, Breast Cancer Awareness Week!* I caught sight of Tina pawing through a sales rack of jackets (her weakness) and waved that I was heading to the back of the store.

There, I presented my number to another woman, who checked off my name, handed me a discount coupon, and ushered me outside, watching to make sure I really entered the trailer-size X-ray vehicle and didn't sneak around to the front of the store with my coupon. (You can't trust anybody these days.) (Including me.)

Once inside the mobile unit, I slipped off my jacket and bra, and a female technician assisted me in getting my left breast into the jaws of torture, which she kept squeezing until I hollered uncle.

She chided me to "take it like a man," and I commented that if a man had to have his testicles squeezed in one of these things, a kinder, gentler machine would be invented pretty darn quick!

She retorted that a little minor discomfort was a small price to pay for possibly saving my life, and I would have agreed, if I hadn't been clenching my teeth in discomfort. Then the tech disappeared behind a protective partition and took the picture.

The other boob getting squished didn't hurt at all—go figure—but I would have bet a hundred smackers that a man held the patent on that machine.

Clutching my 20 percent reward, I passed

Tina coming out of the store just as I was going back in, and gave her a thumbs-up. This was not a gesture of pride in having taken responsibility over the care of my health, rather an acknowledgment that some really serious shopping was about to go down. . . .

Returning to the jewelry counter to close the deal on the Yurman ring, I happened to come upon a certain girlfriend of Peggy Sue's, who was looking at a table display of particularly tacky Halloween sweaters. That a witch was interested in that holiday was no big surprise to me.

Of all my sister's gal pals, Connie Grimes was the most snobbish, conceited, arrogant, botoxed, and bitchy. Unsuccessfully, I tried to slip by before getting recognized.

No such luck.

"Weeeell, *Brandy* . . ." She always smirked when she saw me, like she knew something I didn't, making the very utterance of my name seem like her own special and very hilarious inside joke. As usual, Connie was hiding her heft under voluminous Eileen Fisher.

I smiled sweetly, "Hello, Connie. . . . Contemplating a Halloween sweater? I'd recommend the one with the witch with the rhinestone mole."

Her smirk smirked some more. "And *who* put a little troll like you in charge of fashion in Serenity?"

I smiled sweetly. "Just thought my sister's bestest best friend might appreciate a little help. . . . The large sizes are on the right, there. . . ."

Her smirk turned into a sneer. "I'll tell you

who could use a little *help*—you and that nut-case of a mother of yours!"

She'd barely finished the sentence when I slapped her.

Sometimes the Prozac works, sometimes the Prozac doesn't work.

Barrel-shaped Connie retaliated, bopping me alongside my head with her Dooney & Bourke bag. Head ringing, I punched her in her considerable stomach—that belly could hide underneath that Fisher smock, but it couldn't run. . . .

Connie staggered back into the table display, where she and the Halloween sweaters took a tumble and went down in a blur of fall colors.

Then Tina was holding me back, and a security guard from the store arrived and helped Connie—sprawled down there like a cow giving birth—up onto her feet, while quite a crowd of shoppers gathered. The onlookers' reaction was appropriate to Halloween, too: amusement and horror, in various combinations.

Connie, a hand clutching her tummy, sputtered to the security guy, "I want the *police*! That horrible creature assaulted me, and I'm going to press charges!" To me, she spat, "You're going to be *sorry* you tangled with *me*, sweetheart!"

I already was—I was pretty sure a playback of the department store's surveillance tape would prove that I threw the first blow. Next time I'd have to make sure I wasn't near one of those darn cameras.

Tina whispered in my ear, "Honey, I take it back about the Prozac. . . . In fact, maybe you'd better increase the dosage."

* * *

I wasn't in lockup long.

To pass the time, I was mentally working on my cinnamon-mocha-frappé-with-whippedcream-and-candy-sprinkles defense, when the chief himself came around to spring me.

Tony Cassato looked none too happy.

Without a word, he opened the cell and motioned brusquely with two fingers to follow him, which I did, down one cold corridor, and then another, arriving at his office.

I took the chair in front of his desk, and he sat behind it heavily, eyes boring into me like disgusted lasers.

"What in the hell is the matter with you?" he mused rhetorically. "You're *how* old? Thirty? And yet you act like an immature teenager."

Another dissatisfied customer.

Tony continued: "Mrs. Grimes—Connie—has agreed with my decision not to bring charges. I explained that the shock of finding Mrs. Norton yesterday most likely led to you overreacting in this situation."

I muttered, "Thank you," looking down at my hands in my lap. My nails could sure use a little TLC. That was what I got, giving up manicures to save a few bucks for mall crawling.

"But you're not going to get off so easy with me," he said. "I'm going to see to it that you take an anger management class."

Which really pissed me off, but I held it in and said only, "Okay."

Tony studied me for a moment. Then: "You still seeing a psychiatrist?"

"Psychologist."

"Who?"

"Cynthia Hays."

He jotted the name down. Which meant that if I didn't come clean with her at my next appointment, Tony was going to tattle on me.

"I'm seeing her next week," I said.

"Good. How about your mother?"

"Yeah, how about my mother?"

"I mean," he said tensely, "is she still seeing a psychologist?"

"She sees a psychiatrist. She needs the heavy meds."

"I'm not surprised." He shifted in his chair. "Listen, Brandy—it didn't make it into the reports, but I've been told your mother was . . . acting out yesterday, at the crime scene."

I frowned. "*Was* it a crime scene?"

He just stared at me, the kind of blank expression that precedes an executioner pulling the switch on Old Sparky. "Why do you ask?"

"Uh . . . I just didn't know if a dog was exactly a, uh . . . criminal. And don't you need a criminal to have a crime scene?"

"No criminal," he said slowly, "seems required to have your mother make a scene. I am told she was talking murder and making inappropriate comments and asking inappropriate questions."

I gave him a pretend grin. "Yeah, that's my mother! Would make a pretty decent sitcom, if this were 1958."

He pointed a finger at me—Uncle Tony Wanted Me. "I won't have her sticking her nose into police business. I won't have you helping her, either."

"I'm not! I don't even know that she's . . .

doing anything." I leaned forward and asked, "Can you have a little empathy? Mrs. Norton was a friend, and Mother found the body. Of course that got her going! It was a shock, wasn't it?"

He just stared at me. "You were helpful with that other case, but I don't want you making a habit of—"

"Then it *was* a crime scene! Are you saying this is a murder? Did Mrs. Norton die of something other than a pit bull mauling?"

He closed his eyes. He kept them closed for a long time. When he opened them, he seemed disappointed I was still there.

Then he said, "Brandy, I just finished telling you this matter wasn't any of your business. And you just asked me a series of questions that are none of your business. They are, in fact, police business."

"Sorry."

Tony shook his head, then stood, handing me my purse, which had been taken from me. "Where's your car?"

I told him it was still back at the mall, and he said he'd drive me there in his.

That may have been the most uncomfortable ride I ever took, me hugging the passenger door, my chauffeur staring stonily ahead. By the time we got to my Buick, I had started to blubber, feeling sorry for myself (since no one else seemed willing to).

When I snuffled snot, he snapped, "Do you *have* to do that?"

"I . . . I don't have a tissue."

He reached into his coat pocket, handed me

a tissue, and I blew my nose, with a *honk* his car horn might have envied.

Tony was shaking his head again, but more sad than disgusted. "I don't get you, Brandy. . . . When I first met you, you were professional, focused . . . back when you helped the department initiate our new mental health program."

"Back when I had a life, you mean."

"And whose fault is that?" He handed me another tissue. "Here . . . stop crying, you big baby."

Second person today to accuse me of that.

And I didn't dare tell the chief that the real reason I was bawling was not his lectures about my behavior at the mall and my enabling of my would-be detective mother, rather that . . .

. . . *I didn't get my David Yurman ring!*

I blew my nose again, and promised I'd try to behave myself. Tony spared me any parting words of advice, and I made my escape out the passenger door.

Standing in the parking lot, I watched the chief drive away, then went to my car, where a piece of paper was stuck under one of the wipers.

I opened the note, which read *Brandy—I bought you the ring you were looking at. We'll settle up later. Love, Tina.*

I let out a *whoop-de-do!* What a pal!

My spirits lifted, I hopped in my car and was about to start it when my attention was drawn to a man and woman inside a blue Cadillac, idling a few spaces away. I couldn't make out their words, but they were having what seemed to be a terrific argument.

The woman, behind the wheel, had her back

mostly to me, but the man was visible. Over forty, with greasy black hair, and a two-day growth of beard, he might have been attractive if his face weren't contorted in anger.

Suddenly, the woman threw the Cadillac in gear and pulled away. As she glided by, my mouth dropped.

The woman was Bernice, Mother's old friend turned archenemy.

Who, as far as I knew, had long been a widow. . . .

Was the younger man a paramour? Or a protégé from the playhouse turned lover?

I shrugged, not really interested.

But Mother would be.

And I was too good a daughter not to tell her.

### *A Trash 'n' Treasures Tip*

If you've acquired so many antiques and collectibles over the years that you've had to rent several storage units, it's time to admit you have a problem and seek professional help. (One storage unit is acceptable.)

# Chapter Eight

## Throw in the Trowel

Mother insists on having her own chapter, to help offset what she feels is an otherwise one-sided depiction of herself "through the Brandy end of the telescope," as she puts it.

So here it is, but I feel obligated to warn you that she is not always a reliable source of information. In fact she's seldom reliable. Also, since I have no control over what Mother will say or do, I apologize beforehand to anyone she may offend.

Including me.

My poor, darling daughter—stress and medication do take their toll—had taken my grandson Jake hiking that morning, out at scenic Wild Cat Den State Park. I only hoped the fresh air and exercise would do her good, thinking the dear girl needed to get a grip on herself before going off the deep end.

(On the other hand, I of course didn't tell Brandy—not wanting to encourage her antisocial behavior—that in my heart of hearts I could only applaud her standing up to that snobby Connie. In fact, any time she wants to pick a fight with any of Peggy Sue's friends, it's fine by me . . . they all act so high and mighty and holier than thou. My only regret about that unfortunate incident at the mall was that I wasn't there to see it, or perhaps pitch in and help Brandy. But you didn't hear that here. . . . )

After tending to Sushi, who seems to need an outdoor potty break every hour on the hour (probably because she drinks like a fish), I fetched my pocketbook and wrap and headed out the door into the crisp fall morning.

It took a mere three-block stroll to catch the Serenity Trolley, an old electric converted-to-gasoline streetcar (shouldn't we be considering the opposite transformation these days?), owned by the downtown merchants.

The trolley is free, but a person can only travel downtown (and back), the idea being to spend one's hard-earned dollars with those friendly retailers who'd provided the ride. If ever I *did* want to go someplace off the beaten trolley-track, however, the driver would usually comply, always seeming to be glad to drop me off anywhere at any time.

Mrs. Roxanne Randolf had formerly driven the trolley, until one afternoon she arrived home unexpectedly only to catch her husband in bed with a neighbor young enough to be his daughter. On the spot, Roxanne swore she would take the unfaithful wretch for all he was worth—which she did, only that wasn't much because the unfaithful wretch's business was making and selling ceramic lighthouses out of their basement.

Anyway, after the divorce Roxanne joined her sister in Tucson, having packed up a considerable stockpile of ceramic lighthouses, which they soon began selling out of *their* basement, to great success, I hear. The last I heard they were making their own new and improved models, which is a good thing, because the one I bought right before Roxanne left town went on the fritz, the little light shorting in and out, which in a real lighthouse could lead to shipwrecks, and takes much of the charm out of owning a little ceramic lighthouse at all. (But I digress.)

Maynard Kirby now drives the trolley. Retired from the fish hatchery, Maynard tells everyone who'll listen (and many who don't) that he only took the job because he was bored at home, but I happen to know he needs the money because his wife lost, if you'll pardon the pun, a boatload gambling on the *River Queen* last summer, forcing the Kirbys to take out a second mortgage on their home. (Have you noticed that gamblers love to tell you how much they've won, but almost never share the unfortunate details of what they've lost?)

I climbed aboard, exchanged pleasantries with Maynard, then managed to find a seat on the crowded trolley, which is always full nowadays due to the high gasoline prices. When we made another stop for passengers, I gave up my seat to Billie Buckly the town little person—or is "height-challenged person" the correct term these days for a midget?

This magnanimous gesture on my part was for two reasons: standing Billie and Billie's standing. First, I had once seen the trolley brake suddenly and send a standing Billie flying through the air like a tiny rocketman, sans parachute; and second, I was paying respect to Billie's local standing—he was practically royalty because his linage went back to the original Barnum & Baily Circus; plus, he had a great-uncle who'd been in *The Wizard of Oz* (playing a Munchkin).

The trolley, arriving downtown, drew up in front of the beautiful old courthouse, the very same historical structure that the aesthetically challenged of Serenity seek to tear down over my dead body. Here, everyone disembarked, and I hoofed it another three blocks to Hunter's Hardware Store.

Hunter's hadn't changed since I wore bloomers, and I don't mean in the production we did four years ago of *Meet Me in St. Louis.* Except for the prices, which have skyrocketed, time stands still in this lovely combination hardware store and tavern, with its wonderful wooden floor, classic tin ceiling, and many original Victorian fixtures.

In the back of the elongated space was a scarred mahogany bar and a few tables, an area that could accommodate a good twenty patrons. Hunter's had been serving up liquor and chain saws for years, and it could get quite exciting when a brawl broke out at the bar and moved into the hardware section.

Junior—the owner—was behind the counter

at the moment, polishing tumblers. Fifty years ago, his nickname had accurately described him, back when there were people on the planet who actually remembered the senior who'd preceded him. But now he was balding and paunchy, with rheumy eyes and a mottled nose. He offered up his endearingly grotesque bucktoothed smile as soon as he spotted me.

"Hello, Vivian. . . . Your usual?"

"Please," I said, taking one of the torn leather counter stools. "But only *one* cherry this time. . . . I'm watching my figure."

"Who isn't?" Junior chortled, and I wasn't sure how to take that. He turned his back to assemble my drink, and—just in case he'd been flirting—I asked, "How's Mary?"

"Oh, the missus is fine . . . she's really getting the hang of the new leg."

Junior's wife lost her limb in a freak accident while visiting the *Jaws* attraction at Universal Studios some years back. They got a nice settlement, but spent it all on buying this place, and Mary had to settle for a less than top-of-the-line prosthetic—specifically, a wooden leg the ever-thrifty Junior ran across in a junk shop. (Apparently an eye patch and a parrot weren't available.)

Mary had been game, at first, but her wooden leg kept falling off at the most inappropriate moments—once at the top of an escalator, bouncing all the way to the bottom, kicking another woman on its merry way down—so I took up a collection to buy Mary a more modern prosthetic. With the limited budget my best efforts accumulated, I felt lucky to find something appropriate on eBay.

Of course, no good deed goes unpunished. I'd been confused as to which limb Mary needed—as the kids say, my bad!—and for a while there, she ended up with two left legs, which can not only make it difficult buying shoes, but tends to lead to a lot of walking around in circles.

The happy ending was that Junior was finally shamed into taking Mary for a real fitting and getting an actual prosthetic for the right (that is, correct) leg. So my efforts were well worth the trouble!

But I digress. . . .

The only other person at the bar at this early morning hour was Henry, a once-prominent surgeon who, after a couple of belts of bourbon to steady his hands, removed a patient's gall-bladder, which went swimmingly, except it was supposed to be an emergency appendectomy.

Needless to say, Henry lost his license, and has been a barfly at Hunter's ever since. (I once organized an intervention at my house to get him off the booze, but Henry arrived with four six-packs of what he described as "pop" and turned out to be wine coolers, and the last thing I remember we were all sitting around singing "Row, Row, Row Your Boat," but not as a round.)

Junior set my cherry-bobbing Shirley Temple in front of me. "I suppose there's no sense in asking," he asked, "but you *did* read in the paper about Mrs. Norton . . . ?"

I took a dainty sip of my drink. "No, I did not."

"You *didn't*?" Junior's cloudy eyes suddenly cleared; the old goat thought he had the latest news on me. "Since when does a juicy local death get past Vivian Borne?"

"Why should I bother reading about it," I said, nonchalantly, "when *I* found the body?"

Junior's mouth dropped. "You don't say!"

I frowned. "Wasn't *that* in the paper?"

"No. Just said two of the 'merchants' at the antiques mall made the discovery. Have you joined the ranks of local merchants, Viv?"

Henry lifted his head above the rim of his whiskey glass. "*You* found the old gurrl?" he slurred.

I shrugged, indifferently, stirring my drink with a cherry stem.

Junior said, impatiently, "Well . . . *spill*, Vivian!"

"I thought you read all about it in the *Sentinel.*"

"That write-up said next to nothin'! *How* did she die? The paper didn't say."

The *Serenity Sentinel,* it seemed, had mentioned very little, particularly if *I'd* been left out of the coverage. But perhaps that was my fault . . . I should have called one of the paper's newshounds and given a personal interview.

Live and learn.

Henry hiccuped. "Yeaaaah, Viv. *Tell* us, why don'tcha?"

I had to admit, dear reader, that I was disappointed my only audience was Junior and the hapless Henry . . . but the show must go on, whether playing to a full house or just a couple of rubes ensconced in the front row.

So I launched into a detailed account of discovering Mrs. Norton's mauled body. When I'd finished, I was pleased with my performance . . . they could take the old girl out of the theater, but they couldn't take the theater out of the old girl!

Of course, I left out Brandy's foolish theory about two pit bulls, and downplayed my own suspicions. I didn't have a thing to go on, after all—it did seem that Mrs. Norton most likely had been mauled by her formerly faithful pet.

Still, the Vivian Borne "Spidey Sense" remained a-tingle. . . .

Junior shook his head. "That fool woman," he said. "A pit bull ain't no substitute for a security system."

"Too bad no one advised her of such," I said.

His head shaking continued but picked up speed. "Oh, Viv, I knew all about it, her pit bull 'security' . . . we all did, in the Downtown Merchants Association. Some even tried to talk her out of using that damn dog, sayin' it would lay her open to a lawsuit if the animal ever attacked somebody. . . . But she wouldn't hear of it."

Henry was also shaking his head. "Fell in a pit, did she? Imagine *that*!"

Junior sighed. "Darn shame . . . that antiques mall was a nice addition to the downtown. And Mrs. Norton was a nice lady, taught a lot of us in this town everything we know about math. What's to become of the business?"

"I expect to find out this afternoon," I said. "I'm supposed to go there shortly to take an inventory of our booth."

"Let me know, will you?" Junior asked. "I'd like to tell the members at our next association meeting."

I assured him that I would, then abruptly changed the subject. "Say, Junior . . . Brandy saw Bernice out with a young man yesterday." I did my best to make the inquiry sound as casual as possible. "Don't happen to know who he is, do you?"

Junior's bushy eyebrows crawled up his forehead like caterpillars trying to flee his face. "Can't say that I do. . . . I thought you and Bernice were on the outs?"

"We're not as close as we once were, that's true. Or I wouldn't have to ask you who that young man is, would I?"

Henry contributed to the conversation by belching. Junior picked up. "But I do know Bernice was seeing Ivan for a while."

Ivan, a widower about my age (the exact number of years of which I share only on a Need to Know basis, and you do not need to know), had once been a mayor of Serenity. He did not seem likely to be the "young man" Brandy had mentioned.

Still, I asked, "*Was*? Know what happened to break up the budding romance?"

Junior shrugged. "He called it off, I know that much. Ivan never did say why . . . but you know what I think? I bet she started talking marriage, and scared the old boy off."

Henry slid off his stool. "Bernice, huh? Saw her at the possst office . . . 'fore she come to town. . . ."

I watched Henry stagger back to the bathroom, then turned to Junior. "Something must be done about that poor man. . . . He's losing his mind, Junior, and you're the enabler!"

Junior sighed. "I know . . . but if I refuse to serve him, he just goes someplace else. At least here I can keep his drinks watered, and see that he gets home in one pickled piece."

I nodded. "Do you happen to know where the Romeos are having lunch today?"

Junior thought so hard I was afraid the vein on his temple might burst. Then: "Say, you might check that new vegetarian restaurant on Chestnut and Main. I heard 'em saying they were going to give it a try."

"A bunch of meat-and-potatoes fellas like that?"

"I know. But they're also adventurous old boys. Not as adventurous as you, Viv . . . but adventurous enough. Can I ask you something?"

I slurped my Shirley Temple to a finish. "Within the bounds of good taste."

"Why do I get the feeling, hearing you talk about Mrs. Norton's death, that you think something's more fishy than doggie about it?"

"I said *nothing* of the sort."

"I'm a bartender. I can read people."

"That's fine with me, Junior." I slid off the stool, putting my money on the counter. "But *do* stop moving your lips. . . ."

Eat Healthy or Die, operated by two aging hippies (the wife did the cooking; the hubby ran the counter), was not very busy for the lunch hour. This might have been farm country, but sprouts remained an acquired taste.

Still, I did indeed find the Romeos (Retired Old Men Eating Out) sequestered at a table.

Usually full of piss and vinegar, today the quartet was settling for vinegar and oil, and appeared sullen and unhappy about it, thanks to the (mostly uneaten) rabbit food in front of these aging carnivores.

But I knew their presence was about more than just checking out a new local restaurant.

Vern, a former chiropractor, had recently gone through a triple bypass; Harold, a retired army captain, was diabetic; former hog farmer Randall had high cholesterol; and Ivan, our one-time mayor, was being treated for polyps. Despite what Junior had said, clearly the gents were being less adventurous than trying more to keep the grim reaper at bay.

The way the Romeos perked up at my arrival told me that—unlike Junior—they knew not only the scuttlebutt about Mrs. Norton, but that I had played a major role in the drama.

Normally, women were not welcome at the Romeos' table—welcome to stop and chat for a moment and move on, yes, but not to actually pull up a chair and sit. But these old codgers were always hungry for gossip, and while I have never been one to carry stories myself, I didn't mind humoring the Serenity Rat Rack with what local tidbits I might have happened to pick up. After all, I was their Shirley MacLaine!

Harold was the first to wave me over. He had a face like an old rottweiler's—barked like one, too. After his wife passed away, I went out with Harold a few times, but didn't cotton to taking orders from the retired captain, so I mutinied. We remained friendly, though.

I took the chair that Vern confiscated from a nearby empty table. The former chiropractor reminded me of an English setter, with his big nose, square face, and curly hair.

"How have you been, Vivian?" he asked, dark eyes twinkling knowingly, the outrageous flirt.

"Fine . . . fine. Trying to stay out of trouble."

"But not succeeding, I trust," said former farmer Randall, a Boston terrier with a pug nose and wide-set eyes.

"Maybe I'm not trying very hard," I answered coquettishly.

I waved the waitress over, then ordered a soy burger and carrot juice.

When she'd departed, Ivan—the ex-mayor, who had droopy jowls like a Saint Bernard (but more hound than saint, I assure you)—implored, "Come on, Vivian! You know what we want . . . *give*!"

I sighed, feigning reluctance, making these old dogs beg for my new trick.

After another prodding or two, however, I repeated my performance for Junior and Henry back at Hunter's . . . only this time adding a few revisions to the script—like me jumping up on an antique icebox as the pit bull snapped at my heels . . . and being roughed up (just a little) by Serenity's finest when I insisted on them sparing the animal's life.

I still kept my tingle of suspicion to myself—not to be stingy, rather to give myself time to develop a theory better than Brandy's silly two-pit-bull one.

Vern, Ivan, and Randall seemed utterly enthralled by my one-act play.

But Harold asked impertinently, "Why the hell would you want to save that son-of-a-bitch dog, when it tried to kill *you*, too?"

Annoyed that my motivation had been called into question, I huffed, "Well, first of all, 'son-of-a-bitch dog' is redundant, isn't it? And second of all, Harold, it's not the *dog's* fault he's that way, is it? Any more than it's your fault for being born the brute *you* are? Why should he be punished for not fitting in to a human being's world?"

The above was accompanied by *ooooo's* and *oooooh's* and laughs and nudges Harold's way from the rest of the audience.

Ivan, ever the politician, abruptly changed the subject. "I hear you've retired from showbiz, Vivian," he said.

The waitress arrived with my soy burger and carrot juice. I managed to contain my enthusiasm.

I said, "If you mean by that remark, Ivan, have I stepped down from the Serenity playhouse stage, that is correct."

"Mind telling us why?" Randall asked.

I took a bite of the soy burger, which had all of the taste and texture of an old shoe tongue between two pieces of cardboard.

"Well," I said, after managing to swallow, "you might as well hear it from the horse's mouth. . . . It's because I feel that *I* would have best served the playhouse as its director, *not* Bernice. After all, I've been long associated with the playhouse, and she's only been in town a few years and, quite frankly, doesn't have the background or abilities for the job."

Vern said, "I thought Bernice was pretty good in *Arsenic and Old Lace.*"

"What was *I*?" I ejaculated. "Chopped liver?"

Eyeing his own soy burger, Ivan muttered, "What I wouldn't give for chopped liver. . . ."

"No, no, no, of course not," Vern said, backpedaling, "*you* were good, too."

"Good," I said. "Why, thank you. How could I survive without such lavish praise?"

"Great, I mean," Vern said. "Wonderful. Hilarious?"

"Besides," I said, "Bernice just might be too busy these days to direct new productions, what with her new *paramour*. . . ."

That elicited a few raised eyebrows . . .

. . . and an outright flinch from Ivan.

"I didn't know Bernice had been seeing someone since . . ." Randall began, then stopped dead, avoiding Ivan's stare.

Harold asked, "Who *is* he?"

I shrugged. "Haven't the foggiest. Thought you boys would surely know. But I can tell you this much . . . that 'man' is young enough to be her own son!"

"That," Ivan said quietly, "is because he is."

Well, dear reader, you could have knocked me over with a cigar store Indian's feather!

Blinking, feeling the same rush of panic I had on the three occasions in my career when I've momentarily gone up on my lines, I said, "I, uh, I didn't know Bernice had children. She never mentioned any to me."

"She never mentions much of anything about before she came here," Ivan said with a nod. "She has two sons . . . one dead. The other, Lyle, came to live with her recently. And let me tell you, the kid is no prize."

So *that* was the reason Ivan stopped seeing Bernice. He and Lyle didn't get along. And from what Brandy witnessed, neither did mother and son.

"Ivan," I said lightly, "you remember that Indian statue you were eyeing at our mall stall, the other day?"

"Of course."

"You remember that it was marked 'sold,' and I couldn't let you have it?"

"Surely."

"Well, the buyer was—"

"Bernice," he interrupted. "I knew all about her wanting to get that Indian back, Viv—though I wasn't aware you girls had come to an agreement over it. Didn't know you were even speaking."

But apparently Ivan wanted to be speaking with Bernice again; elsewise he wouldn't have wanted to surprise her with that statue.

I checked my watch. "Oh dear . . . you boys will have to excuse me. I have a very important appointment at the antiques mall!"

"So antique *males* aren't enough, then?" Vern said.

"Nothing antique about your evil mind," I mock-scolded.

But when I reached for my check, it was not Vern, rather Harold, the sweetheart, who beat me to it. I leaned over to give him a peck on the cheek, but he turned his head so my kiss landed on his lips.

The old dog.

And those other mangy mutts all laughed and laughed.

A few minutes later I arrived at the four-story Victorian building on Main and Pine where Mrs. Norton had met her fate (and where Brandy and I had our booth).

Another dealer, Gene Stubbs, was on his way out, squinting at the bright sun like a mole who'd popped ill-advisedly out of his hole. He had the booth across from ours consisting mostly of worn-out old tools.

"Any word on whether the mall will reopen?" I asked.

He shook his head. "Even if it does, I'm moving out."

"Why?" I asked, surprised.

"Who's going to want to shop in there after what happened?"

"I don't know," I said. "A little mishap like that wouldn't scare *me* off, either as a seller or a buyer."

"Besides," Mr. Stubbs went on, "some of my tools are quite valuable, and I want a place that has security cameras going twenty-four-seven . . . not some homicidal hound. I'm *tired* of getting ripped off!"

With that, he turned and strode to his truck parked at the curb.

Mr. Stubbs did have a point. Theft of antiques in shops was increasingly common these days, in particular small items that could easily slip into pockets or purses. And antiques malls were the most vulnerable because of the obscured view of the booths.

I entered the building, expecting to be greeted by a trustee of Mrs. Norton's estate, since the late teacher had owned the building. Instead I was met by Mia Cordona, a female police detective. Mia was a childhood friend of Brandy's; back in the day, the pair got into their share of mischief.

Dressed in a simple white blouse and navy blue skirt, Mia was a lovely young woman with long dark hair, flashing eyes, and an hourglass figure, the kind they now call "curvy."

"Mrs. Borne," Mia acknowledged me, business-like.

"Mia, my goodness . . . why are you here? Is this a police matter?"

Ignoring my questions, she consulted her clip-board. "Your booth is number thirteen. . . ."

"Yes. Over there, just about where Mrs. Norton bought the farm . . . that is, I mean, where the poor dear woman was found."

Mia rolled her eyes (what was *that* about?) and turned on her navy blue pumps. I followed her the short distance to our booth, near which a confiscated, leftover piece of the new gray carpet discreetly covered the stained spot where the body had been.

"Mrs. Borne," Mia said, "I want you to examine your booth, carefully, and tell me if anything is missing. You understand, of course, that some items have sold—I have a list of those obtained from Mrs. Norton's records."

I frowned. "So if you already *know* what has sold, and what money is owed to us, why do you need me to—"

Mia interrupted, "Mrs. Borne, I'd appreciate your cooperation. The sooner we get this done, the sooner you can leave."

The fallacy there was assuming that I *wanted* to leave.

But I said, "Of course, dear . . . always glad to help the Serenity boys . . . and *girls* . . . in blue."

She winced at that (what was her *problem?*) and I turned my attention to the booth. My eyes searched over its displays like the beacon in my ceramic lighthouse (before it quit working).

And what I saw got me boiling mad.

"It's a *crime*!" I said.

Mia frowned. "*What* is? Mrs. Borne, what—"

"Why, it looks like a *tornado* went through here!" I declared, taking in our most untidy booth.

"We had nothing to do with—"

"Oh, I know you didn't, dear. It's the *customers*! Why don't people have the common decency to put things back the way they *found* them? Have they no *manners*? No couth?"

"Mrs. Borne—"

"No consideration for the owner of the booth, who spends hours—"

"Mrs. Borne! May we *please* continue?"

"Sorry. Mia, dear, I know you're working and are trying hard to sound all, all . . . official. But I've known you since you were in rompers. Is it really necessary for you to be so stiff and formal?"

Mia said nothing. Her half-lidded eyes gave her a most unflattering sullen look.

I shrugged. "Oh well. . . . Now, let's see . . . yes, there's an amber vase that's gone. . . ."

Mia rifled through the papers on the clipboard. "That item sold."

I stomped a foot. "*Shit!* Pardon my French, dear. Actually French would be *merde,* but I *knew* I priced that vase too low! To whom did it sell?"

I was at her side now, looking over her shoulder, helping her with the clipboard. "Another dealer? You can *tell* by the discount—"

"Mrs. Borne!" Mia snapped, drawing away. "I'm not here to give you that kind of information! Now, may we *please* proceed?"

Disappointed in my daughter's old friend's bad behavior, I turned back to the booth. "Well . . . the lyre banjo clock is missing."

"That sold as well."

I clapped my hands hard enough to bring Tinkerbell back to life. "Oh, *goodie!*" Then I froze. "Goodie, that is, unless it went to *another* dealer . . . and then I priced *that* too low, too. Oh, this business can drive a person simply insane!"

"So I've noticed. Is anything else gone?"

My eyes swept the booth in another inventory. "No. But I can tell someone was interested in the rolltop desk."

"Why do you say that?"

I pointed. "Because they moved our cigar store Indian out of the way to get a closer look. Does that count?"

"No. I'm not concerned about that."

I asked, slyly, "What *are* you concerned about, Mia? What's *really* going on here? You can tell me. Ask anyone—Vivian Borne is the soul of discretion."

The clipboard slapped down to her side. "*Thank* you, Mrs. Borne. Give my best to your daughter."

"Well, certainly, dear."

"That's all we'll be needing for now. You may go."

"Do you mind if I use the bathroom first? We seniors do the bladder's bidding, you know."

"Thanks for sharing." Mia sighed. "All right, all right, but be quick about it. I have another dealer coming in, in a matter of minutes."

I headed down the aisle to the rear of the store where I opened the bathroom door and let it bang shut. Then I sneaked back along a row perpendicular to where Mia was standing, now talking on her cell phone.

"Yes . . . three more to go," she was saying. "Okay, sure. Here's the rundown to date . . . booth number one reported a gold watch worth three hundred dollars as missing. . . . Booth seven said some comic books totaling about fifty dollars were gone . . . booth twelve, missing an iron. No, used for ironing . . . and the dealer in fourteen claims a hand garden rake was stolen, but the matching trowel was still there. . . . I don't know, how should I know? Maybe he already had one. . . . You tell me why the cash was still in the till!"

*Try Midol, dear,* I thought. *It works wonders. . . .*

I tiptoed back to the bathroom and banged the door again. When I returned to the front of the store, Mia, off the portable phone now, had a wary look.

I said, "Thank you, dear . . . I needed that," giving my girdle a realistic tug.

"*Good-bye,* Mrs. Borne," she said with a smile as frozen as a Popsicle but not nearly so sweet.

Then she walked me to the front door, as if she didn't trust me to leave. Nervy child.

By the time I caught the trolley in front of the courthouse, late afternoon had arrived. I asked

Maynard Kirby for one of those aforementioned off-route "special requests," and he acquiesced, dropping me at the Mabel Streble Animal Shelter, which after all wasn't too far off his beaten path.

The modern one-story tan brick building with its landscaped lawn might well be mistaken for a medical complex or law office, if it weren't for the assorted barking and meowing that drifted from behind the shelter, where dogs and cats frolicked on the green grass in spacious pens during most sunny afternoons.

These poor abandoned animals would still be languishing in the old run-down Quonset hut on the outskirts of town, if it wasn't for me making an unscheduled visit to the Sunny-Side Up nursing home, some years back.

You see, I'd had a flat tire in front of the rest home, so I went inside to use their phone. (This was before I had lost my license for taking a certain shortcut, which was terribly unfair because farmers drive through their fields all the time and don't get arrested. But, again, I digress.)

When the service station told me they couldn't come to change my tire for at least an hour, I decided to drop in on some of the Sunny-Side Up residents to put a little good cheer into their day.

Mrs. Streble was one of several elderly folks I visited on that impromptu call. The widow was what we used to call filthy rich, though her husband had made his fortune in cleaning. Hardly anyone in town knew of her wealth, or the extent of it, anyway, because of the miserly way she lived.

When I entered her room, the poor dear was in such a state . . . crying about how her children and grandchildren never called or came to visit. She was particularly bothered by having been deprived of her pet cats when she'd been brought out to Sunny-Side Up, all of whom had been dispatched to the local pound and . . . dispatched.

So I said, in my cheerful conversational offhand way, that if she were to leave all her money to the local animal shelter, why, that would teach those inconsiderate ingrate kids of hers a good lesson.

And that's exactly what Mrs. Streble did.

The very day after my visit, she called in her lawyer and changed her will. And a week after that the poor woman succumbed to a heart attack.

Of course, the animal shelter was ecstatic about their considerable good fortune—or rather Mrs. Streble's good fortune, which was considerable—and immediate plans were made for a new, no-kill facility to be built in the late benefactress's name.

Mrs. Streble's relatives, needless to say, weren't too happy with me—apparently Mrs. Streble had let it be loudly known that I'd given her the notion to cut the relatives out of her will, and the dogs and cats in—and I received a number of death threats. People can be such animals, sometimes.

Anyhoo, I walked into the cheerful, spotless waiting room of the animal shelter, and approached the young girl behind the counter, whose name tag identified her as Beth. Beth was on the porky side and rather dim, but she loved animals, which was a big plus in this business.

"Why, hello, Beth," I said. "Have you lost weight, my dear? You look wonderful! Simply wraithlike."

The plain-faced, cow-eyed child beamed. "Five pounds, Mrs. Borne. Could you really tell?"

"Of course . . . every pound shows." (Encouragement must be given to the weight-challenged, however hopeless the case.) "Would you be a dear and tell Jane I'd like to see her?"

"Certainly." Beth turned away from the counter and I watched her formidable backside disappear through an archway with little leeway to spare. Five pounds, I'm afraid, was like taking an ice-pick to the floater that took down the *Titanic*.

After a minute and change, the manager of the shelter appeared. In her midforties, with short brown hair and an athletic build, Jane had been a dedicated advocate of the homeless animals of Serenity for twenty-some years. Never married, Jane once told me that she considered these animals to be her very own children—an ever-changing brood—and always took it hard when any had to be (as the terrible phrase so accurately states it) "put down."

Jane came around the counter to greet me. "Nice to see you, Vivian," she said with a winning smile. "You look wonderful. Have you lost weight?"

That was rather too personal and presumptuous a question for her to ask, I thought; so I ignored it and inquired, "How is the foster pet program going?"

Jane had recently initiated this new concept, believing that more animals would be adopted if they were first placed in foster homes where they could get comfortable being around people. Also, the animals would "show" better to prospective buyers, having been in a home setting.

And sometimes the "foster" homes became real ones.

"We have fifteen dogs and twenty-five cats in foster care at the moment," Jane said. "And last week seven others were adopted."

"That's delightful to hear, dear, simply grand."

Jane tilted her head. "Are *you* interested in being a foster pet parent, Vivian?"

"Possibly," I answered slowly. "Sushi might enjoy having a companion. Sushi is my daughter Brandy's dog, you know—she's blind, and diabetic."

"Brandy is?"

"No, dear. Sushi. The dog."

"Are you interested in any particular breed?"

"I understand you have a pit bull."

"Why, no. Other than . . ." Jane's head reared back. "Oh my . . . you don't mean the one that was just brought *in* . . . ?"

"His name is Brad, dear. Brad Pit Bull. Isn't that precious?"

She shook her head. "I'm afraid that's impossible, Vivian—he's scheduled to be put down."

I put on my most indignant expression, which in this circumstance wasn't difficult. "I thought you didn't *do* that kind of thing here anymore!"

Her eyes took on a sorrowful look. "Only when it's necessary—rabid animals, for example. Or if the city orders us."

"And *have* they? Signed Brad Pit Bull's death warrant?"

"No, not yet . . . but they just haven't gotten around to it. They're still investigating, after all."

*And if they were investigating, so should I be! Brandy and I!*

"Well," I said, "then stall them, Jane. . . . Brad's a good dog, who may have made a mistake."

"May have made a *mistake*?"

I waved that off. "Well, even if he did maul Mrs. Norton to death, doesn't everyone deserve a second chance? Even a bad little doggie?"

She was giving me the funniest look, her mouth hanging open. . . .

I asked sweetly, "May I see him? Brad?"

Jane seemed puzzled at my request, but she knew darn well *I* was why this fancy doghouse had ever been built, and finally she said, "All right, but just for a moment." Like a bossy nurse does when you want to visit someone in intensive care, after hours.

I followed Jane through the door to the large concrete-floor area housing the wayward animals. As I walked along, the noise became deafening, each dog barking, each cat meowing, the language of species differing but the translation the same: "*Pick me! Pick me!*"

(Here, by way of full disclosure, I must admit that I've never wanted a pet, being as busy as I am . . . but having Sushi around the house these past months had changed my mind. And it broke my heart to see the hope in the eyes of these discarded animals being dashed as I passed by them.)

Jane halted in front of a large cage, and for a moment I thought it was empty. But then I spotted the pit bull curled in a pitiful ball in a corner.

Jane warned, "He's not been very responsive."

I called his name, and then Brad's head and ears perked, and he jumped up and scampered over.

Jane said, amazed, "He . . . he seems to really like you."

"Yes, dear . . . we're old friends. And he has excellent taste!" I bent and scratched the dog's ear through the cage wire, and he pressed closer for more.

"Do you think you can get him to eat?" Jane asked. "He won't for me."

"I can but try."

Jane gazed down at the dog. "A loss of appetite after being sedated is expected . . . but that's been some time ago."

I straightened to face the woman. "You had to sedate Brad when he arrived?"

"No. Animal Control apparently did, before they brought him over, yesterday . . . and not a very good job, I might add. He wasn't even close to being knocked out."

I said, "No one with Animal Control sedated this dog. I should know!"

"Why is that?"

"If the *Serenity Sentinel* did its job, you'd *know* why! Because, dear, *I* was at the antiques mall when Brad was put into the van!"

Jane shook her head. "All due respect, you must be mistaken, Vivian. There were clear signs that this animal had been drugged when he was brought in—dilated eyes, sluggishness . . ."

I frowned in thought.

Jane sighed, turning her attention back to the pit bull. "But that was long enough ago to be well out of his system. No, I'm afraid he isn't eating right now because he's depressed."

I nodded. "To be expected. Brad misses his mistress."

"Then he shouldn't have killed her."

"Oh, but he didn't, my dear," I said. "I'm quite sure of that now. . . . So, where are the Kibbles and Bits? He'll gobble them down for his old friend Viv."

*A Trash 'n' Treasures Tip*

Sometimes a dealer will mark an antique as "firm," meaning he won't come down on the price. If the item has been gathering dust for a while, however, try making an offer on the day the rent on his booth is due.

# Chapter Nine

## Hike-and-Seek

I'm pretty sure Jake had a good time at Wild Cat Den (I know I did), rediscovering the natural-made attractions at the state park, from "Fat Man's Squeeze" (a fissure in a limestone rock wall allowing a shortcut for the slender) (my son made it, I did not) to "Steamboat Rock" (a gigantic boulder in the shape of a prow that you could climb up on). And of course, every kid's favorite was "the Devil's Punch Bowl" (a small crater that filled with reddish goo when it rained), and Jake was no exception.

Unbeknownst to me, however, my son had an ulterior motive, other than hiking . . . and if I'd had my parental radar up and running, I'd have noticed he *had* agreed to the outing a little too readily.

We were driving along the scenic River Road on our way there, when Jake asked, "Ever hear of geocaching?"

I admitted I hadn't. If it's not fashion-related, I'm pretty much on the outside.

He un-Velcroed one of his many pants pockets, withdrew a small rectangular gadget, and asked, "Know what this is?"

I thought, *Another expensive toy your father bought you?*

But I said, "Plays music, right? Download your tunes?"

How sad when Mom tries to sound "with it" ("with it" by now being a term only a mom would use, by the way).

Jake shook his head. "It's a GPS—Global Positioning System."

"Oh, I have heard of that . . . allows you to track something?"

He nodded enthusiastically. "Yeah, within ten meters."

I took my eyes off the road for a second. "Cool. . . . Uh, what exactly do you track with it?"

He smiled. "That's where geocaching comes in." After a pause, he went on: "Remember you told me how you and Grandma used to vacation every summer at the same place, and how you'd put little stuff in a tin Band-Aid box, then hide it and try to find it the next year?"

Yes, life really was that exciting back in the Olden Days.

"Yeah," I said with a smile, "only sometimes I'd forget where I buried it . . . but somehow, eventually, I always found my precious trinkets—rusted and slimy, but I found 'em." I shot him another glance. "Is *that* geo . . . geo . . . ?"

"Caching. Like in a cache . . . get it? Yeah. It's

sort of a treasure hunt and stuff, only with lots of people playing besides you."

"And how do they do that?"

"Well," Jake explained, slowly, as if to a small child or an imbecile, "once I hide my cache, I post the longitude and latitude points on an Internet site."

"Then what?"

Jake shrugged. "Then anyone with a GPS can try to find it." He reached into another pocket and produced a large plastic aspirin bottle. "This is what I brought along to stash."

"What's in it?"

"Oh, coins and marbles and stickers and stuff . . . just whatever we had lyin' around."

"Won't that disappoint the finder?"

"Naw! Everybody hides that kind of junk. It's more about *finding* the thing than what's in it."

I smiled. "Not much different than when I was a kid."

"Yeah, technology changes but kids don't."

My eyes widened. Nice to have a child this smart . . . if intimidating.

Jake, really talkative for the first time since he'd come to stay with us, was going full throttle: "But sometimes the cache can get muggled."

"Muggled?" What was that, a Harry Potter reference?

"Found and taken by somebody who's not playing the game. So you got to hide it real good and stuff, only you can't bury it . . . that's the rules."

"Sounds like fun. Can I help?"

"Sure . . . especially if you can spot poison ivy. *That* is no fun findin'."

One of the unchanging rules of childhood over the ages: Poison ivy bites.

We'd been all over the park before Jake settled on an acceptable hiding place for his aspirin bottle, in an old oak, just off the main trail. He slipped the bottle into a hole in the trunk, then checked his gadget for the coordinates.

Satisfied, he rejoined me on the path.

We were walking along the pine-needle strewn trail when Jake gave me a sideways frowning look, whispering, "Mom . . . don't look, but there's a guy back there in the woods. . . . I said don't look!"

"Sorry. . . . Is he wearing army fatigues?"

"Yeah, I guess. He keeps ducking and weaving and peekin' out from behind the trees."

"That's Joe Lange."

Another sideways frowning look. "Who's he?"

I sighed. "Just a guy I know."

"What, another stalker like that rolltop-desk freak?"

"No, just a friend of mine, from high school. And, anyway, that other guy isn't a stalker, just another antiques buff."

Our shoes crackled on leaves for a few steps.

Then Jake sighed and said, "Mom, you sure got some weird friends."

I didn't bother trying to deny it. "Joe's a special case," I said. "He kind of lives out here—during the day, anyway. He was in Desert Storm . . . ever hear of that?"

"Nope."

"It was a war before you were born."

"You mean Vietnam?"

"No, Iraq. *First* Iraq war."

Jake shook his head, his expression sour. "That figures. You know what they say."

"What do they say?"

"Sequels always suck."

I guess I could have mentioned *Godfather Part 2*, but his was a point well taken just the same.

"Anyway," I continued, "Joe was in Desert Storm and, well, came home suffering post-traumatic shock syndrome."

"Oh. You mean he's a mental case like Grandma."

"It's better to say 'mentally disabled,'" I suggested, dispensing advice I oftentimes didn't take.

"Whatever," Jake said.

I stopped and pointed to a small boulder by the side of the path that we could easily climb up onto. "Let's sit here. . . . Knowing Joe, he probably just wants to talk to me."

As Jake settled on the rock, he asked, "Should I pretend not to see him? I mean, he doesn't think he's invisible or something, does he?"

Trying to get comfortable on the hard surface, I responded, "Joe marches to a different drummer, is all. Just go with the flow."

"Okay. But if the flow gets too *weird*, I'm goin'."

We sat and waited, now and then glancing over our shoulders as leaves behind us crunched and pine needles snapped.

Suddenly Joe's head popped up alongside the boulder, startling us, even though we knew he was coming. The black and green greasepaint that camouflaged Joe's face made it difficult to see his not-bad-on-the-eyes features.

I said casually, "Hello, Joe, whaddaya know?"

Jake, a little nervous, squeaked, "Hey, dude . . . what's new?"

Joe returned to a crouch, using the boulder for cover. He looked here and there and everywhere (but at us).

"Thought you should know you're under surveillance," he whispered.

Jake, innocently, asked, "By you?"

Joe shrugged. "Counterinsurgency has its place."

*Riiiight,* I thought, but asked, "You mean, someone's following us?"

"Affirmative. Male. Civies."

"Description?" Best to keep it clipped with Joe.

"Negative. Too far."

"Hmmm," I said.

"Hmmm," Jake repeated, playing along.

I said, "Well, thanks for the tip, Joe. By the way, this is my son, Jake."

Joe, dropping the whisper, said, "Thought so . . . can see the resemblance. Nice to meet you, son. Say, you don't happen to have any chew stick or pogie bait on you?"

Jake and I exchanged quizzical looks.

"Beef jerky or candy . . . haven't been able to get to a slop chute."

Jake offered helpfully, "I got some Hi-C boxes."

Joe nodded. "Bug juice'll do."

Out of a cargo pocket, Jake retrieved the small drink carton with its little attached straw and handed it down to Joe.

"Much obliged, bro."

Jake asked, "Where's your gun?"

I glared at my son, who gave me a *What?* look.

Joe spread out his hands, fingers clawlike. "Don't need a Glock *or* a pineapple. . . . *These* babies are registered."

Jake's eyes went wide, and I tried not to smile at this army blarney.

I said to Joe, "We're heading back to our car. Do you want to walk along?"

"Negative. SOP is for me to go on ahead for recon."

"Oh," I said, "sure. Right. Well, thanks for the intel."

Joe gave us a loose salute. "If I get a better read on him, I'll catch you on the AGB."

"AGB?"

"Alexander Graham Bell," he said. "You won't see me, but I'll be around."

*Yeah,* I thought, *like the wind.*

Then, assuming a half crouch, my commando guardian angel ran back into the woods.

"That guy talks way cool," Jake said, sliding down off the rock.

*For a mental case,* I thought.

Walking, Jake asked, "Do you think he's right? *Is* some guy after us?"

I joined my son on the path. "No. He has an overactive imagination, that's all. Joe just likes to play survivalist out here."

But I could only wonder if Joe hadn't spotted a real threat, considering all the strange things happening lately. Maybe, Troy, my rolltop desk picker, really *was* a stalker. . . .

The return to our car was uneventful; we didn't spot Joe again, and no male among the tourists hiking and camping seemed to have anything more than a casual glancing interest in us.

The only bit of unpleasantness came on the drive home, when Jake said I didn't make a complete stop at a four-way sign coming into town.

I said, "I did *too* stop."

He said, "You did not."

"Did too."

"Did not."

"Too!"

"Not!"

"*Too, too, too!*"

"*Not, not, not!*"

I let it drop. Honestly, for a kid his age, Jake could be childish sometimes.

Arriving back at the house, we found a note from Mother taped to the front door, saying she would be back in time for supper. So much for alerting burglars (and stalkers) that no one was home. How did the old song go? *Walk right in, sit right down. . . .*

Inside, on a table in the foyer, we found another missive from Mother—beside a large orange plastic bowl brimming with an assortment of miniature candy bars—telling us to keep our mitts off the treats. This was Halloween, after all.

Out of respect to Mother's wishes, I took only one Almond Joy, and Jake a single Snickers.

My son said, as he tore off the wrapper, "Am I bigger, or are these things smaller?"

"Yes," I said, and popped the candy morsel in my mouth. Talking while I chewed, setting a really splendid example, I said, "Not the big regular candy bars you got when *I* was a kid . . . as the fillings in my teeth can attest."

While Jake retreated to his bedroom, I headed

for the bathroom, because hiking had swathed Brandy in a scent that was not perfume. After a quick shower, I wandered into the kitchen to see what was for supper, and found yet another note from Mother.

> *Brandy, darling, would you please start supper? Remember, the trick or treaters will be coming at five-thirty.*

I looked at the wall clock. *Yikes!* The little ghouls and goblins would be ringing our doorbell in just half an hour. . . .

Mother had set out three ingredients on the counter: spaghetti, V-8 juice, and bacon bits. She had invented this cheap, easy meal back when I was a snot-nosed kid, and this was probably the only food we had left in the cupboard. The concoction doesn't taste too bad, but really stinks up the joint when cooked . . . a terrific houseguest-clearer-outer. (If you make it, I won't be held responsible.)

I broke up the spaghetti, threw it in the frying pan, poured in the juice, tossed in the bacon, slapped on the lid, and let the thing simmer. Remember: I am not liable.

Jake appeared in the kitchen. He wrinkled his nose. "What *died*?"

Didn't I tell you?

"Supper," I said.

"Yuck. I'll just have candy." He tromped out.

Another mother might have called out, "Come right back in here, young man!" Another mother who wasn't competing with Jake's father's money, that is.

I was setting the table with paper plates (this dish didn't deserve china) when I heard someone coming in the front door. Expecting Mother, I went into the living room to greet her, instead coming face-to-face with a furious Peggy Sue.

"How *dare* you attack one of my friends!" Sis shouted, her cheeks nearly as red as her lipstick. She was in an orange silk blouse with signature pearls and tailored black slacks, her upscale idea of a Halloween getup.

I shrugged. "She asked for it."

Peggy Sue stood with her hands on her hips, like Supergirl deciding whether to tear a villain's head off or maybe arms and legs. "How would *you* like it if I—" She stopped and frowned in thought. "Who is *your* best friend?"

My own sister didn't know the name of my BFF? How sad was that? I knew every one of her horrible, despicable pseudo-pals.

"Her name is Tina," I said. "And Tina, not being a sociopath nitwit, would never talk to *you* in the insulting way Connie did *me*. She trashed not just me, but Mother, by the way. Why aren't you mad at your so-called *friend*? Whatever happened to standing up for family?"

"Whatever happened to civility is a better question," Peggy Sue said, and waggled a finger. "I want you to *apologize* to Connie. I don't care if you phone her, or send her a note, or better still go over to her house. . . . *However* you do it, that's your choice . . . but you *will* say you're sorry."

"Will she be apologizing for calling Mother and me whack jobs?"

Peggy Sue's eyes narrowed skeptically. "Connie actually said that?"

"Well . . . I may be paraphrasing a little."

Peggy Sue folded her arms. "All right. What *did* she say? Better still, what did *you* say?"

Another shrug. "All I did was offer her some fashion tips."

"I bet," Sis snapped. "You *will* call her and say you're sorry."

I couldn't remember Peggy Sue more riled up; this was the most emotional I'd seen her since childhood.

"Okay, okay," I said, holding up my hands in surrender. "If it means so much to you, fine! I don't know why you want that backstabber for a friend, anyway. She's *always* treated you terrible. Remember those awful rumors she spread about you, after high school?"

The red had left Peggy Sue's cheeks and now she went deathly pale. "How . . . how do you know about that?"

"I heard you and Mother talking about something like that more than once, when I was little."

"Well, that was a long time ago," Sis huffed. "No one's perfect and the Christian thing was to forgive Connie, and I have. She's been a good, loyal friend ever since."

I grunted. "Some friend . . . insulting your mother *and* your sister." I had to keep bringing this around to being Connie's fault, because, really, *you* know and *I* know the truth: I'd been way out of line.

But now we were at an impasse, glaring at each other . . . and since I would rather cut off my right arm than apologize to that load Connie Grimes, I came at it another way.

"Sometimes," I said, "I think you're afraid of that witch."

Boy, did *that* hit a nerve!

Peggy Sue's eyes widened. "Why . . . why would you say that?"

"Because you *act* that way—scared. What does she have on you, anyway?"

"Nothing!"

Suddenly I could smell blood in the water. "I'm right, aren't I? What is it, Peggy Sue—what does she know? One of those 'What happens in Vegas stays in Vegas' moments? Only it *won't* stay in 'Vegas' if you ever *cross* that monster. . . ."

Peggy Sue stood frozen. The nerve I'd hit had paralyzed her, and now . . .

. . . now I felt sorry for her. *Damn!* Just when I was finally getting on the scoreboard, I had to go and feel guilty and concerned. You can't win.

Thankfully, Mother chose that moment to make her latest grand entrance, fluttering in the front door like a wayward butterfly, putting an end to our sisterly conversation.

"Why, Peggy Sue," Mother said in surprise, "I didn't know you were coming over. . . . Would you like to stay for supper?"

I smiled at Sis, trying to mean it. "I've made Mother's specialty—spaghetti and V-8 juice—I'm sure there's plenty."

My sister did not share my nostalgic love for the nasty-smelling dish.

Peggy Sue backed up toward the door. "No . . . no . . . I'm afraid I have to go. I already have dinner made at home."

Mother said, "Well, then, dear, perhaps some other time."

Sis shot me a *We'll talk later about this* look before making her escape out the front door.

Mother turned her wild, wide eyes to me. "Brandy, I have wonderful news!" she announced. "Mrs. Norton was *murdered*!"

*A Trash 'n' Treasures Tip*

Where can antiques malls be found? Defunct shopping strips, out-of-business factories, old dead churches . . . I once stopped at a former prison that had been converted to retail, only I had trouble wrapping my head around shopping in booths with bars—particularly close to closing. The place enjoyed a low rate of pilferage, though.

# Chapter Ten

# Fire Urn and Cauldron Bubble

Only Mother could think she was bearing good news.

She was saying, "Your teacher was *not* killed by either the first *or* the second pit bull. She was *murdered*!"

"Yeah, I heard you." My eyes narrowed. "Where have you been?"

"Oh . . . out and about."

No words could strike more terror in my heart than those three spoken by Mother.

"Out and about *where*?" I asked.

"Here and there."

Better add those other three words to the terror alert.

I put my hands on my hips and chided, "Now, Mother—whatever makes you think Mrs. Norton was murdered?"

Mother's eyes were dancing a jig. "I don't just *think* it, dear, I *know* it! When I went to the antiques mall to take inventory of our booth, who do you think was conducting it? Your childhood friend, Mia! *Policewoman* Mia!"

Mother began moving around the living room, gesturing like a demented interior decorator.

"Now I ask you, Brandy, dear, what made that a police matter? Certainly not because a few antiques had been reported missing. . . . No! It's because they believe Mrs. Norton was murdered!" She needed a breath and took one. "Then it was out to the animal shelter, to Jane—she runs the shelter, you know—and she told me that when Brad Pit Bull was brought in, he had signs of having been *sedated* by Animal Control, when we know for a *fact* that the animal hadn't been! So you see, Brandy, it all fits!"

So does a straitjacket.

I shrugged. "I don't mean to take the wind out of your sails, Mother, but first of all, it makes perfect sense that the police would be called in to take the mall's inventory, particularly if any antiques had been reported stolen. . . . And second, maybe the Animal Control officer *did* in fact sedate Brad."

"Brandy, you saw it with your own eyes—"

"Granted, we witnessed a docile Brad getting into the van, but who knows what that dog's disposition was by the time it got to the shelter? Think about how Sushi behaves every time she thinks she's going for a car ride, only to end up at the vet's?"

Mother's face fell.

I sort of changed the subject, asking, "What about the rolltop desk?"

She frowned. "Still there, dear. I thought you

said that young man from the auction was going to buy it."

I frowned. "Troy must not have made it in time. It was close to closing when I sent him there."

Was it possible the desk wasn't Troy's main interest? Did I have a stalker, as Joe suspected?

Mother sighed. "Well, now he'll have to wait like the rest of us, until this whole thing is resolved." Her eyes landed on the dining room clock. "Oh my! I have to change."

She whirled and whisked from the room.

I called after her, "*Now* where are you going?"

By the time I reached the living room stairs, Mother had disappeared up them.

I stood at the banister and yelled up the stairwell, "Isn't *anybody* going to eat with me?"

No response from either Mother or Jake.

Grumbling, I returned to the kitchen. Apparently, the gourmet meal was mine alone. I stood and stirred the muck awhile until it looked done—it's not a science. Grabbing the pan handle, I turned away from the stove . . .

. . . and shrieked as I came face-to-face with a witch wearing a pointy black hat and a black caftan!

The pan tumbled from my hand, red spaghetti splattering onto the floor like blood at a vicious crime scene.

The witch cackled. "It's only *me*, dearie!"

"*Mother*," I snapped, "you scared me half to *death*!"

She grinned, showing fake rotten yellow teeth. "No actress could hope for a better review, darling . . . proof positive that my costume and makeup will bode well for tonight's performance."

I stood amidst the mess, hands on hips. "*What* performance? I thought you'd given up acting."

She adjusted her fake nose with its prominent wart. "This is an exception, dear. Two of the girls from my club and myself are replacing the Shakespeare cauldron witches at the Haunted House tonight."

The club Mother referred to was the Red-Hatted League—an offshoot of the Red Hat Social Club—made up of her dearest friends; they read mysteries and got together twice a month to discuss them—although I suspected local gossip was served up between fictional murders.

I asked, "What happened to the other haunted house witches?"

"Oh. Most unfortunate. Toxic poisoning from too much dry ice in the cauldron. But I hear they'll recover."

But would I?

Jake's voice called from the living room. "Hey! There's two ugly old witches in a golf cart sitting in the driveway!"

"Ah!" Mother said. "My ride . . ."

Alarmed, I asked, "You're going in a *golf cart*?"

"They're called *Club* Cars, dear."

"I don't care what they're called, Mother, you're not supposed to drive them anywhere but on a golf course."

She wrinkled the exaggerated wrinkles of her forehead. "Why not?"

"How about," I said slowly, "number one, it's dangerous? And number two, you'll get arrested?"

"Pish posh tosh."

"Pish what?"

"There's no chance of apprehension if we stay on the sidewalk, dear. There's no city ordinance against that."

But there might be after tonight. Mother was, after all, directly responsible for any number of city ordinances.

I touched my forehead as if checking for a fever. "Help me out here. Why aren't you going in one of the *other* ladies' cars?"

"Because, dear girl, we've *all* lost our licenses, for one silly imagined infraction or another." The witch made a clucking sound, and her expression indicated revenge was called for. "Most unfair. Frannie was the last to go, when she knocked over a gas pump. Bad luck, really."

"Bad luck."

Witch Mother nodded. "She should have hit it *before* filling up the tank. What use is a full tank when your license is revoked? And at these prices . . ."

I said, "Please . . . let me drive you in my car."

"Nonsense. We girls must remain independent. Besides, this in no ordinary Club Car! Frannie had it custom-made! It's got headlights, a horn, a radio . . . why, it even has On-Star!" Mother raised a bony finger with a glued-on, warped nail, and pronounced, "They can take away our licenses, they can take away our cars . . . but they can never take away our resolve!"

And with that, Mother was out the front door and down the steps, black caftan swishing, pointy hat bobbing.

Jake and I went out on the porch and watched

as Mother hopped into the front passenger seat of the golf cart. The thinner witch—a woman I recognized as Alice Hetzler, because her makeup wasn't as elaborate as Mother's—had been relegated to the backseat where golf clubs normally were stowed, with Frannie behind the wheel.

"Brandy!" Mother called out. "Do wait up for me. We have much to talk about . . . such as the scarlet claw!"

"The what?"

"Scarlet claw, dear! Later. . . ."

The golf cart—excuse me, Club Car—backed out of the driveway, bumped down over the curb, careened back up, then took off down the sidewalk, horn tooting, a few early trick-or-treaters jumping out of the way, the three witches holding on to their black pointy hats, caftans flapping in the night wind.

"Well," I said, "there's something you don't see every day."

Jake asked quietly, "Is Grandma all right?"

"I think she's just having a good time, honey." Was I kidding him or myself?

He squinted at me. "What's a scarlet claw, anyway?"

I thought for a moment. "You know, I think it's a Sherlock Holmes mystery. One of the old movies, not one of the real stories."

"Sounds like science fiction." His eyes were off me and onto the sidewalk. "Uh-oh . . . here come the trick-or-treaters."

"Could you handle them?" I asked. "I have a big smelly mess to clean up."

Jake nodded and scurried over for the orange

bowl of candy, while I returned to the kitchen where I found Sushi sniffing around the splattered spaghetti on the floor.

I was about to say, "No, girl, that's bad for you," when she turned up her nose at it and trotted away.

Blind but not dumb.

Then I got to work scrubbing the Jackson Pollack off the floor and the lower cabinets, amazed at how far the food had flung. After a short while, an exasperated Jake came in holding Sushi, who was driving him crazy with her yapping every time the door bell rang. I shut her in the kitchen with me, where she drove *me* crazy every time the doorbell rang.

After about three-quarters of an hour of elbow grease, the kitchen sparkled, and I joined Jake to help at the front door. But the onslaught of treaters had slowed to a trickle, and the ones showing up now seemed to be teenagers, whose costumes were more realistic and sometimes as gory as a George Romero movie.

I checked my watch; the two-hour time limit decreed by the city to stuff grocery sacks with free candy was fast approaching. I was contemplating shutting off the porch light a tad early—and risk being egged—because we were down to just a handful of candy, when the bell rang again.

I opened the door to a tall trick-or-treater wearing jeans and a tattered dark gray hoodie over a torn black sweatshirt . . . and a hockey mask.

I waited for the evil Jason from *Friday the 13th* to say "Trick or treat," before offering the paltry remains of sweets; but when he didn't speak (maybe the plastic mask prevented it), I held out the bowl anyway.

But Jason ignored the candy, his eyes behind the mask's slits, cold and dark, as he studied me . . .

. . . and then Jake.

"Go on and take it," I said, indicating the candy.

He just stood and stared. Now and then a teenager liked to really creep out the poor candy givers on Halloween, but this was getting weird. Really weird.

Sushi, let loose from the kitchen on account of good behavior, took an instant dislike to this Jason, even though she couldn't see him. She made little stops and starts toward his feet, barking wildly as she advanced and retreated and advanced.

Jason reacted by trying to kick her!

Jake snatched Sushi out of harm's way. I yelled, "Creep!" at the guy, then slammed the door in his hockey-masked face and threw the bolt.

I went to the front window and looked out.

Jason remained standing on the porch for a few more seconds, then turned and walked calmly down our front steps, disappearing into the night.

"What a jerk!" I said.

Jake, putting Soosh down, nodded. "You were right the first time—he's a creep . . . and *creepy*. Didn't even want any candy! How old you think he was?"

"*Too* old! There ought to be an age limit for

this. . . ." I went back to the entryway, turned off the porch light with an indignant click, then joined Jake, who had gone over to the couch.

We sat in silence for a few minutes, sharing a disconcerted feeling.

Jake was the first to throw it off. "Let's do something."

"Okay, what?"

"I dunno, anything."

I reached for the evening paper on the coffee table, and scoured it. Serenity was host to numerous Halloween haunted houses.

"How about going to the Field of Screams?" I suggested.

"What's that?"

"Another maze."

"Been there, done that."

"All right, then . . . the Haunted Forest."

"Naw . . . too buggy."

"Okay. What about Sleepy Hollow?"

"What happens there?"

"A headless horseman chases you down a dirt road."

Jake made a game show "buzzer" sound. "Next!"

I thumbed through the paper. "We're running out of options. The only thing left is the JC Haunted House . . . sounds lame, but it really is always pretty scary."

Jake smiled wryly. "How can it not be? That's where Grandma's working, isn't it?"

"Good point. Let's go!"

Complete with multiple towers and broken-out windows, the Haunted House was an abandoned dilapidated mansion on West Hill that had once belonged to one of the city's pearl button barons.

Over the years, however, the mansion had fallen into such disrepair that no one could afford to buy it to sink a small fortune into fixing it up, so eventually the city claimed it for back taxes. Then the Junior Chamber of Commerce got the bright idea of renting the mansion each October and transforming it into a real moneymaker, incorporating high-tech animatronics, set design, music, and live actors in ghoulish makeup.

I had to park about a mile away—we should have just walked from our house!—but once Jake and I reached the rusted, iron-gate entrance to the old mansion, we were glad we'd made the trip.

First, I paid our admission (ten dollars each, so it had better be good) to an evil-looking clown who I'm pretty sure was Mr. Evans, the high school marching band director, who made us perform one time in one-hundred-degree heat, even though half the percussion section had fainted.

As Jake and I walked with the others up the winding drive, fog machines hidden in the bushes spewed out white smoke that stalked us, ghostly fingers grabbing for our ankles. Out on the front lawn, red-spattered white-faced zombies wandered among a makeshift graveyard, some coming alive and rising up out of the ground, while the organ music of Bach's *Toccata*—punctuated by bloodcurdling screams—poured from loudspeakers positioned on the roof of the house.

At the front door, a mob was waiting to get in,

and I stood in line behind a young girl with long red hair and glasses, who looked about Jake's age. My son was ahead of me in line, pretending not to know his mother.

The girl seemed nervous, and we hadn't gone inside yet, so I asked, "Are you here with anyone?"

"My older sister, but she ditched me."

I knew how that felt. "Do you want to go through with me? My name is Brandy."

She nodded. "Thank you. I'm Amanda." She got a good grip on my arm, and we went in, as Jake disappeared ahead, wanting no motherly chaperone.

The JC Haunted House's rep proved to be well earned.

The library featured a spiral staircase you had to go up, which swayed and wobbled as if it might break away at any moment (kind of like climbing any flight of stairs after three margaritas).

The dentist's office was genuinely gross, with blown-up images of oral diseases playing on the wall, while a demented dentist—who actually *was* my dentist—worked on a screaming patient with a horrible old rusty drill (I'm gonna cancel my appointment for a cleaning next week).

The second-floor hallway had framed portraits of people who suddenly reached out for you (even though I saw that coming a mile away, I allowed a handsome Civil War soldier to grab me and hug me . . . can't let the kids have all the fun).

But my favorite scare was in the first-floor bathroom. When I peered in the mirror, a half-eaten-away skull replaced my face in the glass (although it was kinda what I look like first thing every morning, anyway).

At the basement door leading to the torture chamber, Amanda ran into her sister, and I said good-bye to my new young friend. Opting to skip the chamber (I couldn't imagine anything down there more torturous than my root canal), I headed to where I thought I might find Mother and her friends.

The three witches were in the main tower, and since they were on their feet, the amount of dry ice in the cauldron must have been correct. A crowd of fifteen to twenty people were gathered around them, listening to their oratory, and I waited until they had finished before butting in.

"Have you seen Jake?" I asked Mother.

Mother, stirring the pot with a long stick, cackled, "Round about the caldron go, in the poisoned entrails throw, is the boy with friend or foe, in a moment you shall know. . . ."

"Just *tell* me, already."

"Brandy," Mother said, sotto-Vivian-voce, "I *have* to speak in rhymes! Not doing so is the worst of crimes!"

I sighed. I knew Mother hated to break character, but this was ridiculous.

She cackled again: "Now about the caldron sing, like elves and fairies in a ring. The boy was here whom you do seek, and went to the portable potties to take a leak."

I didn't know who to feel more sorry for, Jake or Shakespeare.

I tried my hand at it. "Double, double, toil and trouble, fire burn and cauldron bubble, when

Jake returns from near or far, tell him I'm going to wait in the goddamn car."

"Brandy!" Mother gasped. "How randy!"

Anyway, I trouped to the Buick, got in, and leaned my seat back as far as it would go before closing my eyes.

Knuckles rapped on the car window, jolting me awake, and I turned my head to see Mother's witchy face in the glass.

I powered down the window.

"Don't tell me you're still waiting for Jake," she said.

"What *time* is it, anyway?" I yawned.

"After one, dear."

I bolted upright. "What!"

God, had I conked out *that* long?

I put my seat up. "Where is *Jake*?"

"I don't know, dear," Mother said, shaking her head. "The boy never came back. . . . I just assumed you'd found each other and gone home."

"I have to go back to that mansion!"

Mother shook her head harder, pointy hat flopping. "It's locked up. . . . We were the last to go!"

By "we" she meant her two witch friends in the club car parked behind me, on the now otherwise deserted street. Mother signaled to them that she was staying with me, and they rumbled off as she came around and got in on the passenger side.

"Nothing to worry about," Mother said. "Jake probably walked home when he couldn't find you. He's a big boy."

"But . . . I was right *here*. . . ."

"Dear, *I* couldn't see you with your seat back

like that, not until I looked in the window. Come now, let's go . . . Jake's probably wondering where *we* are."

This was the second time I'd been worried about my son going through one of these stupid Halloween concessions, and I knew Mother was probably right—my paranoia at that maze had been unfounded—but, even so, the short drive home seemed interminable.

Then, when I wheeled into our drive, my panic eased when I could see that my son's bedroom light was on.

Only when we got inside, Jake was not in his room . . .

. . . or anywhere else in the house.

"I'm going to call the police," I said, pacing furiously, getting out my cell.

Mother, seated on the couch, said, "Perhaps you should."

I stopped midpace, expecting her to have pooh-poohed the idea.

"Then you *do* think something's wrong!" I said. "That something *has* happened to Jake!"

Still in witch's drag, she smiled feebly. "Of course not, dear . . . but you're obviously upset. And it *is* nearly two in the morning. . . . Perhaps you *should* call."

Did Jake cause his father this kind of parental agony?

*Roger!*

I used my cell.

My ex's sleepy voice answered. "Brandy," he groaned. "Do you have any idea what time it—"

"It's two in the morning, and time your son

should be in bed but he isn't because I can't *find* him!"

A woman's muffled voice in the background asked, "Who is it, Roger?"

"Nobody," I heard my ex whisper. Then he said to me, "Okay, all right, now settle down . . . *what* happened?"

Quickly I told him about going to the Haunted House.

"Look," Roger said, placatingly, "the boy's just out having a little Halloween fun. . . . He'll turn up pretty soon, full of apologies."

"Roger! He's only ten!"

"I stayed out all night once at that age."

"That was thirty years ago! Times have changed. Why aren't you *upset?*"

He sighed. "I'm sure there's nothing to worry about. . . . Tell you what . . . when Jake turns up, have him call me. I'll talk to the boy."

I was so furious I couldn't speak, and flipped my phone shut, which is not nearly as effective as slamming down a receiver in someone's ear.

Mother asked, "What did he say?"

"Basically, boys will be boys, and I'm just being an uptight mom. Also, I'm 'nobody.'"

Mother said slowly, "I'm sure Roger is right about Jake. . . . Still . . ."

"What? You're *scaring* me, Mother."

"I don't mean to, dear. It's just that . . ."

"*What?*"

Mother took a deep breath. "I really do think there may be a connection between the federal auction, Mrs. Norton's death, and Jake's disappearance."

I shook my head disbelievingly. "Mother, I'm in no mood to listen to any of your wild theories right now, your stupid, crazy mystery games. . . ."

As absurd as her witch's outfit was, what she said next was credible: "Brandy, hear me out. What if one of the antiques we bought at the auction had something valuable hidden in it?"

"Like what?" I was frantically pacing. "The Hope Diamond? A map to the Flying Dutchman's ghost mine?"

Mother said patiently, "It's the *Lost* Dutchman's *gold* mine . . . and if you're going to be facetious, I won't continue. Go ahead and call the police."

I swallowed. "All right. All right, I'm listening."

She sat forward. "What if someone broke into the antiques mall to get the . . . whatever it is, diamond, map, we don't know . . . but that someone *didn't* find it, and in the process of that failed search was surprised by the unfortunate appearance of Mrs. Norton, who he then had to silence?"

"But the dog . . ."

"Was framed. Never mind how, for the moment—our concern now is Jake."

"It sure as hell is! But . . . how does *he* fit into this fanciful conjecture?"

Her witch's face was grave. "He may have been taken for leverage, dear . . . to get back from us what that person believes we have."

"But we *don't* have it . . . whatever it is!"

My cell phone trilled.

Roger.

His voice was alert now. "Brandy, is there an airport in Serenity?"

"Yes . . . a small one used by corporate types and flying clubs. Why—"

"I want you to meet me there in an hour. I'll call you as I'm coming in."

That seemed a little extreme, and I said, "Roger, I'm just about to call the police about Jake. There's no need for you to coming flying here in the middle of the night—"

"Yes, there is." His voice quavered. "Brandy, stay calm . . . but I just received a text message from Jake on his BlackBerry . . . and he says he's been kidnapped."

*A Trash 'n' Treasures Tip*

Half the fun of buying antiques is discovering new ways to use them once their original purpose has gone out of fashion. A pair of "sad" irons make great bookends, and an antique scale can hold fruit or potted plants. Mother once took an old bedpan, filled it with water and floating candles, and used it as a centerpiece. But I think she went too far, because the guests had trouble eating.

# Chapter Eleven

# In the Kill of the Night

As I remembered it, the Serenity Municipal Airport—I hadn't been there for years, not since taking a flying lesson on a whim and nearly hitting the white beacon tower—resided in a flat field about ten miles south of town, and consisted of a hangar, an airstrip, and a wind sock.

So I was surprised by how the tiny airport had expanded; even in the darkness I could make out a modern main building, four or five more hangars, a second landing strip, and a prominent new boldly red painted beacon tower that you couldn't miss (or maybe the idea was a beginning flier like me couldn't hit).

I squealed my car to a stop in the small empty parking lot right up by the one-story brick administration center. At this ungodly hour (3:00 AM), this main airport building—along with every other one—was locked up tight for the night. The airstrip landing lights, however, were on, as a courtesy to unexpected drop-in guests.

I got out of the car onto shaky legs and took several big gulps of cool air, trying to calm my nerves—sometimes Prozac just wasn't enough. Then I made my way over to the fence that cordoned off the two airstrips, stepped through the gate, and waited, eyes searching the inky sky.

Roger had celled me at home when he and the pilot were close to town, allowing me enough time to make it down to the airport before they arrived. And his calculation (as usual) was correct, for within minutes I could hear the faint drone of the plane's single engine, and begin to see the lights of the aircraft as it dropped lower and lower in the night sky.

The pilot—considering the short notice, either a friend of Roger's or someone from his company, I would guess—circled once, picked out an airstrip, then set the small plane down with ease.

I folded my arms across my chest as chill air from the propellers blasted my way. Then the plane taxied toward me, and the pilot—only a dark form behind the controls—cut the engine, and Roger hopped out holding the Louis Vuitton brown leather carry-on bag I had given him two Christmases ago (bought with his money).

Until I saw my ex, I had been doing okay, not great, but hanging on; but as Roger rushed toward me, my legs turned to jelly, and if it weren't for his arms drawing around me, I would have crumbled.

I laid my head on his chest and blubbered.

"Shhh . . . shhh," Roger said soothingly, stroking my hair. "We'll find him."

I pulled back. "I'm so glad you're here," I sniffled.

"Me too."

The plane's engine wheezed and coughed back to life, and as the pilot taxied for his return flight, Roger taxied me with an arm around my waist, toward the parking lot.

"You okay to drive?" he asked, holding me out in front of him with a hand on each of my arms.

"Yes."

"You sure?"

"Really, yes. You don't know your way around Serenity."

He couldn't argue that point.

Calmed down enough to drive, I got behind the wheel, and as I pulled on to the highway, asked, "Any more text messages from Jake?"

"No. Just that one he sent from his Black-Berry."

"But *who* in God's name would kidnap our son? And *why*? It's not like Mother and I have any money!"

"No." He was looking out the window at the dark countryside gliding by. "But I do."

Roger ran his own investment company in the prosperous Chicago suburb of Oakbrook.

In the empty backseat of my Buick sat the proverbial elephant neither one of us wanted to acknowledge: that Jake might have been abducted by a sexual predator. Our son was, after all, a very handsome boy, quite the spitting image of his father.

Roger said, "There is another possible answer to Jake's disappearance."

"What?"

"It's a rather more . . . benign one."

"What, Roger?"

"Our son may be trying to bring us back together."

"By pulling a prank, you mean? Kind of extreme, don't you think, even for Halloween?"

My voice had more of an edge to it than I intended.

Roger was shaking his head glumly. "Brandy, he's been very unhappy lately. He doesn't like my new . . . friend."

Another pachyderm had joined us: that this was somehow all *my* fault. . . .

I am guilty of my share of sins, but playing Jake off against his father, or even trying to undermine my new replacement, was not among them.

With a tinge of acid, I asked, "Is that why you keep buying him all those expensive toys?"

Roger stiffened. "That's unfair."

"Yes, it is unfair that I can't compete with the things you give him," I said. "If he didn't have that *BlackBerry* . . ."

"Let's not."

"Not what?"

"Waste time with the blame game."

". . . Okay."

"We'll get Jake back, and we'll go from there. If he's pulling something on us, we'll deal with it."

We'd be furious with our son as soon as we got over being ecstatic that it had been nothing worse. *Please, God, make it be nothing worse. . . .*

We rode the rest of the way in strained silence. As I pulled into our driveway, I warned,

"Mother has her own harebrained notions about Jake's disappearance."

"Now, there's a shock."

"Don't be mean. You have my permission to ignore her. Just don't . . . goad her."

"She's not that easy to ignore, Brandy."

"Roger. Please? For Jake's sake."

He nodded, and a tightness around his eyes eased. "Sure. United front."

"Thank you."

Inside, we found Mother, still in her witch costume but with the makeup washed off and her thick-lensed glasses on, seated by the phone on its stand near the stairs.

Roger set down his bag. "Hello, Vivian . . . you're looking lovely as ever."

"Why, thank you, Roger," Mother said, not rising from her chair, or to her ex-son-in-law's bait. "Sorry about the unfortunate circumstances." Whether she was being bigger than my ex, or just oblivious of her current attire, I have no idea.

I nodded toward the phone. "Anything?"

"No, dear, I would have called you on your cell, if there had been. . . . But I did take the liberty to call that nice young Officer Lawson of yours . . . at his home?"

Roger frowned just a little at that.

"And?" I asked anxiously.

"He said that we should sit tight, dear," Mother said, "and that he would come over to hear the whole story, before deciding what should be done."

"*We'll* decide what should be done," Roger said firmly.

I said, "Roger, Brian's a friend. He'll only help."

Roger asked Mother, "When do you expect him?"

On cue came a sharp rap at the back door.

We moved collectively through the kitchen, but I reached the door first, and opened it to Brian Lawson, who stepped in.

Not surprisingly, he looked like someone who had been dragged out of bed; but in spite of the cockeyed-buttoned flannel shirt, slacks sans belt, and uncombed hair, the officer's eyes were alert, and his jaw set.

I introduced Brian to my ex and suggested everyone move into the living room; Mother returned to the chair by the phone, Roger and I took the couch, and Brian sat across from us in an antique Queen Anne needlepoint chair as valuable as it was uncomfortable.

The clock on the mantel chimed four times.

Brian began, his eyes focused on Roger and me. "I'm sure you're familiar with the Amber Alert. . . ."

We nodded.

"In order to put that in motion, we must have a description of the person your son was seen going off with, and/or the car he got into . . . and as I understand it, from my conversation with Vivian, you don't have any such information. . . . Is that correct?"

"Yes," I said, "Mother was the last to see Jake—around midnight at the Haunted House. . . . He knew where our car was parked and was supposed to me meet there—and I was *waiting* in it. He never showed up."

"This was around one a.m.?"

"Yes."

Roger asked, with a burr in his voice, "Are you telling us, Officer, that there's nothing that can be done at the moment?"

"Not at all," Brian said. "I've spoken to the dispatcher and given a detailed description of Jake. . . . I'm familiar with your son, sir."

"I gathered."

"And the patrol cars that are out cruising have been notified to be on the lookout for him." Brian paused. "But yes, as of now, I'm afraid that's all we can do."

Choking back tears, I sputtered, "Till he shows up dead in a ditch, you mean!"

Roger touched my shoulder and said, "Brandy—please . . ."

"We can't just *sit* here!" I insisted to my ex, getting right in his face. "If Jake *has* been kidnapped, every minute that goes by puts our son in greater danger. He's out there somewhere, *and we have to find him*!"

Roger sucked air in sharply, as something flashed in his eyes. "Brandy! Do you know if Jake had his Global Positioning System with him?"

I blinked back tears. "He . . . he *could* have . . . he usually carries all that portable electronic gear around in his pockets."

Roger was on his feet. "Can I use your computer?"

"Of course."

"Or maybe—do you have wireless?"

"Yeah, we have wireless." I couldn't see where this was going.

Roger strode over to his carry-on, abandoned by the front door, unzipped it, and withdrew a sleek gray-and-blue laptop computer.

I said, "I thought a GPS was only used for *locating* things . . . not to *be* located."

Brian, right with Roger on this line of thought, said, "Unless it has its *own* tracking device. . . ."

"It does," Roger replied, returning to the couch. He opened the computer on his lap. "I wanted to be able to find Jake if he ever got lost doing his geocaching."

*Or if his mother ever took off with him?*

Even if that were the real reason for the tracking device, I didn't care; it was a line of approach, and a smart one.

Brian sat on the other side of Roger, and we both looked over my ex's shoulders as Roger's fingers danced nimbly on the flat keyboard, going first to the Internet tracking site, logging in his account number, then clicking on Track Now.

Almost instantaneously the screen filled with a map. Roger pointed to a flashing red star. "There he is!"

I stared at the screen. "*Where* is there?"

Brian, leaning in for a view, eyes narrow, said, "That's Tipton Road, west of town. . . . Let's take my unmarked car."

And the two men stood, in lockstep.

I got to my feet, also, and started to follow them; but Roger stopped me, putting his hands on my shoulders.

"No, Brandy. You should stay here, in case Jake calls."

"But he's *my* son, too! What if . . . ?" I couldn't finish the unthinkable.

Roger was shaking his head.

I said, "If he calls on my cell, I'll have it with me. The phone here, Mother can watch, and—"

Roger gave me a look that said: *Do you really want to leave your mother in charge of that important duty?*

And I had to admit, in the echo chamber of my mind, that he was right.

Mother, who had been listening all this time, said softly, "Roger's right, dear."

My ex gave Mother a grateful look.

Brian touched my arm and his warm eyes did their best to reassure me. "We'll call you when we get there."

Then the two most important (adult) men in my life exited through the kitchen, leaving Mother and me behind.

Mother came to join me on the couch. "We must put our trust in the Lord, dear," she said, patting my hand.

I had no such instinct. The Lord helped those who helped themselves, as far as I was concerned, and I was sick at heart and literally sick to my stomach, stuck here next to my eccentric mother in her witch's costume while somewhere out there in the darkness my son's fate was being decided. Without me.

My cell phone rang shrilly.

I jumped to my feet and got it out and open, and the voice on the other end was faint, but oh so familiar. "Mom? It's me. . . ."

"Jake! Where *are* you! We've been so worried!"

"Mom . . . you have to stay cool. Can you do that for me, Mom?"

"Jake—"

"You really have to do what this guy says, okay?"

"Jake! Where—"

A male voice, low and coarse, said, "As you heard, your son is fine."

My knees buckled and I sank back into the nearby couch.

I managed to ask (keeping perhaps 50 percent of the hate out of it): "What do you want?"

"Something that belongs to me."

"What in hell?"

"Just listen! Your son claims it's under his mattress. I want you to put it in a grocery sack and go out to Weed Park, where you'll place the sack in the trash can—next to the band shell. Then you're to leave . . . got it?"

"I think so. . . ."

"Say it back."

"Under his mattress, grocery sack, Weed Park, trash can by the band shell. Leave."

"Good. This smart kid has a smart mom."

*Go to hell, you bastard! Go to hell, you bastard!*

"Now listen with both ears, lady—you're to do this alone, within the hour. You're not to call the police or tell anyone where you're going or what you have with you, and what you have to do. You up to that?"

"Yes! And then you'll let Jake go." I didn't want it to be a question.

"Yeah, unless you cross me. . . ."

"I won't, I won't! I'll do *exactly* as you say . . . and after you let Jake go, we won't say any—"

The phone clicked dead.

Mother said, "Then Jake *has* been kidnapped."

I nodded numbly. "I need a grocery sack, Mother."

As a frowning mother went into the kitchen, I bolted upstairs to Jake's room.

I didn't know what I'd find hidden beneath my son's mattress—money? jewels? drugs?—but when I lifted the bottom corner exposing the box spring, I could only gasp.

A gun.

Not unlike the paint gun I took away from Jake. But this gun was all too real; the only color it would splash was deadly red, and, as I learned upon closer inspection, the awful thing was loaded with five bullets.

*Where on earth did Jake get it?*

And what was so important about *this* particular weapon that somebody would risk kidnapping a child for its return?

I didn't have the luxury of time to explore possible answers to these questions. I ran downstairs where Mother was waiting with a brown paper bag.

When she saw what was in my hand, her eyes behind the thick lenses popped. "My goodness! Where did *that* come from?"

Carefully placing the weapon in the sack, I said, "It's what the kidnapper is after. How or why Jake had it, I have no idea. And I can't tell you any more than that."

Mother followed me to the front door. "What if Roger or Officer Lawson calls? What should I say?"

My words came out in a tumbling rush: "You

need to say something that's very unusual for you, Mother. But you have to do this and be letter perfect. If you ever remembered your lines in any play, remember them in this one."

"*What*, dear? What would you have me say?"

"Nothing."

I was halfway out the door when she pleaded, "Can't you tell me where you're going, dear?"

"No, Mother."

"Just a little hint," she begged. "Is it in Serenity? Just nod, you won't really be telling me—"

"Mother! Jake's life is at stake! Stick to the damn script!"

"Yes, dear . . . you . . . you're his mother. And you know what's best. Mothers always do."

I left her on the porch and hurried to my car.

Weed Park—my destination—was so named after the Weed family who donated the land and provided these largely weed-free grounds with their ironic designation. Sprawling over rolling hills on the bluff of the river, the park had a state-of-the-art aquatic center, multiple tennis courts, a baseball diamond, numerous playgrounds, a large duck pond, plus the usual array of picnic shelters, benches, and outdoor grills.

Also a band shell.

I followed the winding, one-way, single-lane road through the dark deserted park, with only my headlights and my combination of fear and rage to guide me. Finally I came to the ancient stone-and-cement bandshell where a teenage Brandy once played her trumpet in a much nicer small-town world, one that seemed a lifetime ago now.

Leaving my Buick idling at the curb, I walked purposefully to the trash can in front of the band shell, lifted the metal lid, placed the brown paper bag inside, and replaced the cover.

I returned to my car and drove off.

But the moment I rounded the next hilly curve and was out of sight, I wheeled off the road, drove behind a picnic shelter, and cut the engine.

Then I jumped out and, keeping low, running as quietly as I could, headed back through the wooded park . . .

. . . toward the band shell.

Not far from the trash can was a large hydrangea bush, and I crawled inside it and waited.

And waited.

Had the kidnapper seen me?

Would my actions compromise my son's life?

I was being eaten alive—mentally with fear, and physically by mosquitos who had found a tasty early morning victim. As I screamed at myself in my mind for being such a fool, not doing exactly as I'd been told by my son's captor, another voice screamed back: I was Jake's mother, and I would do *whatever* it took to get him back, safe and sound.

Then headlights appeared around the curve in the road, moving stealthily, glowing like the eyes of a nocturnal beast stalking its prey. The late-model sedan slowed, then came to a stop at the curb in front of the band shell.

The engine died.

A man got out.

From the womb of my hydrangea bush, I

watched as the apparently male figure walked cautiously toward the trash can, looking around for witnesses. He had cause for concern: The moon still provided enough light to allow me to see his features.

I covered a gasp with a hand.

The man seeking a handgun ransom was the one I'd seen in the mall parking lot, arguing with Mother's old friend-and-enemy Bernice, and—judging by the clothes he was wearing—he was also the creepy Jason who had come to our door, obviously to get a good long look at Jake.

Jason lifted the trash can lid, and as he bent to retrieve the sack, I crawled out of the hydrangea bush.

Mother was correct to have trust in the Lord . . . but, like I said, helping Him help you couldn't hurt. . . .

"This what you're looking for?" I asked, showing him the gun grasped in my right hand.

Startled, he jumped back, dropping the lid, which clanged noisily against the metal can.

"Don't do anything stupid!" he said.

"You shouldn't have done something stupid," I said, and shot him in the left foot. "*Now where's my son!*"

*A Trash 'n' Treasures Tip*

Secondhand stores, such as Good Will and the Salvation Army, are great places to shop for tomorrow's antiques at yesterday's prices, today. I once found a vintage Chanel bag, but they wouldn't take a check, so I ran home to get cash, and by the time I got back . . . you guessed it. *Adieu.*

# Chapter Twelve

# Down by the Old Mill Scream

Like the world's worst Riverdance audition, Jason hopped on one shoe and shrieked, "You *bitch!* You *shot* me! In the goddamn *foot!*"

I pointed the gun below his belt buckle. "Guess where the next one goes?"

"You crazy bitch!"

"You're repeating yourself."

I aimed straight at his zipper; my hand was trembling but that only made it more threatening, so I was cool with that. Owning the fear.

Adrenaline trumps Prozac every time.

"*Where* is my *son*?"

Now he was hopping and holding up his hands at the same time, choreography that would have been a laugh riot if I had been in the mood, and he hadn't been bleeding.

"Okay! Okay, lady—take it easy! Your kid is fine, I swear, I would never—"

"*Where*, I said!"

"The . . . the old mill."

"More specific."

"The Old Mill at Wild Cat Den! My God, it hurts! I need a hospital! Listen, I think I'm gonna pass out or something. . . ."

"Fine," I said, "but, first, empty your pockets."

Still one-legged hopping, he had his hands down now, on his waist—more Riverdance. His forehead was contorted and his eyes were woozy. "Wh . . . what?"

"You heard me . . . quit hopping like a wounded rabbit and take out everything in your pockets and toss them on the grass, one at a time. And don't make me shoot you again."

With his weight on his good foot, he fished in his jeans, then dropped a cell phone, car keys, and a wallet onto the ground.

"Now back up two or three feet. Do it!"

He did.

My eyes remained glued on him as I bent at my knees, snatching up the keys, then, straightening, pointed the remote at his car and popped the trunk.

I gestured with the gun. "Hop on over," I said, "and get inside."

His forehead creased with disbelief. "What are you, high? You can *see* I'm hurt!"

"Sure. I remember doing it to you."

He was afraid, truly afraid now; maybe as afraid as I was. "What, do you want me to bleed to death in there?"

"Is that a trick question?"

"I'll suffocate!"

"Not my problem. *Move!*"

He hobbled over to the car, dragging the injured foot, more Mummy walk than Irish jig now.

Finally, he paused at the trunk's yawning mouth and stared at it in horror, as if it were the jaw of a beast waiting to devour him.

"Look, lady." He craned to look at me, pleading, getting a pathetic smile going. "Your son is fine . . . just tied up, not real tight or anything. He's great."

"Who's watching him?"

"I was! I left him there—by himself!"

I wasn't sure I believed him, but short of shooting him again, didn't know what to do about it. . . .

He was saying, desperately, "I really was gonna let him go . . . I needed what he took! You're *holding* it—holding what I need!" He nodded to the gun in my grasp.

"That's why I gave you some," I said sweetly. "*Inside.*"

Now he tried a smile—and it was the sickliest smile I ever saw. "We're both, you know, reasonable people. Why don't we just discuss this calmly?"

But he was anything *but* calm, brow sweating, eyes darting, searching for a way out. The man was a head taller than me and way heavier, and really was dangerous; gun in my hand or not, I had a shiver of fear—who knew what this shifty SOB would do to me, given half a chance?

So I took my best shot—literally.

I put on my crazy face, reserved for full-scale mental meltdowns, and fired the gun again, this time hitting one of his back tires, bullet thunking into the rubber and initiating a hissing worthy of an audience at a meller-drama letting the villain know what they thought of him.

"What the hell!" he blurted.

If he was wondering why I'd done that, I didn't bother telling him. For your edification, the why was (1) to disable the car, and (2) to throw another scare into the creep.

"Okay, okay! Jesus, lady! I'm getting in!" He swung the good leg in first, easing into the trunk, then, flinching, pulling the wounded limb in after.

"I'm in, okay? I'm in!"

"Make like a fetus," I told him. "And, hey. Feel free to suck your thumb."

He curled up, and I slammed down the lid. I had a momentary flash on that old James Cagney gangster movie where Cagney put a traitor in the trunk of a car and then provided plenty of air holes with his pistol. Those were the good old days. . . .

Then I threw Jason's car keys in the hydrangea bush and took off, sprinting back toward my car. On the go, I fumbled to turn on my cell phone and speed-dialed, frantic with concern.

Roger's voice came on immediately. "Brandy! Where *are* you? We didn't get anybody at the house, just the message machine."

"Mother . . . Mother didn't answer?"

"No!"

"Don't . . . worry . . . about that."

"Don't worry about that!"

I was sprinting, so my words were halting. "I mean . . . remember it's . . . it's Mother. . . . She must've . . . must've figured the best way . . . way to handle any incoming calls . . . with questions . . .

regarding my whereabouts? . . . Was just to never . . . never take them . . . in the first place."

Obviously working not to lose his temper entirely, Roger said, "What *are* your whereabouts?"

"Weed . . . Weed Park."

"Are you all right, Brandy? You sound like you're having a heart attack!"

"I'm . . . I'm running. . . ."

And as I did, I filled Roger in on everything, right down to shooting Jason in the foot. For some reason my ex didn't seem at all surprised by that.

"I'm . . . heading . . . heading out to the . . . old mill now," I said.

"What, are you gonna run all the way?"

"Just . . . just to my . . . car."

"Brandy, *stop* a second!"

I didn't.

Roger was saying, "Please, please, *please*, when you get out to the mill, wait for me. We'll go in together . . . face whatever we have to, together. We're in this together, babe, remember that."

*Babe?*

Had Roger already given up hope that our son was alive?

I said, "Of course . . . of course, I'll wait."

But, of course, I wouldn't.

Brian got on the cell. "Brandy, I'll call a squad car to Weed Park to handle the kidnapper."

"Better . . . better send an . . . ambulance, too."

"Right. Then I'll notify the county sheriff to meet us at the mill. . . . Roger and I should be there in no less than . . . make it fifteen minutes."

I'd reached my Buick. Breathing hard, I leaned

against the door. "What about Jake's GPS? Did you find it?"

"Yes, right where the computer said it would be."

"At the mill?"

Brian's voice was wry with disgust. "No—it was with Jake's BlackBerry, along the roadside. Most likely tossed there to send us on a wild-goose chase."

By now I was in the Buick and behind the wheel, backing it out from behind the picnic shelter. "Never mind that," I said. "Makes no difference, now that we know where he is. See you in a few minutes."

"Why don't you wait for us, Brandy? This could be dangerous. That guy may not be working alone."

"He said he was."

"Hell, you know that doesn't make it so!"

"What I *know* is, my son is out there. Don't think like a cop, Brian—you're a parent. What would the father part of you do?"

He didn't answer the question, just said quietly, "I'll see you out there." Maybe he did answer the question, at that.

"See you out there," I said.

"But, Brandy! Be careful. People get hurt in situations like this."

I laughed, once. "You're telling me? Wait'll you open that car trunk."

The first purple-pink rays of dawn were streaking across the horizon as I sped along winding River Road, my vision imperiled by lingering ground fog. On one tight curve, I nearly lost control of the car, tires squealing, the long drop-off way too close.

I slowed.

A dead mom wouldn't do Jake any good at all. . . .

After about five minutes, the sign to Wild Cat Den materialized through the drifting fog, and I turned onto a secondary road, kicking up dust, lending some brown to the ground-cover gray.

And in another few minutes, the old mill loomed on my right, silhouetted against an ever-brightening sky.

Pine Creek Gristmill was built in 1848 by Benjamin Nye, who came west from Massachusetts shortly after the war with Chief Black Hawk. The three-story mill is one of the finest examples of . . .

Hell with it. No time for history lessons. Do your own color commentary—I have a son to save.

I wheeled into a gravel pull-off where, later today, tourists would park and then walk their leisurely way down the sloping landscape to the old gristmill.

Only I kept right on driving, including over a border hedge and down the incline, nothing leisurely about it, and right up to the front door. Mother had worked very hard to raise money for the restoration of the old mill, so I figured the Borne girls had a perk or two coming.

I got out of the car, the gun in my right hand—it was starting to feel really heavy now—and, finding the main door locked, circled around to the back of the mill. The stream was catching glimmers of the growing sunlight, gurgling in good-natured response, water spilling over the concrete dam to turn the huge wooden wheel, just as it had a century and a half ago, in a day where a frontier mother might take up a gun to protect her child from Native Americans who weren't selling cigars.

I could relate.

The back door was unlatched, and I entered quietly, pausing to adjust my eyes to the darkness, a gloom aided and abetted by the boarded-up windows. The first floor, however, was empty . . . nothing more than the scarred wooden floor and few vertical beams, and a few streaks of mote-mottled sunlight finding their way in through cracks and crannies.

Moving deeper into the room, shaking with a bizarre mingling of hope and dread, I finally tossed caution aside, and called out: "*Jake!* It's *Mom!*"

Almost immediately came a *thump!*

Right above me.

Off against the wall at left, I found wooden steps leading up and again caution didn't enter in—I rattled up the ancient plank stairs, my footsteps sounding like rapid gunfire.

On the second floor, the haphazard slats on windows weren't keeping the sunrise out much at all, and I spotted Jake instantly—he was seated on the floor, tied to a metal grain grinder, blindfolded, and his mouth duct-taped.

"Jake, I'm here!" I said, moving toward him.

His head jerked my way.

I rushed to my son, fell to my knees, set the

gun on the floor, and removed the blindfold, a red western bandanna.

He tried to talk behind the duct tape, but no words were discernible, just an urgent mumble.

"It's all right, sweetheart . . . everything's fine now . . . Mother's here. . . ."

But my soothing words did not have a calming effect on my son.

If anything, his eyes revealed more terror as he continued to struggle to speak and be understood. My heart ached at the thought of the ordeal he'd suffered over these last hours.

As I peeled off the tape, Jake shouted, "Mom! *Behind* you!"

Clumsily, I whirled in a half crouch only to see Bernice Wiley—chic in a white silk blouse and cream-colored slacks—almost on top of me, holding the gun that a moment ago I had placed on the floor while I attended to Jake. Backing away, putting a good six feet between us, she wasn't exactly pointing the weapon at us; but she wasn't exactly *not* pointing it at us, either.

Slowly, making nothing close to a sudden movement, I got to my feet, blocking my still-seated son with my body, keeping my voice level, which was a trick, I'll admit.

"Why, Bernice . . . what in heaven's name are you doing here?"

The forced innocence of that sounded lame even to me, and as for Bernice, nothing doing—she had a cold, calculating look as she leveled the weapon at me, witchier than any of the cauldron girls at the Haunted House.

"Where is Lyle? *Where is my son?*"

No use for pretense. "I, uh . . . he's still out at Weed Park."

"*Go on*!"

"I kind of faked him out—I left a package but I held onto the gun . . . the, uh, gun you're holding on to right now."

"Where is Lyle, you stupid moron?"

That was a little redundant, wasn't it?

"He's in his car."

"In his *car*?"

I wasn't in a hurry, about filling her in. Roger and Brian should be here any moment, right?

Right?

"What is Lyle doing in his car, you dolt? Start making sense or—"

"He's locked in the trunk." I thought it best not to elaborate, such as mentioning sonny boy's shot-up foot.

Bernice shook her head, gray arcs of hair swinging like scythes. "That *idiot*!" she said.

Seemed like everybody was a dolt or an idiot or a moron to the director of the Serenity playhouse.

Raging, eyes wild, she all but yelled, "I *knew* I should have handled this myself!"

I risked a tiny shrug. "Look, Bernice, you've got what you want—that gun—and I've got my son. . . . I've told you where *your* son is, and I assure you he's alive and . . . so why don't we just write this off to a couple of moms under a good deal of stress, and just call it a day? Morning. Whatever."

"You're an even less convincing actress than your ridiculous mother," she said with a sneer. "Well, even if I believed you, it's not that simple.

Not now that you've seen me, here . . . now that you know my son took *your* son. You tell me, Brandy Borne—if *your* son faced the kind of penalties that a kidnapping brings, would you—"

I lunged for the gun.

A shot shattered the silence, echoing off rafters, seemingly making every board in the old building groan.

And Bernice Wiley, knocked back a step, gasped and dropped the gun, which clunked heavily to the wooden floor. Frightened and aghast and confused, she stared down at the splotchy red circle on the left side of her blouse.

A second shot sent the woman staggering back, her skirt splashed green now.

"Hit 'er *again*, Grandma!" Jake whooped.

Still in witch's drag, Mother, holding Jake's paint gun, complied with her grandson's wishes, and hit Bernice with a shot in the forehead, which caused the kind of expression to bloom that in the old cartoons was usually accompanied by tweeting birdies. Appropriately, Bernice's face was now splattered a gaudy purple.

"Nice *shot*, Grandma!" Jake called.

"I rather thought so," Mother said, comically blowing on the end of the paint gun.

Bernice was staggering, only to finally lose her balance and sit down, hard, legs sprawled, clearly dazed.

As I untied Jake, I asked Mother, "How did you know where to find us?"

Mother was stooping to retrieve the real gun from the floor where it had tumbled from the paintball-assaulted Bernice's fingers.

"Elementary, my dear Brandy," Mother said

with a patronizing smile. "I simply followed you in my own car, as soon as you left the house."

Jake, quickly and gladly getting to his feet, said, "But you're not supposed to drive, Grandma."

Mother said, "Perhaps the court will take exception in this case. After all, it was an emergency. Anyway, Jake, you will learn that certain of society's laws are more . . . guidelines." Then she added cheerfully, "But driving again was really a treat—I'll have to get myself one of those souped-up club cars like the other girls!"

"If you do, Grandma," Jake said, rubbing a wrist where duct tape had been, "you can have my GPS, and then you'll never get lost."

Mother came over and patted her grandson's head. "Why, how sweet, Jake . . . but, frankly, I'd rather have something else of yours."

Jake raised his eyebrows.

Mother held up the paint gun. "This powerful little baby! It's more fun than driving, any day!"

Mother hugged Jake, and I hugged Mother and Jake.

Then Mother broke away from us and crossed over to Bernice, still sitting on her keister, wiping purple paint out of her eyes with the tail of her blouse.

Mother stared down at Bernice and, in her best Bette Davis voice, said, "Well! How the mighty-full-of-themselves have fallen. Looks like *I'll* be the new director of the playhouse now! On the other hand, I've never seen you look better—*real* color in your cheeks, for a change."

Bernice, looking defeated beneath the purple paint, said, "I loathe you, Vivian Borne. I've always loathed you."

Mother sniffed. "How terribly unkind. I've always rather liked you. It was merely your acting I loathed. As long as I've known you, Bernice, you've been a bad actor—but *this* bad act . . . helping your son kidnap my grandson? You've outdone yourself."

"Mother," I said, tugging on her sleeve. "Let's go. We'll leave the colorful diva here for the police."

"Yeah, Grandma, come on," Jake huffed. "Let's leave *her* to the law!"

As we exited the mill and stepped out into the cool, crisp morning, we found a sun shining brightly and a sky as blue as a robin's egg and, best of all, a small regiment mostly in shades of brown that came loping down the sloping lawn toward us: County sheriff, state troopers, along with Brian and Roger in plainclothes.

Jake broke into a run.

Roger, tears rolling down his face, did likewise, and father and son embraced.

Forehead tight with concern, Brian strode over to me. "Brandy, you're all right?"

I nodded. "We're all fine . . . but there's a woman inside—the kidnapper's accomplice—who might possibly need some medical attention."

Mother said proudly, "I pelted her with a paint gun. Three times! Might have knocked a little sense into her, but mostly just painted her the felon she is. Right about now that woman is as harmless . . . *Oh!* Who wants *this*?"

And she held out the real gun by two fingers on its snout, distastefully, as if the weapon were a dead mouse she had by its tail.

The sheriff himself took charge of the thing, and I was shaking my head and laughing a little when someone right behind me barked: "*Brandy!*"

Startled, I turned and beheld a familiar figure in khaki and green-and-black war paint, his eyes glittering: Joe Lange.

"Can I be of assistance?" he asked crisply.

"Well, uh . . . no. But thanks. The sheriff and the police are taking care of the situation."

Frowning, his eyes swiftly scanned the perimeter. "What went down?"

"I, uh, rescued my son from a kidnapper, Joe."

"Outstanding!"

Bernice Wiley was being walked out of the mill by deputies.

I pointed. "And that's his accomplice, over there—see her, lady with the paint splotches?"

"Affirmative."

"Well, she was the kidnapper's accomplice. His mother actually. And my mother helped disarm and capture her."

He called over to Mother: "*Mrs. Borne!*"

Eyes blinking behind the thick lenses, Mother said, "Why, Joseph! Nice to see you. Lovely war paint, I might say."

"Thank you, ma'am! Just wanted to say, first-rate job!"

Mother, oblivious of how weird she looked in the witch's dress, touched her hair and blushed. "Why, thank you, Joseph. Means a lot, coming from you."

Joe turned to me and said, "Everything seems

to be squared away. But if you ever need me, I'll be there."

"Right, Joe. Like the wind."

He smiled tightly, saluted, and said, "Remember, Brandy, I've always got your back!"

"Nice to know," I said.

And Joe took off running, in a half crouch.

Both Brian and Roger were looking at me.

"Don't ask," I said.

*A Trash 'n' Treasures Tip*

When having a garage sale, be sure to lock up your house. A lady I know was thrilled when she sold most of her unwanted garage sale items . . . until she went inside and discovered her entire collection of Hummel figurines had been stolen while she was busy with customers. There are all kinds of collectors in this world.

# Chapter Thirteen

## Eat, Sink, and Be Merry

Less than an hour after returning home from Pine Creek Gristmill, Mother—still in the witch's dress, which suited her sense of melodrama—was serving up a hearty breakfast buffet off an old dry sink in our dining room to a large and hungry group consisting of Brian, Roger, Jake, Peggy Sue, and myself, all salivating (in the most genteel fashion, of course) around the Duncan Phyfe table.

As Mother placed a plate of her famous crepes with boysenberries and powdered sugar in front of Brian, she said, somewhat disappointedly, "Too bad the sheriff and his deputies couldn't join us . . . the more the merrier, I always say. . . ."

Mother, of course, would've loved to have a larger audience for the "Big Reveal," i.e., the explanation she had promised us of what had transpired over the last few days. With all of the Nero Wolfe audios we'd been listening to lately, not to mention the Stout novels the Red-Hatted

League had been reading, I figured we were in for one of what Archie Goodwin called Wolfe's "charades."

Brian managed to look up from the steaming, fragrant plate to smile wryly. "Why do I think *I'm* here, just so you can pump me for information, Mrs. Borne?"

Mother, taking no serving for herself and then settling into the only empty chair at the table (at the head, of course), pretended to be hurt.

"Why, Officer Lawson," she said, "I'm dismayed that you question my motives. . . . As a matter of fact, I just may be able to tell *you* a thing or two about the murder of Mrs. Norton, and the kidnapping of Jake—which are related, of course."

Brian blinked and said, "We've been working on the Norton case as a homicide, but we haven't released that fact to the media. How did you deduce the mauling was a murder?"

Mother had blossomed into a smile at the officer's use of the word "deduce."

"Now, let's not get ahead of ourselves, young man. Eat your breakfast—we'll save crow for dessert."

Brian shook his head, laughed good-naturedly, and dug in.

"If you don't mind, Viv," Roger said, looking stern, "I'd like to start. I want to ask my son just what he was doing with that gun"—he shifted from Mother to Jake—"and how did you *get* it?"

All eyes went to Jake, who choked on a mouthful of food—whether the bite was too big, or guilt had tightened his gullet, I won't venture to say.

Jake swallowed, then said sheepishly, "I . . . I didn't take it or anything. I *found* it."

His father, still stern, demanded, "*Where* did you find it?"

"In that cigar store Indian statue thing. It has a secret compartment and stuff. Ask Mom."

I said crossly, "I *distinctly* remember asking you if anything *else* was in there besides the statue's cigar."

Jake spread his hands, a fork in one. "I didn't lie to you, Mom. I *didn't* say, 'No, there isn't anything else in there,' I said, 'Do you *see* anything else in there?'"

Nobody can split hairs like a ten-year-old.

"You mean *after* you'd already removed the gun," I said.

"Well . . . yeah. But it still wasn't a lie, right?"

"Not technically," I said. "But you misled me, on purpose, which is the same thing."

Jake shot back, "Well, you *did* take my paint gun away!"

"Son," Roger said sharply, "you know a real gun is hardly a paint gun."

"Well, yeah. Sure. I just . . . it was an impulse, okay? I know I shouldn't have done it, but after I did it, what could I do about it?"

That, too, was the kind of bewildering but at heart utterly accurate statement that only a ten-year-old could make.

His father said, "Your mother did the right thing, taking that paint gun away—you shot it inside, at that helpless dog, didn't you?"

Jake's eyes were starting to tear up.

I gave Roger a look, and he said to his son,

"Jake . . . I'm not going to beat up on you. All I ask is you reflect on one thing—that none of this would have happened if you hadn't taken that weapon."

His chin crinkling, Jake said, "You mean you're not gonna beat up on me except saying that everything's all my fault!"

Mother jumped to her grandson's defense. "Just a moment . . . let's not forget who is *really* to blame—a certain Lyle Wiley, who hid the gun in the statue in the first place, believing it to be a safe hiding place. . . . And imagine his surprise when, after his recent return from a stay up the river, he discovered that not only had his mother, Bernice, given *me* that statue, but Brandy and I had put it in our booth to sell."

I said, "So your suspicions were right, Mother—Lyle Wiley killed Mrs. Norton."

My sister's forehead creased. "Didn't a pit bull do that?" she asked. "How can a mauling by an animal be a murder?"

Mother was shaking her head. "Lyle broke into the antiques mall to retrieve the gun, only to have Mrs. Norton interrupt him in the act. He killed the poor woman by hitting her on the head with an antique iron—which he snatched from nearby booth number twelve. Then he used an old hand rake—from booth fourteen—to make it appear as if the bit bull had mauled her to death."

"My God," Roger said.

"How awful," Peggy Sue murmured.

"*The Scarlet Claw*," I said.

Everybody looked at me curiously, except Mother, whose smile was knowing.

I said, "Last night Mother referred to *The Scarlet Claw*—it's an old Sherlock Holmes movie with Basil Rathbone. You see—"

"*Spoiler alert*!" Mother blurted.

I sighed and went on: "The murderer used a garden implement to imitate the claw of a Baskervilles-type hound, and divert blame and attention from himself."

Peggy Sue mused aloud, "Whatever was Mrs. Norton doing there so late at night?"

Mother waved a dismissive hand. "Maybe she was still somewhere in the building and had never gone home that evening. She was a workhorse, cleaning and putting up signs and generally being a benign mother hen . . . or perhaps someone called her about seeing a light on in the building and she went to investigate . . . we may never know. Have you learned anything on that score, Officer Lawson?"

"No," he admitted. "But Mrs. Norton *was* known to work there late at night, doing just the sort of things you said. It was a new business and she was putting her all into it."

Roger asked, "Then why didn't the dog attack Lyle?"

Jake, his tears a memory, popped in with a possible answer. "I saw this movie once? Where a bad guy got past a guard dog by feedin' 'im a steak."

"Very astute," Mother said proudly to her grandson. "But in this case the bribe of food was not just a temporary distraction. Lyle drugged whatever-it-was that he fed Brad Pit Bull."

Peggy Sue asked, "Is that a guess, Mother?"

"No. Jane at the animal shelter stated that the

dog had been sedated before he was brought to her. And Brandy and I saw how sluggishly he acted when we discovered Mrs. Norton's body—mutilated by the most vicious animal on earth—a human being."

Mother paused for the melodrama to sink in; then she smiled slyly at Brian. "How am I doing, Officer Lawson?"

Brian, a piece of sausage halfway to his mouth, paused to say, "Fine, Mrs. Borne. Very impressive performance, so far."

Mother's smile broadened as she basked in the praise. Then she frowned. "But what I *don't* understand is the importance of the gun. . . ." Her eyes were trained on Brian. "Perhaps I need to share the stage with you for a moment, Officer."

Brian rested his fork on his mostly clean plate. "I suppose this is where I sing for my breakfast."

Mother said sweetly, "A brief but telling solo, if you don't mind."

He sighed. "Well, I guess I can limit myself to a supporting role . . . but only because these are the best crepes I've ever eaten."

Everyone waited with boysenberry-crepe-bated breath.

Brian, dabbing his mouth with a napkin, sat back in his chair. "The gun was very important to Lyle—easily important enough to risk kidnapping Jake here, to get it back. You see, Lyle had used it to kill his partner after a bank robbery some years ago, and if the weapon was found, it could tie him directly to that murder, a crime on which there is no statute of limitation."

Murmurs all around.

Brian went on, "After the robbery, the getaway car was traced to Lyle's mother's home in Kansas City. But before law enforcement could apprehend him—and with his mother nowhere around—he had a chance to hide the gun where he thought it would be safe until he could retrieve it again."

"In the secret compartment in the cigar store Indian!" I said. I leaned an elbow on the table and rested my chin in my hand. "Then Bernice must not have known the gun was in the statue . . . or else she would never have given it to Mother!"

Peggy Sue said, "So Lyle didn't trust her? His own mother?"

"Possibly," Brian said. "Or maybe he felt it wise that she not know where the gun could be found, and thus implicate herself."

Sis muttered, "The lengths parents will go to, to protect a child."

Roger and I looked at each other; the irony was not lost on either of us.

Eyes tight with thought, Mother said, "There may be another reason for Bernice's ignorance of the gun's hiding place—her son never had the chance to tell her. She was not home when he was apprehended, and any visits they had at the prison were monitored, just as all mail was censored."

Jake asked, "What happened to the money stolen from the bank robbery? Maybe it's in the statue, too—in another compartment—and it's finders keepers!"

Brian laughed and shook his head. "Sorry,

Jake, the cash was recovered years ago, in Lyle's possession—he took it all after double-crossing his partner. And, uh, by the way—finders keepers doesn't exactly work like that, in bank robbery situations."

I asked, "So what happens to Lyle now?"

Brian said, "He'll be charged with murdering his partner, and with kidnapping your son." He sighed deeply and frowned. "But there's one unresolved aspect about that robbery . . . the identity of the person who waited in the getaway car, while Lyle and his buddy went into the bank. A witness passing by claimed it was a middle-aged woman."

Mother slammed both palms on the table, causing everyone to jump and every dish to rattle. "*Bernice!*"

Once again, all eyes were on her.

"*That's* what poor Henry meant! Remember, Brandy? He told me at Hunter's that he'd seen Bernice at the post office *before* she came to town, which I felt was merely one more of Henry's rambling drunken manglings of the King's English. He must have recognized Bernice from a wanted poster in the post office lobby!"

Roger asked, "Then why didn't this Henry come forward, when he thought he'd spotted a wanted woman?"

Brian said, embarrassed, "I, uh . . . believe that he did. She only moved to Serenity a few years ago, and I seem to recall that Henry stumbled into the station spouting a bunch of what we thought was drunken nonsense. We sent him on his way with the city's thanks."

Peggy Sue made a scoffing sound. "Surely the

police who picked up Lyle at his mother's house would've quickly tracked Bernice down. They would have had descriptions of the female bank-robbery accomplice."

Mother raised a gently scolding finger to her older daughter. "You forget, Peggy Sue—Bernice Wiley, if indeed that is her real name, is an actress, albeit not a very good one, and a terrible ham."

No one at the table gave in to the temptation to say, *Takes one to know one.*

Mother was saying, "Bernice could quickly change her looks with a wig and stage makeup." She shrugged. "And besides, folks don't usually think of someone's mother being a wheelman at a bank heist . . . even though Ma Barker made the Ten Most Wanted list in her day, with great regularity."

"Well," I said, "it certainly explains why no one in Serenity seemed to know anything about Bernice's past."

Brian, who was looking at Mother with the same expression many an audience member had (a sort of appalled admiration), said, "Mrs. Borne, I think your theory that Bernice was involved with her son in that robbery just might have validity. . . . And if it does—"

"There'll be a reward?" Jake interrupted.

Brian laughed. "I was going to say 'You'd have the sincere gratitude of the Serenity PD,' but I can see where money would be better. But the bank's cash was returned, and I'm afraid no reward was posted."

The doorbell rang. Which made sense, coming at the end of Mother's Nero Wolfe charade. . . .

Mother jumped up from the table, announcing, "Ah! Just in time . . . our cozy little family of three expands to four."

I didn't like the sound of that; neither did Peggy Sue, and we exchanged alarmed looks.

Quickly I got up from the table and followed Mother to the front door, which she opened onto a trim, middle-aged woman with short brown hair and casual clothes. The lady looked pleasant and unpretentious enough to join our little party, but I wasn't enamored of the idea, particularly since I didn't know why she'd been invited.

Then my eyes traveled down from her face to her navy blue sweater, to the brown slacks, and the Nike-clad feet . . . where Brad Pit Bull, on a leash, sat patiently, his tongue lolling.

Mother was saying, "Brandy, this is Jane from the animal shelter."

And Jane was smiling. "Hi, Brandy. I want to thank you and Vivian for your willingness to—"

"Mother!" I spewed. "We're not . . . *he's* not . . . you *haven't* . . . ?"

Mother said cheerfully, "Now, dear, we're not adopting Brad Pit Bull . . ."

"Thank God!"

". . . merely pet-fostering the misunderstood creature until Jane can find a more permanent family."

I was aghast. "What about *Sushi*? You *know* she'll have a conniptions fit."

"Nonsense," Mother said dismissively. "The little darling will get used to having a big brother around. And you will, too, dear. You also never had a big brother."

"But will *he* think of Soosh as a little sister?" I asked with trepidation. "And, if so, will he have incest on his mind?"

Jane said, "Brandy, Brad's been fixed. Not to worry."

Mother put hands on hips. "Brandy, *you* have a pet . . . why shouldn't *I*? Even if it's only temporary."

During this entire exchange, Jane from the animal shelter remained steadfast, smiling pleasantly, sure that the outcome would be in Mother's favor. Brad Pit Bull wasn't so sure, his head tilted, his expression pitiful, as he listened intently during the determination of his fate by a species deemed to be superior to his (though sometimes I wonder).

And Sushi?

By now she had smelled Brad, and come running from the dining room, trotting right up to our guests. The two dogs faced each other and began doggie-speak. This is my best translation:

SUSHI. What are *you* doing here?

BRAD. Bitch, I was invited. ("Bitch" meaning female dog, of course).

SUSHI. Well, you're not staying, if that's what you think!

BRAD. Don't get your cute little tail tied up in a knot. . . . Say, what's wrong with the peepers?

SUSHI. I'm blind, you moron.

BRAD. Gee, that's a tough break. Maybe youse could stand a strong dog around.

SUSHI. I already *have* a dog-friend!

BRAD. Funny. Don't seem to see her around.

SUSHI. It's a *he*, and he works for the police station, and it just so happens he's *crazy* about me.

BRAD. Okay. I ain't askin' you to have my puppies. I got a bad feelin' I'm shootin' blanks, anyway. Hey, I just want us to be pals.

SUSHI. Well . . . maybe . . . as long as you put it *that* way . . .

BRAD. As long as I'm here, cutie-pie, why don't ya show me around the joint?

SUSHI. All right . . . but keep your paws to yourself. And if I catch you tryin' to mark *my* territory . . .

BRAD. Sure, sure, sweet-cheeks, whatever you say.

SUSHI. We'll start right here—this is the living room. Keep off the needlepoint furniture. . . .

While Sushi took Brad Pit Bull on a nickel tour, Mother and Jane moved to the couch, where the latter gave the former instructions on her role as foster pet parent. I stepped out onto the porch for some much-needed fresh autumn air.

After a moment, the screen door swung open and Roger slipped out to join me. He placed his hands on my shoulder, and—to my utter shock—bent and kissed me, warm and sweet, like it used to be.

When our lips parted he looked deep into my eyes and said earnestly, "Jake's welfare and happiness are more important than anything that happened between you and me, understand?"

"Yes."

"Where our son is concerned, we're a team now . . . not adversaries."

I nodded. "I'm . . . I'm sorry I made such a mess of things."

His one-sided smile was melancholy. "Perhaps . . . you were too young. I'm not letting you off the hook, mind you . . . but, well, maybe our marriage was ill-fated because of the difference in our ages."

"The age difference didn't stop us from producing a terrific kid."

"No, it didn't. And Jake's great. Not perfect, as we've seen, but considering the competition? We produced one of the good ones."

"Couldn't agree more."

He put a finger under my chin and lifted it. "And, Brandy? We must do everything we can to make sure he has the best life possible. . . . And to do that, we have to be supportive of each other."

This logical side of Roger had been a lot of what made me fall in love with him, eleven years ago. I got on my tippy toes and kissed him back—on the lips, not passionate, just friendly, sealing the peace treaty.

As I pulled back from Roger, I noticed Brian watching through the screen door. How long he'd been there, I didn't know.

Brain stepped out on the porch.

He stood there awkwardly, eyes on Roger, then on me. "I, uh, have to report back to the station."

Roger went over to him and held out his hand. "I want to thank you, Officer Lawson, for everything you've done. I really do appreciate it. We made a pretty good team, I think."

"Me too. But we're nothing compared to the Borne girls."

"No," Roger admitted. "Nobody is." Then he

looked back over at me. "And I know when I return to Chicago, I'll be leaving Brandy in good hands."

My ex was just being pleasant, of course. But something in and around his eyes told me it was okay that I move on. That first kiss had been nostalgia; and nostalgia just wasn't what it used to be. . . .

I asked Brian, "Mind if I escort you to your car?"

"I wouldn't mind at all."

Roger headed back into the house, and Brian and I went down the front steps together. As we walked I could almost hear what he was thinking.

*Does she still love him? Are they back together? And where does that leave me?*

To clear up the one dark cloud hovering over us in an otherwise cloudless blue sky, I asked, "Why don't you come over some evening next week? Say, Thursday? Jake will be back home with his dad, by then . . . and Mother will be off to her mystery book club meeting."

Brian's puppy-dog brown eyes seemed to like the bone I'd thrown him. "You mean it?"

"Sure. I think we've been sniffing around each other long enough, don't you?"

He smiled, showing off his dimples.

We were at his car. I put my arm in the crux of his. "Tell you what," I said, leaning against him. "I'll even cook for you."

The dimples deepened. "Well, I'd like that. Yes, by all means."

"Italian okay?"

"It's my favorite."

"Good. I have this yummy old family recipe for spaghetti. . . ."

If Brian could stomach *that*, we might have a sporting chance together.

Brian had barely driven away when another car pulled in, a black Mercedes.

I was thinking, *Who in the world . . . ?*

And then Troy Hanson, the antiques picker, stepped out and called, "Brandy—hi!"

Well, my B-cup runneth over. Another hunky male had come calling. . . .

"Hi!" I called back.

He was in a powder-blue polo and black slacks and Italian loafers, and he looked great, from his dark pomaded hair to the fashionable two-days' growth of beard.

He made a little jog up to the porch and joined me.

"Hope you don't mind my dropping by," he said.

"Not at all."

"I was in town checking out an estate sale, and wondered if you still had that rolltop desk."

Clearly he was using the desk as an excuse to see me again. . . .

"Well, we do. But I'm not sure when it's going to be released to us by the authorities. Everything's on hold, because of Mrs. Norton's death."

"Yes. That was a shame. A real tragedy. Well." He got a card out of his pocket. "Let me know if it comes available. I'll make you an excellent offer, one nobody can beat."

Well, maybe it *was* the desk he was interested in. . . .

"You mind my asking," I said, "what it is about that desk that's so important to you?"

Those piercing eyes narrowed and he let out an embarrassed little laugh. "Well, I guess I did misrepresent things a little. I am a picker, and I do have clients . . . but that particular desk? It's exactly what my partner, Bruce, and I have been looking for, for a little alcove in our apartment."

"Oh." Should've known from the Italian loafers.

"Let me know!" He winked, said, "*Ciao.*"

And ran to his Mercedes and was gone.

I returned to the house, where Mother was showing Jane the album of autographed movie stars she had collected over the years; Roger was giving Peggy Sue some investment advice at the dining room table; and Jake was in the kitchen playing with Sushi and Brad Pit Bull.

Jake looked up with a grin. "Hey, Mom!"

"Hey."

He left the dogs, who were flirting, and came right up to me. "Listen, uh . . . you were great today. This morning."

"Thanks."

"I mean—you really went all out and stuff."

"Well, you're my kid. I'm your mother. I love you."

"Yeah, uh, well, me too. And I'm sorry if I've been a jerk and all."

"No problem."

"Can I tell you something? Something private?"

"Sure."

"Promise not to tell Dad?"

"I promise—as long as it's not something else you found in that secret compartment."

"No! Not that. Nothing like that." He looked around to make sure nobody could see or hear us. "I just wanted to say . . . I kinda hate to leave. I like it here. It'll be cool, next break, staying with you guys."

And he gave me a hug.

Funny thing, I didn't even tear up. Not a drop.

And if you believe that, Mother and I have a number of nice things at very reasonable prices in our booth at the mall that I'm sure you'll adore.

Exhausted, I sneaked off upstairs to plop down on my bed for a nap. I had been conked for a while, when my cell phone trilled on the nightstand.

I fumbled for it and checked the number.

Tina.

"Hi, honey," she said. "Heard you've been through quite an ordeal! Jake all right?"

"Everything's hunky-dory," I said sleepily. "Tell you all about it later over a latte. . . . Right now I'm way too tired. Forgive me?"

"Always."

The silence lingered.

"Everything okay on your end?" I asked out of courtesy.

"Uh, kinda not really. . . . There's just something . . . I just didn't want you to hear this from anybody else."

I sat up, suddenly wide awake. "What, Teen?"

Deep breath. "Don't get all weird on me, sweetie, but it looks like I, uh . . . I have cancer."

"Oh my God. . . ."

"No, no, be cool! It's early *stages*. Good prognosis."

I breathed a sigh. "Well, thank God you got that mamogram."

"Funny thing is, it's not that . . . it's cervical. See, I had a Pap test last week."

I tried to process what this meant to my best friend and her husband who so desperately wanted children.

"How's Kevin taking it?" I asked.

"He's a rock, or anyway he's pretending to be. But he's taking time off from work to go through this with me. . . . In fact, we're leaving in a few minutes to see a specialist. I'll call you when I get back."

"Tina?"

"Yes?"

"I'm here for you . . . you *do* understand that? Whatever you need, whenever you need it, whatever it takes . . . day or night."

"Thanks, Brandy. I knew . . . knew I could always count on you."

I returned the cell phone to the nightstand and sat on the edge of the bed, feeling like a clubbed baby seal.

Mother entered the room.

"Fan mail from some flounder," she said in her best *Bullwinkle* cartoon voice. She tossed a letter in my lap and traipsed out, still in her witch's garb—would she ever take it off?

I don't know how it is where you live, but in the Midwest, bad news travels in pairs, misery loving company.

I picked up the plain white envelope with no

return address, my name computer-printed on the front. I opened the letter and unfolded the single sheet.

Only one sentence—also computer printed. It read *Wouldn't you like to know who your* real *mother is?*

Don't you just hate those season finale cliff-hangers?

*A Trash 'n' Treasures Tip*

A few dealers do not bother to tag their merchandise. Instead, they will quote you a price, depending on what they think you can pay. . . . So go wearing your worst clothes and carry your money in an old gym sock. That's me right behind you, in the baggy running suit.

Here's a sneak preview of Brandy's next
Trash 'n' Treasures mystery,
ANTIQUES FLEE MARKET.
A Kensington Publishing hardcover,
available in October 2009.

Please turn the page.

# Chapter One

## Market in the Book

The snow had begun falling in the late afternoon—big, wet flakes that stuck to the rooftops of houses like dollops of marshmallow cream, and coated bare branches with hardened white chocolate, and covered the ground in fluffy cotton candy. (I've been off sugar for a while and it's just *killing* me.)

I was sitting in the living room on a needlepoint Queen Anne armchair, gazing out the front picture window at the wintry wonderland, waiting for Mother to come downstairs. Sushi, my brown and white shih tzu, lounged on my lap, facing the window, too—but she couldn't see anything because the diabetes had taken away her vision.

Soosh, however, seemed content, and any impartial observer who hadn't caught sight of the doggie's milky-white orbs would swear she was taking it all in. I imagine she could still picture what was going on outside, her ears perking every now and again at the muffled rumble of a snow plow, or the scrape, scrape, scraping of a metal shovel along the sidewalk. (Mr. Fusselman, who lived across the street in a brick Dutch Colonial, had been coming out of his house every half hour to keep the pesky snow off his front walk; I, no fool—at least where shoveling was concerned—wasn't about to tackle ours until the very last flake had fallen.)

I sighed and gazed at the Christmas tree that was in its usual spot next to the fireplace. The fake tree, with fake white tipping (which made Sushi sneeze), had been up since early November, as Mother jumps the gun on everything. (Christmas cards go out in October.) She still decorated the tree with things I had made since the first grade, and many were falling apart, like the clay Baby Jesus that had lost its legs (makes walking on water way tougher). But mostly, hanging from the branches by green velvet ribbons, were small antique items, like red plastic cookie cutters, Victorian silver spoons, floral china teacups, and colorful Bakelite jewelry. One year, however, when I was in middle school, Mother went overboard with her antiques decorating and jammed an old sled in the middle of the tree, and it fell over knocking our one-eyed parrot off its perch.

For those just joining in (where have you been?), I'll lay in some backstory—all others (unless in need of a refresher course) may feel free to skip ahead to the paragraph beginning, "I stood, giving my butt cheeks a break," etc.

My name is Brandy Borne. I'm a blue-eyed,

bottle-blond, thirty-one year-old, Prozac-prescribed recent divorcée who has moved back to her small, Midwestern Mississippi River hometown of Serenity to live with my widowed mother, who is bipolar. Mother, a spry seventy-four—she claims she's seventy and from here on probably always will—spends her time hunting for antiques, acting in community theater, and reading mysteries with her "Red-Hatted League" gal-pals. Roger, my ex (early forties), has custody of Jake (age eleven), and they live in a beautiful home in an upscale suburb of Chicago, an idyllic existence that I forfeited due to doing something really stupid at my ten-year class reunion two years ago (involving an old boyfriend, alcohol, a condom, and poor judgment).

I have one sibling, an older sister named Peggy Sue, who lives with her family in a tonier part of town; but Sis and I have an uneasy relationship, due to the span of our ages (nineteen years) and difference in politics, temperaments, and lifestyles—not to mention clothing styles (hers, high fashion; mine, low prices). Therefore, a truce is the best we can hope for. Peggy Sue, by the way, is still ragging me for not getting a good settlement out of my busted marriage, but everything Roger and I had—which was substantial—had been earned by his brain and sweat, and I just couldn't ask for what wasn't mine. I do have *some* scruples, even if they didn't extend to ten-year class reunions. . . .

I stood, giving my butt cheeks a break from the uncomfortable antique chair, and replaced Sushi on the hard cushion—she jumped down, not liking it, either—and then I wandered into the library/music room to check on my latest painting.

Was I, perhaps, an artist? Someone who toiled in oil on canvas, waiting for her genius to be discovered? Hardly. Unless you count covering the bottom soles of an inexpensive pair of black high heels in red lacquer to make them look like expensive Christian Louboutin's. (I don't know why I bothered; I'd always know they were as cheap inside as me.)

I picked up a shoe to see if it was dry, and left a fingerprint in the still-gooey paint. (Sigh.)

Mother, who also had a painting project in progress on the plastic-protected library table, was having more success. She had taken the little dead bonsai tree I had given her during her last bout with depression (I didn't *give* it to her dead—she forgot to water it) and had resurrected the tiny tree (or entombed it?) by covering the brown branches with green spray paint. Brilliant!

I returned to the living room to see what was keeping Mother. We had preshow tickets this evening to the winter flea market event, and should have left a half hour ago for the county fairgrounds.

Mother and I maintained a booth at an antiques mall downtown and desperately needed to restock it with new merchandise for the holiday season. We also desperately needed to make a buck or two, since she was on a fixed income, and I wasn't working. (Okay, I did receive alimony—*that* many scruples I haven't.)

I crossed to the banister and gazed upstairs,

where a good deal of banging and thumping had been going on.

"What are you doing up there?" I hollered.

Mother's muffled voice came back. "Be down in a minute, dear—keep your little drawers on!"

In Mother's eyes I was perpetually five. I guess if she could be perpetually seventy, I could be perpetually a kindergartner.

So I stood and waited, because there is no other choice with a diva, and in another minute Vivian Borne herself descended, wearing her favorite emerald-green velour slacks and top. Coming straight down would have lacked drama, however, and Mother halted on the landing and, with hands on hips, cast me an accusatory glare through thick-lensed glasses that magnified her eyes to owlish dimensions.

"*Where,*" she demanded regally, "is my raccoon coat?"

The hairs on the back of my neck began to tingle. I narrowed my eyes. When in doubt, answer a question with a question: "Why?"

"*Why?* Because I want to wear it, that's why! What have you *done* with it?"

This was not as unreasonable a question as you might suspect. I had been known to take certain measures with that particular garment.

Displaying the confidence and grace of a child with a chocolate-smeared face being asked about the whereabouts of a missing cake, I said, "I . . . I, uh, I put it in the attic . . . in the trunk . . . ."

"What? *Why?*"

"To store it," I said lamely.

Mother sighed disagreeably. "Dear, you know I like to keep that coat in my closet where I can get to it. It's my favorite!" She turned on her heels and marched back up the stairs.

I shivered.

You would, too, if you'd spent your formative years in that house with that woman. Nothing could strike more terror in little Brandy's heart than the sight of her mother in that raccoon coat.

I don't know when Mother had bought it . . . probably in the 1940s (judging by the severe shoulder pads) when she was in college and Father was off being a war correspondent in Germany. I'd always pictured Mother wearing the raccoon coat while riding around in an open jalopy with ten other kids, waving a school banner and shouting "Boola-boola" into a megaphone, like in an old Andy Hardy movie. (Not that there are any new Andy Hardy movies out there.)

But over the years, the coat—besides keeping moths fat and harvesting bald patches—had taken on a more disturbing significance than just the benign symbol of the bobby-soxed, jitterbugging Mother who once walked the earth with other hepcat dinosaurs. From the dawn of Brandy, that coat had been the magic armor Mother always insisted upon donning at the beginning of her manic phase (this included summer!).

Once, during my teen years, after Mother got better, I threw the coat out with the trash . . . then retrieved it before the garbage truck came around. After all, I reasoned, what better early warning system was there to alert me of her deteriorating condition?

And so, perhaps you now have a small understanding of just how worried I was at this moment. If not, let's just say if we were on a submarine, a horn would be blaring *ah-OOO-guh! ah-OOO-guh!* and Brandy would be yelling, "Dive! Dive! *Dive!*"

So when Mother tromped back down the stairs wearing the full-length ratty raccoon coat, I hadn't moved from my frozen spot by the banister. Again, she paused on the landing, this time to look at me intently.

"Brandy, darling, if you're worried about my mental health, you needn't be," she said. "I am quite current on my medication."

"I . . . ah . . . er . . . ah . . . ."

And, having said my piece, I shut my mouth.

Mother was frowning thoughtfully and raising a theatrical finger. "We can't look like we have any *money,* dear. You know how some of those dealers are at a major flea market like this one! They'll send the price sky-high if they think we're women of means."

I nodded, sighing inwardly with relief.

An eyebrow arched, Mother was studying my designer jeans and cashmere turtleneck. "What are you going to wear, dear? I mean, which coat? I suppose they won't see what we have on underneath. . . ."

I said, "I only have my black wool."

Mother made a scoffing sound. "Far too good . . . I'll find something for you in the front closet."

Which was better than something from the attic.

While Mother rooted around raccoonlike in the entryway, I took the time to put Sushi out again. Diabetic animals have to pee a lot because they drink so much, and Soosh was no exception. The nice thing about winter is that she can't stand the cold, and when she does her business, she's quick about it—no sniffing each and every blade of grass, or checking to see if any other animal had dared trespass and soil her sacred ground.

I returned to find raccoon-coated Mother holding aloft a sad-looking, strangely stained trench coat, which I dutifully put on so we could get the heck out of there.

As we exited out the front door into the chill air, I suggested, "Let's take your car. It hasn't been driven in a while."

Mother had an old pea green Audi that was stored in a stand-alone garage. "Stored" because she lost her license to drive it. Several times, however, she had used it for "emergencies"—once to help me (*Antiques Roadkill*) and again to help her grandson, Jake (*Antiques Maul*)—which caused her suspended license to become a revoked license.

I turned the key in the ignition and the Audi whined. How dare we wake it from its deep slumber on such a cold winter night? The car shuddered and shook and wheezed and coughed, but I forced it to life, and we backed out of the garage and into the street. I turned the Audi toward the bypass, which would lead us to a blacktop road that would then take us to the fairgrounds.

Five minutes into the trip, I sniffed the air and asked, "What smells?"

Mother was studying the winter landscape

gliding past her mostly fogged-up window a little too intently. "Pardon?"

"What . . . *stinks*?"

Overly casual, Mother replied, "Oh . . . that would be the hamburger grease."

"Hamburger grease."

"Yes, dear. Hamburger grease."

"*What* hamburger grease?"

She was pretending to be enthralled by the vista barely visible out her frosted view on the world. "Why, the hamburger grease I smeared on your coat."

"*What!*"

"It looked far too pristine, dear—I told you, we mustn't appear as if we have much money."

"Well, we *don't* have much money!" I snapped, then grumbled, "Great. Now I look poor *and* smell. I love it when a plan comes together." I powered down both front windows to get rid of the odor.

"Brandy!" Mother protested. "I'm *cold.*"

"Good! I hope you catch one."

For the next ten minutes, all that could be heard was the howling wind blowing in from my window (Mother had rolled hers up) and the castanet chattering of our teeth. But before icicles had a chance to form on the end of our noses, in that jaunty Jack Frost fashion, the bright lights from the county fairgrounds could be seen, and I wheeled off the highway and into the snowy drive leading up to the main building. As I slowed to a stop in front of the large, one-story, maintenance-type structure, Mother hopped out like a hobo from a train and I proceeded on to find a parking spot in the already filled lot.

Man may be able to fly to the moon, clone animals, create bionic body parts, and keep his balance while exercising on a Body Dome. But he (or she) remains powerless to park in a straight row once the snow has obliterated the lines.

After dead-ending down two different lanes, I gave up and added to the confusion, inventing a spot along a far fence.

The temperature had dropped, and my breath mocked me by making smoke worthy of the warmest fire. Hunkered over, I trudged through the white toward the welcoming lights of the building, big wet flakes clinging to my hair and shoulders like the dandruff of a giant.

Just a few hundred feet away from the sanctuary of the building, however, I heard a long, low growl behind me. Then another. And another.

I turned.

Darting out from a row of parked cars came a pack of wild dogs. They were heading straight for me and didn't seem friendly, so I began to run (well, first I went, "Yikes!"), but the snow—nearly four inches deep now—impeded my flight, and even though the front door to the building seemed close, I knew I couldn't make it before the dogs were on me.

I tore off my coat as the lead dog—a black mongrel apparently pissed for being passed over for the movie version of *Cujo*—snapped at my heels. Then I whirled, throwing the garment on top of him, and made my final dash toward the building. Reaching the door, I risked a glance over my shoulder. The pack, five in all, were tearing my trench coat to pieces!

What if I'd still been inside the thing?

As I stepped into the safety of the building, shivering with more than the chill, it finally dawned on me that the *coat* was what the dogs had been after—drawn by the smell of the hamburger grease.

And the scoreboard reads: Mother, one; Brandy, zero.

The flea market preshow was in full swing, and I was a little surprised by the good quality of the merchandise—these were some high-class fleas! (I'd been to some where I really had gone home with fleas.) There were at least one hundred dealers hawking their wares—furniture, china, pottery, vintage clothes, jewelry, books, toys, and assorted collectibles. The sight was dizzying, the sounds deafening, as a sea of winter-clad shoppers scurried about, trying to beat the other guy out of an early bargain.

I took a moment to gather my thoughts. Before we'd left home, Mother and I had devised a game plan and divvied up the money. Since she was the expert on glassware—that is to say, more expert than me (which isn't saying much)—Mother was to look for such items. I, on the other hand, had more knowledge about collectibles (which also isn't saying much) and was to cover that ground.

And because our booth already had enough furniture to sell, we agreed to ignore anything along those lines, particularly if bulky—unless the item was a steal, of course.

Antiques dealers—like all store retailers—depend on good pre-Christmas sales in order to make money. It can mean the difference between dealers keeping their heads above water for the entire year, or going under. But trying to figure out what tickles the public's fancy around Christmastime is difficult; buy the wrong thing, and not only has a dealer laid out good money, he's stuck with the item.

But before jumping into the frenzy and fray, I first had to find a new coat . . . because, in spite of the number of people in the building, it was freezing inside! I doubted there was any heat going at all.

I zeroed in on a table of women's fur coats that shared space with a collection of Annalee Christmas dolls, and seeing so many of the Elves and Mice and Santas grouped together with their demented expressions was decidedly unsettling.

I pointed to the fur coats that were piled on top of each other like a bunch of sleeping critters, and asked the middle-aged lady attending the zoo, "How much?"

She studied me through her outdated, oversized round glasses, the bottom halves of which were tinted a pale pink so she didn't have to wear blush (who came up with *that* dumb idea?).

"Twenty-five dollars each," she said.

I showed disappointment in my face.

She held her ground.

I stood mine.

Then she must have taken pity on me—anyway, on my dripping wet hair and shivering body—because the woman said, "I . . . I do have one other fur that I didn't put out because I'm sure it wouldn't sell . . . ."

"How much?"

"Oh, you can have it."

I brightened. "I'll take it! Whatever it is . . . ."

The lady bent and rummaged under the table and then dragged out the freebie: a ratty raccoon coat, bald-patched, moth-eaten, and nearly identical to Mother's.

I reached for my karma gratefully and thanked her.

It wasn't until two hours later that I finally crossed paths with Mother. She was standing by a table of old toys and memorabilia, multiple bags of her flea market finds dangling from each arm while she chatted with a pudgy middle-aged man wearing a plaid coat.

As I approached, it became clear, however, that their exchange was more confrontational than conversational.

Mother was saying, "That book of Mr. Yeager's is worth *far* more than one hundred dollars! That's a famous title and it's a first edition. Clearly, he didn't know what he had, and you are simply out to take advantage of him."

Mr. Yeager, I deduced, was the elderly frail-looking gentleman in a black parka, seated behind the table, and looking increasingly uncomfortable at the unfolding drama. On stage and off, Mother was famous for creating memorable scenes.

Pudgy tightened his grip on the item in dispute—a hardcover book that said *Tarzan of the Apes* on its dust jacket, and featured its branch-swinging hero in silhouette.

"It's marked one hundred dollars," he snapped at Mother, "and that's what I'm going to pay for it!" Then he looked pointedly at Mr. Yeager, saying, "There *are* certain rules that dealers have to abide, you know."

I butted in. "Just a moment . . . has Mr. Yeager accepted any money yet?"

Mother turned to see me, gave my raccoon coat a double take, but wasn't thrown enough to stop her performance. (Once, when Mother was doing *The Vagina Monologues,* some unfortunate woman in the front row was so rude as to have a heart attack and keel over, and the paramedics came, performed CPR, then carried the revived lady out of the theater on a stretcher, while Mother never missed a line.)

"My daughter has a point," Mother snapped back at Pudgy. "The transaction has not yet been completed, and therefore can be taken off the table, so to speak, *if* the dealer wishes it."

All eyes turned to the elderly Mr. Yeager, who said in a frail voice, "I . . . I . . . *do* want to withdraw the book."

"Well!" huffed Pudgy, his fat fingers still clutching the object of his desire. "This is quite unheard of, and I feel compelled to report your conduct, sir, to the organizers of this flea market."

Now might be a good time to mention that Mr. Yeager had a helper seated beside him behind the table. She was about twenty, wearing all black, which extended from her jeans and leather jacket to her short, spiky hair. Her elfin features were not unattractive, though certainly not helped by multiple piercing (ears, eyebrows, nose) and a tattoo of barbed wire that encircled her neck.

At the threat of discrediting the old man, Goth Girl bolted out of her folding chair and flew around the table to face Pudgy.

"Oy!" she shouted in a thick Brit accent, her dark tinted lips peeled back revealing the metal grillwork on her front teeth. "You 'eard me, Grandad! 'E don't wanna sell it!"

And she snatched the book out of Pudgy's hands.

Pudgy's mouth dropped open, closed, then opened again. "I . . . I'm going to report you *both!*"

Goth Girl, who was a good foot shorter than the portly man, shouted up into his red face, "That's a load of bullocks, you dodgy ol' punter! Now *piss* off!"

Pudgy backed away, turned, and fled, pushing his way through a number of folks who had gathered in the aisle drawn by the impromptu skit.

Impressed by Goth Girl's moxie, I stuck out my hand. "Hi. My name's Brandy."

She extended one black nailed hand. "Chaz."

Mother beamed royally at the young woman, and said, "And I'm Vivian, my dear, Brandy's mother. You handle yourself *quite* well . . . . Have you ever heeded the siren song of the footlights?"

Chaz screwed up her face. "Put me foot *where?*"

"Theater," Mother explained, pronouncing it *thee*-ah-tah. "I'm the current director of the Playhouse and wish to know if you've ever acted."

"Oh, yeah, sure," Chaz nodded. "This one time, I did the Artful Dodger at Holloway's, innit?"

Mother frowned curiously. "Holloway's? I'm not familiar with that theater . . . . Is it in the West End?"

"Naw," Chaz said, "Islington." She made a face like she'd sucked on a lemon. "Place is a pile of piss, man . . . full of rats and cockroaches."

Mother gave a short laugh. "Well, many of the older buildings are like that . . . but still, they do have their charm."

Chaz made the face again. "Eh? Wha' you on about?"

I intervened. "I believe Holloway is a women's prison, Mother—isn't that right, Chaz?" It pays to watch BBC America.

Chaz smiled, showing the metal grillwork. "That's right, Bran . . . . Mind if I call you that, luv?"

Chaz didn't wait for my reply before going on, "Anyway, when I got outta that dump, I come straight to the States to find me granddad, yeah?" She beamed back at Mr. Yeager, who had remained seated behind the table.

Mr. Yeager nodded, smiling shyly. "That was three months ago," the old gent said softly, "and Chaz has been living with me ever since."

The gawkers had moved on, now that the conflict had ended, except for a man Mother's age named Ivan Wright, who had once been mayor of Serenity, and was among the many old boys in town who Mother was convinced had the hots for her—or anyway, the warms.

Ivan interjected himself into the conversation. "Wasn't that quite a shock, Walter?" the ex-mayor asked Mr. Yeager, his friendly tone taking the edge off his words. "I mean, having this young lady show up on your doorstep claiming to be your granddaughter? How did that happen, exactly?"

Chaz, annoyed by the intrusion—and perhaps the negative content of what Ivan said—snapped, "Well, 'e shagged me grandmum *exac'ly,* didn't 'e? That's 'ow it 'appened, innit?"

I stifled a smile. Mother didn't, letting a grin blossom; she had something like admiration in her big eyes.

"Very succinctly put, my dear," Mother told our newfound friend.

Walter Yeager said proudly, "My granddaughter may be blunt, Ivan, but she's also correct. I met Elsie, her grandmother, when I was stationed in England during the Second World War. After I came back home, she wrote me that we had a son . . . but since I'd married, and Elsie had also found someone, we decided to keep our love child a secret." He paused, then added, "She and I stayed in touch for a while, through the mail . . . but, well, as they say, time marches on. . . ."

Chaz had gone back around the table to stand next to her grandfather; she put one black-nailed hand on his slight shoulder. "I located Granddad from some old letters in a trunk, yeah?"

Yeager looked up adoringly at the girl. "Now that my wife has passed on," he said, "I'm thankful Chaz and I—a couple of lost souls—have found each other." He gave her arm a squeeze. "And I'm relieved that the secret I've carried with me for so many years is finally out."

Ivan smirked, just a bit. "Well, in your case it worked out, but sometimes secrets are best kept secrets . . . especially when nothing good can come of it."

The remark reminded me of something that had been troubling me for weeks on end, thanks to an anonymous letter that had questioned my own parentage. I sneaked a glance at Mother. *Was she keeping a secret from me?* But her face looked placid, even serene.

Walter shook his head. "I used to think that way, Ivan . . . but not anymore . . . not since this little bundle from Britain appeared on my doorstep. Now I want to make it up to her, give her things I couldn't before . . . and that takes money. That's why I'm selling all my old collectibles—memories, if you will."

Ivan's smirk morphed into a smile. "Well, hell, I'll buy this Hopalong Cassidy coffee mug, Walter . . . if that will help. A friend of mine has a son who grew up on Hoppy who'll get a kick out of this."

Yeager smiled, "It's a start. . . ."

The ex-mayor brought out his wallet, but the transaction was interrupted by a commotion nearby, punctuated by shouts of *"Thief!"* and *"Stop him!"*

Sprinting toward me came a young man in torn jeans, a navy sweatshirt, and with a stocking cap pulled down low to right above wild wide eyes. While everyone else jumped out of the young man's way, I positioned myself so I could, at just the right moment, stick out my foot and trip him.

But the second I lifted my leg, Chaz whispered out sharply, "Bran!" and I hesitated just long enough to miss my chance.

The thief whisked by, shoving patrons out of his way, some clearing the path on their own volition—and no other would-be heroes (or heroines, either) risked tripping the kid or tackling him or otherwise keeping him from bolting out the front door. Which he did.

I frowned at Chaz, more in confusion than irritation.

She shrugged. "Sorry, Bran . . . thought 'e might 'urt you, mate."

Or that I might hurt *him*?

In short order, the floor manager had called the police, and in less than ten minutes, a uniformed officer arrived. I wasn't surprised that the representative of Serenity's finest who answered the call was none other than my boyfriend, Brian Lawson, who worked the Serenity PD night shift.

As soon as Brian stepped inside, he spotted me and Mother, and shook his head as he approached us down the aisle.

"I might have known," he said with a tiny, wry smile forming on that handsome mug. "If the Borne girls aren't in the middle of trouble, they're bound to be somewhere on the fringes. . . ."

Among those who stood shivering in the blast of cold air that had come in with Officer Lawson were Chaz and the dealer who had been robbed—a gray-bearded, potbellied guy in a plaid shirt and jeans who ran a local antiques shop. Mr. Yeager remained back at his table, and Ivan had moved along.

Brian asked our group, "Who's making the complaint?"

"Complaint, my foot!" the dealer fumed. "I want to make a charge! And I want you to actually *do* something about it!"

Complaint, his foot? Funny he should say that, because I'd never seen this guy on his feet before. Whenever you entered his shop, he was sitting in a rocker, reading a newspaper and letting his wife handle the customers. I figured he was more irritated about having to exert himself than getting robbed.

"All right, settle down," Brian said, not unkindly, patting the air with a hand, "I'm here to help." He withdrew a small tape recorder from his jacket pocket. "Let's start with your name, and then tell me what happened."

The dealer took a deep breath. "I'm Claude Anderson and I have one of the dealers' tables over there . . ." He pointed. ". . . and I'd just turned my back for a second when that punk stole my money!"

Brian asked, "He came around behind the table?"

"Yes! I had the money in a plastic zipper bag—you know, like the bank gives you. . . ."

"And where was the bag?"

"On the seat of my folding chair. I'd gotten up to make change for a customer . . ."

Wow, the guy was going all out all tonight.

". . . and then put the bag down on it while I wrapped the purchase . . . and the next thing I know this thief is running off with it."

"Can you describe him?"

Anderson said in frustration, "I only saw the back of him!" He pointed an accusatory finger at me—apparently the front of my face resembled the back of the thief's head. "But that girl must've gotten a good look! He ran right past her!"

I started to say something, but shut my mouth because Chaz had moved close to me and surreptitiously took hold of my hand at my side and squeezed it. Hard.

Brian looked at me. "Well?"

"I really didn't get *that* good a look," I said. "He went by so fast—dark jeans, sweatshirt, stocking cap—that's all I remember."

Brian asked Chaz. "How about you?"

Chaz made an exaggerated frown and shook her head. "Seen one bloke you seen 'em all, innit?"

He turned to Mother. "What about you, Mrs. Borne? You're generally observant."

Mother gestured to her thick glasses, "Oh, well, I appreciate the compliment, Officer Lawson . . . but honestly, I didn't see a thing . . . not with *these* poor old peepers."

Brian sighed, hit the stop button on the recorder.

Mother added, "However, I do have one important question. . . ."

Officer Lawson raised his eyebrows. "Which is?"

"Is there any truth to the rumor that you're going to stop using the ten-codes like some other police departments?"

Brian gaped at Mother at this non sequitur; I stifled a groan and faded back behind Chaz.

"No, Mrs. Borne, we haven't dispensed with them yet."

"Good," Mother said approvingly, tossing her head back. "It's a most efficient system—if it ain't broke, don't fix it!"

Why did Mother care? Because Vivian Borne had her very own code number unofficially assigned by the Serenity PD; when the police radioed "ten-one-hundred" it meant that Mother was on the scene and to proceed with extreme caution.

Anderson said irritably, "Look, can we get back to my stolen money?"

Brian nodded, and told our little group, "All right, you can all go except for Mr. Anderson." Then he took the dealer by the arm and walked him over to his table to finish the interview, leaving Mother, me, and Chaz.

Mother said to me cheerily, "Well, wasn't that exciting? We haven't been involved with a crime for *months*!"

"We're *not* involved."

"We're witnesses, aren't we?" She leaned close and whispered theatrically: "Incidentally, why are we covering up, dear?"

"What?"

"Why aren't we telling your nice young officer what we saw? I was simply following your lead, dear."

"Follow this lead," I said, and made a "zip" gesture across my mouth.

I told Mother to wait while I went to fetch the car, then turned to Chaz with a forced smile. "Can I see you outside for a moment?"

She swallowed and nodded and we stepped out into the cold and stood under the scant protection of the tin awning, our breaths pluming.

Chaz spoke first. "Thanks for keeping your gob shut, Bran, and not grassing."

I said testily, "I know you're involved somehow in that theft."

"Wha'? No way, man!"

I ignored her. "And if you don't want me to

'grass,' that money better be returned to me tomorrow, or I'm gonna suddenly remember all kinds of details about that boy, and no doubt so will Mother—including the spider tattoo on the side of his neck."

Chaz spat, "Bloody hell! I told *'im* to cover up that bugger!" She sighed resignedly. "You win, mate. I'll make 'im give back the money. He just did it for me because—"

"I don't want to know," I snapped. "I've already lied once to my boyfriend, and I don't want to do it again."

Her eyes widened. "That screw's your bloke?"

That sounded backward somehow.

But I said, "That's right . . . so you know I mean business, 'mate.' I'll come to your house tomorrow, around noon, and you'd better have that cash—every bleeding quid! Where do you live?"

"Grandad 'as a caravan at Happy Trails Trailer Court . . . Number 21. But I don't want me grandad to know!"

"Don't worry . . . I'll bring some information on the value of that Tarzan book along, as an excuse."

"Okay." She cast her eyes downward. "Thanks, luv."

"Why don't you find some nice friends?"

Chaz looked up again. "Wha'? A ex-con with a funny accent like me? Who's gonna wanna be mates with me?"

"Well . . . me, for one. *If* that money's returned . . . and if you stay out of trouble, Chaz."

"A posh lady like you?"

I snorted. "I'm not posh. Far from it. Take a

closer look at this raccoon coat." We were both shivering, so I said, "Remember, Chaz . . . noon tomorrow."

She said, "I won't let you down," and her smile had a shyness at odds with the spiky hair, multiple piercings, and public theft.

She slipped inside.

I trudged into the snow to get the car, wondering if I'd done the right thing.

On the drive home Mother was a chatterbox, carrying on about her fabulous finds, interspersed with melodramatic rambling about poor Walter Yeager having to sell all his childhood memories. I concentrated on keeping the car on the snowy road, grunting every now and then to show I was listening, even though I wasn't, really.

As we pulled the Audi into the garage, Mother suddenly asked, "Why did you cover up for Chaz, dear?"

I'd hoped we wouldn't be returning to this subject, that I'd ignored her sufficiently to put it out of her mind. Out of her mind was right.

Mother sighed. "Well, I'm sure you have your reasons, and you know I'm never one to pry. . . . By the way, where did you get that wonderful coat? We could be twins."

I shut off the engine and smiled nastily. "Yes, Mother, I feel like your twin . . . . And from now on, whenever I wear this coat, you should be afraid . . . you should be very, very afraid."

Mother frowned and opened her car door. "I don't know what's gotten into you lately, Brandy . . . but I'm glad we're both seeing our therapists tomorrow."

"Me, too," I said, meaning it.

Because Mother was keeping something from me that was way more important than withholding a little information from the police.

And Mother had been keeping her secret a whole lot longer.

*A Trash 'n' Treasures Tip*

Shopping can be daunting at a flea market, where treasures are often hidden among the trash—like the rare photo of Edgar Allan Poe some lucky buyer purchased for a pittance and then sold for thirty-five thousand. Bet that dealer's kicking himself. So am I—I passed it up!

## BARBARA ALLAN

is the joint pseudonym for husband-and-wife mystery writers Max Allan and Barbara Collins.

**BARBARA COLLINS** is one of the most respected short story writers in the mystery field, with appearances in over a dozen top anthologies, including *Murder Most Delicious*, *Women on the Edge*, and the best-selling *Cat Crimes* series. She was the coeditor (and a contributor) to the best-selling anthology *Lethal Ladies*, and her stories were selected for inclusion in the first three volumes of *The Year's 25 Finest Crime and Mystery Stories.*

Two acclaimed hardcover collections of her work have been published—*Too Many Tomcats* and (with her husband) *Murder—His and Hers.* Their first novel together, the baby boomer thriller *Regeneration*, was a best seller; their second collaborative novel, *Bombshell*—in which Marilyn Monroe saves the world from World War III—was published in hardcover to excellent reviews.

Barbara has been the production manager and/ or line producer on "Mommy," "Mommy's Day," and "Real Time: Siege at Lucas Street Market," and other independent film projects emanating from the production company she and her husband jointly run.

**MAX ALLAN COLLINS**, a five-time Mystery Writers of America "Edgar" nominee in both fiction and nonfiction categories, has been hailed as "the Renaissance man of mystery fiction." He has earned an unprecedented fourteen Private Eye Writers of America "Shamus" nominations for his historical thrillers, winning twice for his Nathan Heller novels, *True Detective* (1983) and *Stolen Away* (1991), and was recently presented with the Eye, the Private Eye Writers of America's Lifetime Achievement Award. His other credits include film criticism, short fiction, songwriting, trading-card sets, and movie/TV tie-in novels, including *Air Force One, In the Line of Fire*, and the *New York Times* best-selling *Saving Private Ryan*. His graphic novel *Road to Perdition* is the basis of the Academy Award–winning DreamWorks feature film starring Tom Hanks, Paul Newman, and Jude Law, directed by Sam Mendes. In addition to his nominations for both the Eisner and Harvey awards (the "Oscars" of the comics world), Collins has many comics credits, including the "Dick Tracy" syndicated strip (1977– 1993); his own "Ms. Tree"; "Batman"; and "CSI: Crime Scene Investigation," based on the hit TV series, for which he has also written five video games and an internationally best-selling series of novels.

One of the most acclaimed and award-winning independent filmmakers in the Midwest, he wrote and directed "Mommy," premiering on Lifetime in 1996, as well as a 1997 sequel, "Mommy's Day." The screenwriter of "The Expert," a 1995 HBO World Premiere, he wrote and directed the innovative made-for-DVD feature "Real Time: Siege at Lucas Street Market" (2000). A DVD boxed set of his films appeared recently on the Neo Noir label and includes "Shades of Noir" (2004), an anthology of his short films, including his award-winning documentary, "Mike Hammer's Mickey Spillane." He recently completed "Eliot Ness: An Untouchable Life," the film version of his Edgar-nominated play.

"BARBARA ALLAN" live(s) in Muscatine, Iowa, their hometown; son Nathan graduated with honors in Japanese and computer science at the University of Iowa in nearby Iowa City and recently completed postgraduate study in Japan.